THE ADVENTURES OF

RIVELLA

THE ADVENTURES OF

RIVELLA

Delarivier Manley

edited by Katherine Zelinsky

broadview literary texts

Canadian Cataloguing in Publication Data

Manley, Mrs. (Mary de la Riviere), 1663-1724
    The adventures of Rivella

(Broadview literary texts)
Includes bibliographical references.
ISBN 1-55111-121-7

I. Zelinsky, Katherine Elizabeth. II. Title. III. Series.

PR3545.M8A65 1999   823'.5   C99-930195-0

Broadview Press Ltd., is an independent, international publishing house, incorporated in 1985.

North America:
P.O. Box 1243, Peterborough, Ontario, Canada K9J 7H5
3576 California Road, Orchard Park, NY 14127
TEL: (705) 743-8990; FAX: (705) 743-8353;
E-MAIL: 75322.44@compuserve.com

United Kingdom:
Turpin Distribution Services Ltd.,
Blackhorse Rd., Letchworth, Hertfordshire SG6 1HN
TEL: (1462) 672555; FAX (1462) 480947; E-MAIL: turpin@rsc.org

Australia:
St. Clair Press, P.O. Box 287, Rozelle, NSW 2039
TEL: (02) 818-1942; FAX: (02) 418-1923

www.broadviewpress.com

Broadview Press gratefully acknowledges the financial support of the Ministry of Canadian Heritage through the Book Publishing Industry Development Program.

Broadview Press is grateful to Professor Eugene Benson for advice on editorial matters for the Broadview Literary Texts series.

Text design and composition by George Kirkpatrick

PRINTED IN CANADA

Contents

Acknowledgements

I wish to thank Rosalind Ballaster and Isobel Grundy, both of whom readily pointed me in fruitful research directions as I macheted my way through the often contradictory Manley biographical terrain; James Black, Anne McWhir, and David Oakleaf for their editorial advice; Myrna Sentes for her intelligent and timely help with preparing this edition; and Don LePan of Broadview Press for his endless understanding and patience. No editor of Manley's work can ignore the enormous contributions to Manley scholarship of the late Patricia Köster, whose facsimile versions of Manley's novels and comprehensive index provided me with invaluable assistance, and from whose edition I derived all excerpts from *New Atalantis* and *Memoirs of Europe*.

I am also grateful to Oxford University Press for granting me permission to reproduce extracts from *The Correspondence of Richard Steele*, ed. Rae Blanchard (1941), and *Journal to Stella*, by Jonathan Swift, ed. Harold Williams (1948). Thanks are also due to Garland Publishing, whose facsimile reprint provided the source for my extracts from Mary Hearne's *The Lover's Week*.

Introduction

Background to the Composition of *Rivella*

> "[W]oman has remained culturally silenced, denied authority, most critically the authority to name herself and her own desires."
>
> Sidonie Smith, *A Poetics of Women's Autobiography* (1987).

> "She understood that if she was going to hold on to her life at all, she would have to rescue it by a primary act of imagination, supplementing, modifying, summoning up the necessary connections, conjuring the pastoral or heroic or whatever ... getting the details wrong occasionally, exaggerating or lying outright."
>
> Carol Shields, *The Stone Diaries* (1993).

IN early 1714, the year of *Rivella*'s publication, Delarivier Manley learned that the hack writer, Charles Gildon, was at work on a forthcoming biography of her life.[1] The publisher, Edmund Curll, through whose advertisements Manley became aware of the project, and who supposedly commissioned the book, later claimed ignorance about Gildon's personal motivations for embarking on what promised to be a hostile account. In his brief record of the events leading up to the novel's publication with which he prefaces the fourth edition of *Rivella* entitled *Mrs. Manley's History of her Own Life and Times* (see Appendix A), Curll reveals that Gildon wrote "upon a pique, the cause of which I cannot assign ... some account of Mrs. Manley's life, under the title of, *The History of Rivella, Author of the Atalantis.*" Curll is unequivocal, however, in his assessment of Gildon's two printed sheets, which proved to confirm Manley's fears that the narrative would be, in the publisher's words, "a severe invective upon some part of her conduct." Although she would herself see Gildon's preliminary

---

1   Gildon was also the "biographer," who masqueraded as "One of the Fair Sex," of *Memoirs on the Life of Mrs. Behn.* See Appendix H. 2.iv.

work only after receiving his permission, Manley's faith in her suspicions (likely bolstered by both Gildon's and Curll's dubious professional reputations,[1] as well as her own disrepute) was evidently strong enough for her to intervene, since, according to Curll's records of his correspondence with her, she appealed to him to defer the biography's publication until they had at least discussed the matter in person.

Curll's narrative of the ensuing events transverses generic boundaries, oscillating between history and romance, as the prospect of conflict vanished amidst outpourings of mutual generosity and good will. Performing the role of intermediary, Curll arranged a meeting between himself, Manley, her sister Cornelia, and Gildon, which resulted in a reconciliation between Manley and Gildon, who was "so generous, as to order a total suppression of all his papers," and in Manley's "generous" resolution "to write the history of her own life, and times, under the same title which Mr. Gildon had made choice of." According to Curll's record, Manley went on to produce her memoirs under strict time constraints, presumably in an attempt to meet the publisher's deadline originally set for Gildon, submitting "the greatest part of the manuscript" to him "[a]bout a week after" her letter of March 15th in which she promised to "have it out as soon as possible." Exactly when she completed the manuscript remains uncertain. The "translator" of the first edition provides the publication date of June 3, 1714, only about two months after Manley sent the above letter to Curll. She probably completed the work shortly after the March letter, since the second edition, dated 1715, had already been published in September of 1714.[2]

Curll's long-deferred "history" of *Rivella*'s authorship, which finally appeared ten years after the novel's original publication, in fact leaves a number of questions, such as the dates of manuscript completion and publication, unanswered. Dated 29 September 1724, a little over two months after Manley's death, Curll's account seems expiatory, as

---

1   See Appendix A, notes. Also see Ralph Straus, *The Unspeakable Curll*, for a full discussion of Edmund Curll and occasional references to Gildon.
2   Number 11050 of *The Post Man: and The Historical Account*, from Thursday, September 2 to Saturday, September 4, 1714, records the publication of the second edition of *The Adventures of Rivella*, with a complete key, printed for J. Roberts.

though he were finally released from his onerous promise to conceal her identity as the author of her own life story. Deploying the evidentiary tropes of juridico-theological discourse, after a ten-year silence he at last makes his confession, revealing "the fact[s]," "the truth," and "sufficient proof of her being the genuine author." But Manley's injunctions to keep "this affair ... a secret" remain forceful. As if still under oath of secrecy, Curll furnishes a testimony that hesitates between disclosure and restraint, provoking as many questions as it provides answers. Why, for example, did Gildon approach the biography of Manley with such virulence only to acquiesce so readily to her request to write it herself? And were there perhaps other reasons besides the professional rivalry between printers John Barber, with whom Manley was living in 1714 (see Appendix E), and Edmund Curll, why she so clearly feared Barber's discovery of her authorship of *Rivella*? Equivocal itself, *Rivella* raises questions about its own truthfulness, obscuring clear distinctions between fact and fiction in its complex interplay of the discrete discursive modes and practices – historical, juridical, romantic and otherwise – with which Manley constructs her self-portrait. Both a factitious historical account and a wishful tale of male desire, a record of Manley's *bios* and a testimonial to her "biographer's" bias, *Rivella* coheres and fragments, discloses and witholds, confesses and qualifies, deftly eluding generic definition while exposing the discursive and cultural conventions by which subjects and subjectivities are fashioned. Perhaps, then, the "history" of *Rivella's* composition corroborates Manley's efforts to reclaim the prerogative to self-representation from the male cultural judges by whom she was scrutinized and defamed. Curll's curious narrative restraint may, ultimately, signal not only his reluctance to "tattle of [Manley's] frailties" (*Rivella* 108) but also his deference to a woman writer who, in her determination to right/rewrite (his)story, asserted her own authority to judge for herself.

Delarivier Manley's Readers and Reputation: An Overview

Years before she wrote her biography, Manley had achieved widespread fame as a writer of scandal fiction. Her best known-novel, *New Atalantis* (1709), which became "the most sensational bestseller of the eighteenth century" (Morgan, *Autobiography* 20), riveted the attention of her most acclaimed contemporaries, inspiring Alexander Pope's allusion to it in *The Rape of the Lock*[1] and providing Lady Mary Wortley Montagu with the subject of an indignant letter to Mrs. Frances Hewet, in which she petitions for a copy of the second volume, decries Manley's imprisonment, and speculates that the author "will serve as a scarecrow to frighten people from attempting any thing but heavy panegyric" (I.18). Although Manley's fame would never again reach its *New Atalantis* peak, she remained throughout her life (and after) a noted literary and cultural presence, an innovator in the areas of political journalism, scandal writing, and amatory fiction.[2] That Manley "enters history primarily on the periphery of the lives of her more remembered male colleagues Swift and Steele" (Todd, *The Sign of Angellica* 84) may be largely true; also true, however, is that she earned the respect of such luminaries – Steele paid her public tribute with his prologue to her last play, *Lucius*, after a fifteen-year quarrel,[3] and Swift was so confident in her "good sense and invention" (see Appendix D.1.v) that he sought her assistance in completing his preliminary sketch of the Marquis of Guiscard's attempted assassination of the Lord Treasurer, Harley, and also turned over his editorship of the *Examiner* to her from 14 June to 26 July 1711 (see Appendix D.1.i. iii). Even her would-be vilifier, Charles Gildon, earlier acknowledged her talents, exalting her as a "lady [who] has very happily distinguished her self from the rest of her sex, and gives us a living proof of what we might reasonably expect from womankind, if they had the benefit of those artificial improvements of learning the men have ..."[4] Similar effusive praise marked the occasion of Manley's death, as recorded in *The Historical Register* of 1724, whose author eulogized her as "a person of a polite genius, and uncommon capacity, which made her writings naturally delicate and easy, and her conversation

---

1 Cf. Canto III, lines 160-70.
2 See, for example, Gwendolyn Needham, "Mrs. Manley: An Eighteenth-Century Wife of Bath"; Jane Spencer, *The Rise of the Woman Novelist*; and Marilyn L. Williamson, *Raising their Voices: British Women Writers, 1650-1750*, all of whom argue that Manley broke new historical/literary ground.
3 See Appendix C.4.ii.
4 The *Lives and Characters of the English Dramatick Poets*, published in 1699, was begun by Gerard Langbaine and completed by Charles Gildon.

agreeably entertaining."[1] Continuing to reap her share of accolades well into the nineteenth century,[2] Manley clearly appears, in the face of such evidence, to have been "widely read and well loved" despite "political and personal grievances" (Morgan, *A Woman of No Character* 18).[3]

As twentieth-century overviews of Manley criticism indicate, however, political and personal grievances in fact define much of the tendentious Manley canon, providing evidence that while she was widely read she was also widely condemned. Gwendolyn B. Needham, Dolores Palomo, and Jacqueline Pearson, for example, point out respectively that: "Manley's notoriety as an 'old sinner' was not interred with her bones, but continues to colour her evaluation by later writers ..."; "it is constantly insinuated that Mary [sic] Manley was an immoral woman who (therefore) wrote immoral books"; and "[a]s a result of her irregular life and her allegedly immoral work her reputation, in her own time and since, has been scandalous."[4] While many of Manley's opponents condemn her sexual improprieties, as these critics suggest, an appreciable number also dispute her credibility. As Gwendolyn Needham notes, Manley's *New Atalantis* "established her reputation as a defamer," and the effect on her critical legacy of this tag, coupled with her own "ill fame as a 'fallen woman,'" is that she is recalled "either as an unfortunate woman or as a mere scandalmonger" ("Mary de la Riviére Manley" 253). Inspired, in part, by Restoration and eighteenth-century identifications of woman writer and whore, such concerns with Manley's sexuality and veracity underscore the enduring authority with which culturally-

---

1 Cf. *The Historical Register*, vol. 9, "The Chronological Diary for the Year 1724," 35.

2 Adolphus William Ward, for example, casts Manley as "the great society novelist of an age to which she should not be too severely condemned for having held up a mirror. Of her cleverness there can be no doubt, and if she had little consideration for the good fame of others, she had at least the courage of her intentions, and held her own not only by the fear she inspired" (*A History of English Dramatic Literature to the Death of Queen Anne*, 1899, III.432).

3 Fidelis Morgan, who, while she concludes that Manley was "widely read and well loved," also provides a summary of critics whom she condemns as misogynistic for criticizing achievements in Manley "which in a man would have been acceptable and even laudable" (*A Woman of No Character* 17).

4 Cf. "Mrs. Manley: An Eighteenth-Century Wife of Bath" 259; "A Woman Writer and the Scholars" 38; and *The Prostituted Muse* 170-71, respectively.

sanctioned equations of female textual and sexual practice have largely determined the parameters of Manley criticism.

Paradox thus marks a critical legacy both perpetuated and contained by its blindness to its own conceptual paradigms. Among Manley's more ideologically conscious readers, Henry Fielding, in *Joseph Andrews* (1742), reflexively situates Manley squarely within his narrator's polemical discussion of biographical fiction:

> I would by no means be thought to comprehend those persons of surprising genius, the authors of immense romances, or the modern novel and *Atalantis* writers;[1] who without any assistance from nature or history, record persons who never were, or will be ... whose heroes are of their own creation, and their brains the chaos whence all their materials are collected. (184)

Four decades later, Clara Reeve again decries Manley's scandal writing in her quasi-fictional anatomy of literary history, *The Progress of Romance* (1785). This time, however, the authoritative commentator, Euphrasia, is also a mirror of contemporary codes of literary propriety:

> She [Manley] hoarded up all the public and private scandal within her reach, and poured it forth, in a work too well known in the last age, though almost forgotten in the present.... I am sorry to say [her works] were once in fashion, which obliges me to mention them, otherwise I had rather be spared the pain of disgracing an author of my own sex. (I. 119)[2]

---

1   In his note to Fielding's phrase, "modern novel and *Atalantis* writers," R.F. Brissenden, in his 1977 edition of *Joseph Andrews*, identifies specifically Manley and the *New Atalantis*. However, Fielding may also be alluding to Eliza Haywood and her *Memoirs of a Certain Island Adjacent to the Kingdom of Utopia* (1724-5). Immediately following this passage, Fielding's narrator goes on to say of such writers that they "perhaps ... merit the highest" honour for their "human genius" (184), though he goes on to praise the greater achievements of Cervantes in *Don Quixote*.

2   Reeve's Euphrasia echoes, to some extent, John Duncombe's association of Manley and her ilk with moral degeneracy in his poem *The Feminead* (1754). Duncombe deplores the contaminating effects of such writers on the entire sex, as he follows his praise of Catherine Cockburn with the lines: "The modest muse a veil with pity throws/O'er vice's friends and virtue's female foes;/Abashed she views the bold

Increasingly vitriolic, Manley's nineteenth- and twentieth-century opponents continue to advance the cause of literary and moral rectitude in the broader cultural interests of "honesty" and "decency." Writing in 1856, Augustus deMorgan reviles Manley as "[t]his demirep – to give her a name exactly as much above her deserts as it is below those of an honest woman" (265). Over half a century later, the renowned historian George Macaulay Trevelyan characterizes Manley as "[t]he professional libeller" (*Blenheim* 184) and as "a woman of no character" who "regaled the public with brutal stories, for the most part entirely false, about public men and their wives, especially Whigs and above all the Marlboroughs" (*Protestant Succession* 38). So incensed is Marlborough's indignant descendant Winston Churchill that he not only disparages Manley as a "woman of disreputable character paid by the Tories to take part in the campaign of detraction which ... was organized against Marlborough," but he also consigns her to the "cesspool from which she should never have crawled" (*Marlborough* I.53; 130). In her critical study *Women Writers* (1945), Bridget MacCarthy accuses Manley of having "collected filth with the relentless energy of a dredger, and aimed it with the deadly precision of a machine gun" out of "revenge on a condemnatory world" (216). And, finally, in his impressive critical survey of early fiction, *Popular Fiction before Richardson* (1969), John Richetti writes:

> [I]f we approach the enormously popular work of writers such
> as Mrs. Manley and Mrs. Haywood with the high-mindedness
> that literary history has traditionally required, our mood must
> change to dismay at the corruption of popular taste." (119)

While, clearly, Manley has not earned an elevated status in the historical annals of the "high-minded," one should recall the admiration she received from such contemporaries as Swift, Montagu, and Steele. Manley herself appears not to have needed reminding of the ideological underpinnings of all histories – literary, political, and personal – and of the cultural dimensions of objectivity and truth. Indeed, her (auto)biographical *Rivella*, in which the fictional biographer provides

---

unblushing mien/Of modern Manley, Centlivre, and Behn;/And grieves to see one nobly born disgrace/Her modest sex, and her illustrious race" (ll.139-44).

a testimony to the heroine's love of truth and justice, continues to preoccupy its readers with questions of historical accuracy.[1] Again, critical opinion remains sharply divided. Writing in 1929, Walter and Clare Jerrold regard the autobiography as pure invention, insisting that Manley "tells what she pleases – and leaves out very much more than she tells" (84), a sentiment echoed by Bridget MacCarthy, who offers a memorably ungenerous commentary on Lovemore's description of Rivella's feet:

> Small and pretty – those swollen, dropsical feet! Few things are sadder than a woman who knows, but will not own, that her day is done. So it is with this entire autobiography. It is the expression of a life foolish, immoral, revengeful, brave. We watch her juggling with words, talking feverishly on, building up an illusion of beauty, brilliancy and success, but we are no more deceived than she. (230-31)

Fortunately, within the larger critical picture, MacCarthy's sentiments remain extreme. Numerous readers, in fact, celebrate Manley's fictionalizations as imaginative flourishes which ultimately reveal an underlying foundation of truth. Two early Manley biographers, Paul Bunyan Anderson and Gwendolyn B. Needham, for example, argue respectively that "[t]he most casual reader can discover open self-glorification in Mrs. Manley's autobiography, but ... [b]eneath the alluring surface of her narrative lies a structure of objective fact" ("Mistress Delariviere Manley's Biography" 262), and "[t]he autobiography has beneath its cover of romance a solid basis of truth; from it a reader can get the main facts of her life and the best impression of her vigorous personality" ("Mrs. Manley" 275-76). Later biographers Patricia Köster and Fidelis Morgan largely concur, Köster pointing out that while Manley "wants to present herself as favorably as possible ... aside from calculations which bear on her age she does not seem to make

---

1   Until quite recently, *Rivella* has received relatively little critical attention, much of it concerned with its factual value. For more incisive readings of the work, see, for example: John J. Richetti, *Popular Fiction before Richardson* (1969); Lennard J. Davis, *Factual Fictions: The Origins of the English Novel* (1983); Janet Todd, "Life after sex: the fictional autobiography of Delarivier Manley" (1988); and Rosalind Ballaster, *Seductive Forms: Women's Amatory Fiction from 1684 to 1740* (1992).

any gross inaccuracies" ("Introduction," *The Novels of Mary Delarivière Manley* xx), and Morgan asserting that "in her autobiographical sketches she may have embroidered and elevated, [but] she never evaded the truth of her situation" (*A Woman of No Character* 20).

Rivella and the Facts of Manley's Life

"Biography," John Batchelor writes, "is a searching genre; it strives for infinite complexity, hesitant before obscurity of motive where the subject stands in shadow" ("Women's Lives" 97). In the case of Manley, one might argue that biography has not been hesitant enough in its attempts to define its shadowy subject. Unfortunately, so much critico-biographical attention turns on the truth or deceptiveness of Manley's autobiographical writings[1] that she has become a virtual locus of juridical enquiry and debate, her life and works often reduced to questions of evidence and fact. In the face of such reductionist biographical tendencies, it is worth remembering that, while a considerable amount of information is available about her life, a great deal of it comes from Manley herself, and though much of it has been corroborated by external historical sources, she remains her primary historian. But it is even more important to remember that a life is more than a series of events, more than the facts that history can provide, more than even the one who has lived that life can recreate through the collaborative processes of memory, imagination, and desire. In the closing lines of the preface to her painstakingly researched biography of Manley, which remains the most definitive and comprehensive to date, Dolores Diane Clarke Duff concedes: "Mrs. Manley is at best an elusive figure, partially because she wished to be" (vi). This unassuming insight may finally number among the most valuable contributions to Manley scholarship. For in the face of all the facts, truth, and evidence, there is no *one* Manley but rather a plurality of Manleys – protean, diffuse, contradictory. And there is no greater testimonial to her complexity than the story she writes of herself. With its intricate bricolage of discursive and cultural conven-

---

1   Although *Rivella* is Manley's most sustained autobiography, as Rosalind Ballaster points out in her introduction to *New Atalantis*, Manley scatters "inset narratives relating to her own intellectual and personal life through much of her writing (vi).

tions, and in its tricky interweavings of fiction and history, fantasy and fact, Manley's own elusive "biography," *Rivella*, still remains the truest memorial to her life.

Indeed, it is by constructing a self-portrait that contests its own coherence and centredness that Manley achieves this paradoxical quality of truth. From its very outset *Rivella* problematizes conventional reductions of the "self" to a *bios*, a collection of life experiences that can be verified by means of authoritative sources,[1] through which personal "identity" can be traced, understood, and, ultimately, inscribed. The "history" is, in fact, a playful testimony to the uncertainty of origins and the unreliability of sources, claiming to be a translation derived from a French publisher, former Gentleman of the Chamber and amanuensis to Chevalier D'Aumont, who himself derived Rivella's biography from his English friend Sir Charles Lovemore. *Rivella* further mystifies questions of source by neither affirming nor denying the possibility that Lovemore may have related the "adventures" to D'Aumont in English, and, thus, that the biography was not simply translated once, from French to English, but also earlier, from English to French. In any case, the final English translation, which clearly bears the linguistic traces of French influence, may serve a twofold function: reminding us on the one hand of the cross-cultural sympathies between Lovemore and D'Aumont, and on the other of the possible cultural and ideological gaps between these apparently kindred speakers. In confronting the uncertainties of origin, *Rivella* thus also confronts fundamental epistemological and ontological uncertainties. For in posing the possibility that either the quixotic D'Aumont, who meets Rivella only in the realms of imagination and desire, or the enamoured Lovemore could vie for the role of Rivella's biographer (or conceivably even D'Aumont's amenuensis or the English translator), Manley poses crucial questions not just about the authority of the portrait but also about the very "subject" of the portrait. One might well wonder whose vision (and version) of Rivella this is and whether this vision is as much the "subject" of this (auto)biography as Rivella herself.

That Manley complicates the biographical process by introducing

---

1   See Sidonie Smith, *A Poetics of Women's Autobiography*, 1-19, for further elaboration of the constituent elements of self-representation: *autos*, *bios* and *graphia*.

the possibility of D'Aumont's (and perhaps others') interventions in Lovemore's account of Rivella suggests that the narrative persona, through whose perspective we glimpse the elusive historical subject, may in fact be multi-visioned and multi-vocal, a divided and contradictory consciousness through whom Manley mediates her polyphonous, densely textured life story. Complicating questions of narrative consistency even further, behind her dubiously coherent "biographer," Manley is, of course, her own historian, exerting final puppeteer-like authority over her constructed biographer. Even Manley's status as ultimate self-historian, however, generates questions about biographical authority and truth, for while she authors her author's visions of her, it is clear that his visions are not always hers, though not always clear what vision of herself she in fact has. Underscoring these interpretive difficulties is not only the gap between Rivella (as fictional subject historicized) and Delarivier Manley (as historical subject fictionalized) but also between Sir Charles Lovemore, Rivella's putative biographer, and Major General John Tidcomb, whom Edmund Curll identifies in his key as Lovemore's real-life counterpart. At once an actual figure in history[1] and a product of Manley's creative imagination, Lovemore is himself a site of contradiction and ambivalence: the pesty, rejected suitor who condemns Rivella for her imprudent disregard of appearances and her unladylike intrusions into the realm of party politics, and the ever-loyal admirer who praises Rivella for her deep commitment to the principles of integrity, truth, and justice. Indeed, according to Dolores Diane Clarke Duff, Lovemore is a convention-bound departure from, as well as a genuine counterpart of, the actual Tidcomb. Gentle in his moral judgments like Tidcomb himself, Lovemore may even have been a kind of joke between Tidcomb and Manley, both of whom, in Duff's words, likely "enjoyed the publication of Rivella the more for its sentimentalized portrayal of the clumsy soldier as a dashing, lovable rake, gambler and

---

1   While the scholarly community appears to agree with Curll's identification of Lovemore with Tidcomb, Patricia Köster remains skeptical, pointing out that he was "far too old in 1685 for the description of a 'meer Lad' of sixteen, too young to court the eighteen-year-old sister Maria...." She goes on the say that "Although we can well believe that Mrs. Manley has somewhat falsified all the ages, we can hardly think that she would describe as a 'meer Lad' a man of forty-three. Furthermore, Tidcombe came from Calne, Wiltshire, not from Suffolk" ("Introduction" xxi).

follower of an author who styled herself an expert in the softer passions" (289).[1] Lovemore, in whom Manley both incorporates and repudiates cultural, social, and literary conventions, thus not only mirrors the discursively pluralistic "history" and "adventures" of Rivella, but also provides a complex narrative consciousness through whose visions and representations Manley inscribes as well as resists such conventions.

At one revealing juncture in the biography, Lovemore interrupts his story to assure D'Aumont that he is Rivella's "impartial historian"(74) despite having once been her unrequited lover. Significantly, it is this same "impartial historian" who frames much of Rivella's "history" in terms of romance, and whose account of her life is, as Rosalind Ballaster observes, "marked throughout by an attempt to impose a definitive amatory 'form' upon Rivella's literary and personal activities" ("Seizing the means of seduction" 105). Lovemore's amatory bias does, however, serve an additional, alternative function. For if romance conventions restrict Lovemore's vision, they expand Rivella's (Manley's). Exploiting the very conventions that contain her, Manley constructs a mitigating counter-narrative to what was (and might have been) written about her (by Gildon and others), unleashing romance's liberatory, and comic, potential as she reimagines, reenvisions, and reinvents both her person and her past.

Two years before *Rivella's* publication, Jonathan Swift, in a frequently quoted letter to Stella, described Manley as "about forty, very homely and very fat" (see Appendix D.1.v), a description clearly untrammelled by the euphemistic and transformative elements of romance which underpin Lovemore's portrait of Rivella as "inclined to fat; whence I have often heard her flatterers liken her to the Grecian Venus" and as having "scarce any pretence" to the smallpox to which she succumbed in childhood (47). Indeed, Lovemore immediately reintegrates not merely the "fat" and pock-marked but also the "old" heroine into the romance realm by obscuring the date and

---

1   Duff goes on to cite some of Alexander Pope's letters in which he characterizes Tidcomb as living a colourfully dissolute life. See, for example, his letters to Henry Cromwell of 25 April 1708 and 29 August 1709, respectively, in which he associates Tidcomb with the whores of Drury Lane, and says of his life that it is "beastly [and] laughable ... not unlike a Fart, at once nasty & diverting." Cf. George Sherburn, ed., *The Correspondence of Alexander Pope* (1956), I.46-48 and I.70-71.

details of her birth. Rivella, he claims, "was born in Hampshire, in one of those islands, which formerly belonged to France, where her father was governour" (50). According to these details, Rivella must have been born sometime between 1667 and 1672, the period when her father, Sir Roger Manley, was stationed in the Channel Islands where he served as lieutenant-governor of Jersey. These dates conflict, however, with Lovemore's subsequent account of Rivella's youth at Landguard Fort, Suffolk, "Rivella's father's government" (52), where he [Lovemore] "a meer lad" of sixteen, became captivated by the twelve-year-old heroine (52). In fact, Sir Roger Manley came to Landguard Fort, with his sons Francis and Edward and daughters Mary Elizabeth, Delarivier, and Cornelia, in February of 1680, where he served as governor until his death in 1687.[1] It was in 1685 that the Twelfth, or Suffolk, Regiment, led by Mary Elizabeth's future husband Captain Francis Braithewaite, came to the Fort, apparently also the year when, according to Lovemore, Rivella fell in love with the ensign James Carlisle. If Lovemore's statement that Rivella "had just reached the age of twelve" (52) in 1685 is historically accurate, then obviously she could not have been born either between 1667 and 1672, or in Hampshire.

At the level of pure story, such contradictions serve a vital narrative function, for Lovemore can sustain his romantic vision of the ever-youthful heroine (and her spurned but ever-loyal suitor) only by muddling the historical particulars of birthdate and place of birth. Beyond the story, however, Lovemore's contradictions suggest the playful quality of Rivella's history and of Rivella's wilful attempts to confuse her readers; after all, as Dolores Diane Clarke Duff reminds us, "it was she who created the legend of her birth at sea, and consistently reduced her age by ten years" (14, note no. 44). According to Duff's convincing account of the writer's birthdate and place of birth, Manley was born on the Continent in 1663, the third of six children born to Sir Roger Manley and a Walloon gentlewoman. Though little is known of her mother, as Duff points out, the Calendar of State Papers Domestic for 1666-67 records Sir Roger referring to her and

---

1   As Fidelis Morgan points out, Sir Roger's wife and son Roger were likely dead by
    this time, since neither is mentioned in either Sir Roger's or Edward's wills. See *A
    Woman of No Character* (37).

her parents as "subjects of the Spanish Netherlands"(quoted by Duff, 14). Exactly when she died remains uncertain. Lovemore makes only a brief mention of Rivella's mother, a palpable and poignant narrative absence, whose children "had lost [her] when very young" (53). Equally reticent, Rivella's counterpart Delia in *New Atalantis* simply claims that her mother died when she was "yet an infant" (II.181). According to Duff, however, Delia (Manley) was more than an infant when her mother died: "her mother was alive in 1669, visited the Manleys in Wales and put Mary Elizabeth in school in England, but disappears by 1671, when her husband visited England alone" (52).[1] That at the age of fifty one, when she wrote *Rivella*, Manley still makes only a cursory reference to her mother suggests that her death likely left her emotionally scarred and perhaps wishing, well into her adulthood, that she could conjure away this painful memory as easily as Lovemore conjures away the physical scars of childhood smallpox.

If Manley's hauntingly absent mother assumes a kind of spectral quality that places her outside of history, within a timeless spiritual and mythological realm, her father, Sir Roger Manley, is a distinct textual and historical presence, firmly situated within the context of specific seventeenth-century historical events. Again, however, history merges with fantasy as Lovemore creates a figure of almost mythic status, perhaps yet another function of Manley's attempts to conjure away painfully unromantic historical and personal realities. Lovemore provides several facts about Sir Roger, who, in keeping with *Rivella's* account, became a Cavalier soldier loyal to the Stuart cause for which he spent many years in exile on the Continent, where he became a "scholar in the midst of a camp" (51).[2] Repeatedly, however, Lovemore imbues the events surrounding Sir Roger's life and career with cosmic, indeed fatalistic, significance, representing Rivella's father as a hapless victim of social injustice, whose Royalist convictions became his lifelong nemesis. Corroborating Delia's tragic narrative of her father's loss of and failure to recover his estate in *New Atalantis*

---

1 Cf. *Calendar of State Papers Domestic: Charles II, January-November 1671*, 296.
2 Dolores Diane Clarke Duff points out that "Manley [Sir Roger] wrote *A History of the Late Warres in Denmark* and probably part of his *History of the Rebellion in England, Scotland and Ireland* while in Holland" where he moved in 1646 following the First Civil War (11).

(II.182), Lovemore deplores that "the better part of the estate was ruined in the Civil War by adhering to the Royal Family, without ever being repaired, or scarce taken notice of, at the Restoration" (50-51). Lovemore goes on to praise Sir Roger who, he claims, nobly resisted the trappings of power and ambition despite his many years of loyal service to the Court: "His great vertue and modesty rendered him unfit for solliciting such persons, by whom preferment was there to be gained; so that his deserts seemed buried and forgotten" (51). As Dolores Clarke Duff reveals, however, according to the Calendar of State Papers Domestic for 1665-1666, Roger Manley in fact complained bitterly about not having received preferment. Apparently, too, in 1675 Manley wrote jubilantly to his brother-in-law, Isaac Dorislaus, that he had been knighted in the King's bedchamber, and in 1680 applied, albeit unsuccessfully, for the position of receiver general of Cornwall only three weeks into his governorship of Landguard Fort (25-26). Further distorting the facts of history to complete his heroic portrait, Lovemore suggests that Sir Roger, whose death occurred "soon after" (60) the 1688 Revolution and James II's deposal, died of excessive grief, the result of "the misfortunes of his Royal Master" and "in mortal apprehension of what would befall his unhappy country" (60). In fact, Roger Manley died over a year before the King's abdication, probably in March of 1687 (see Fidelis Morgan, *A Woman of No Character* 38), and thus not in the martyr-like manner of Lovemore's sentimental fashioning.

Perhaps more than simply an expression of Lovemore's quixotic sensibility, the sentimentalized Sir Roger Manley, political victim and martyr to the Royalist cause, may well be, too, a fictional embodiment of Delarivier's profound ambivalence toward her ambitious father, whose family, in Dolores Clarke Duff's words, "cannot have been the happiest," considering that he "never gained the position which he desired, nor received the recompense which he expected for loyal service" (25). Manley's portrait of the governor's household at Landguard Fort (from where Sir Roger had for the last time sought preferment) provides telling clues to her own unhappiness within the patriarchal family structure; suggestively, it is in this sequence that Rivella steals from her father in order to assist her love object, Lysander, who has gambled away "all his small stock at backgammon" (56). A conventional narrative of the force of passion versus the claims of filial duty, it is also a covert plot of overweening paternal authority in which the governor, "by the interest [he] made at Court ... procure[s] that battalion to be recalled, and another to be deputed in [its] place ..." (55), thereby thwarting Rivella's growing passion for the young ensign. It would appear, then, that in Lovemore's sentimentalization of this powerful, and power-mongering, figure of patriarchal authority, Delarivier Manley attempts to expose the pretense behind her father's martyr-like persona. Couched within the conventional rhetoric of romance, Manley deploys her plot of filial rebellion, in which she literally pilfers her father's economic power, not only to reveal the power structures behind cultural discourses of male victimization, but also to undermine those structures.

It is through this story of filial rebellion, which Lovemore claims he "had from [Rivella] her self" (56), that Manley unmasks the power politics beneath the guise of benign paternalism, uncovering the "law" behind the innocuous veneer of paternal solicitude, and exposing a culture governed by and obsessed with appearances. Significantly, immediately following the death of Rivella's father, from which event Lovemore traces her "real misfortunes" (60), Manley suggests another plot of misused paternal authority, which Lovemore once again refers to Rivella, namely the events surrounding her bigamous marriage to her cousin, John Manley, in 1689, an account of which Delia provides in the *Atalantis* (cf. Appendix B.iv.). As with her representations of life events in *Rivella*, Manley organizes the details of her marriage to John Manley by means of fictional structures and strategies, anticipating Delia's seduction by her villainous guardian, Don Marcus, with three similar stories – all based on actual seventeenth-century cases – of female innocents betrayed by guardians or lawyers (see Patricia Köster, "Introduction," *The Novels of Mary Delarivière Manley* vi-vii). Moreover, as several critics point out, Delia distorts the facts to create a coherent tale of beleaguered female virtue, obscuring not only chronological dates and details but also the very real possibility that she may have entered the bigamous union knowingly. Dolores Clarke Duff, for one, argues persuasively that Manley, who takes up the subject of polygamy recurrently in *New Atalantis*, likely consented to the arrangement with the full knowledge and perhaps even support of her family (65). Still, Delia's story, like the companion stories of Manley's other victimized heroines, may be more than a conventional period piece. As Rosalind Ballaster suggests, Manley may have been duped by her cousin's compelling arguments in favour of polygamy "[j]ust as [her] heroines [Louisa, Zara, and Corinna] are duped by a rhetoric which claims to represent the ideals of virtue, freedom and innocence ..." (Introduction ix). Whether or not Manley knew her union was bigamous, as Lovemore, who believes "all [Rivella] said," points out: "some part of the world ... not acquainted with her vertue, ridiculed her marriage ..." (61). It is the worldly Hilaria, however, through whom Manley most starkly limns the moral texture of her culture: "She read her [Rivella] a learned lecture upon the ill-nature of the world, that would never restore a woman's reputation, how innocent soever she really were, if appearances proved to be against her...." (62). But if Hilaria is a shrewd witness of the social laws and conventions that determine questions of inno-cence or guilt, Lovemore is an adept practitioner and judge. It is not so much Rivella's "ruin" as her ability to recuperate her reputation for virtue and honesty in the midst of gossip and rumour that concerns him.

It is also arguably because of his obeisance to the social laws of preserving reputation and maintaining appearances, rather than to an established set of moral and ethical codes, that Lovemore subordinates the details of Rivella's bigamous marriage to the events surrounding her six-month residence with Hilaria (Barbara Villiers), with whom Delarivier Manley found refuge upon leaving John Manley in January 1694, and to her relationship with Sir Peter Vainlove (Thomas Skip-with), who helped produce her early plays and whom, according to rumour, she repaid with sexual favours. Both narratives wax prolixly on the dangers of lost reputation. Rivella first falls victim to the machinations of Hilaria who, incited by Rivella's enemy, "the man Hilaria was in love with" (64), accuses her of having an affair and later running off with her son. Significantly, Lovemore, "who knew Rivel-la's innocency," seizes the opportunity by asking her to "retire to [his] seat in the country," reasoning that "this offer ... could no longer do her an injury in the opinion of the world which was sufficiently prej-udiced against her already" (67). Rather curiously, while Lovemore has no qualms about making a mistress of the "innocent" Rivella, since she is already deemed guilty by "the world," he readily condemns both Sir Peter Vainlove, who cultivates his reputation as a rake by circulating the rumour that Rivella has given him venereal disease, and Rivella for her folly: "the world found out the cheat, detesting his vanity and Rivella's folly; that could suffer the conversation of a wretch so insignificant to her pleasures, and yet so dangerous to her reputation" (74). Lovemore, however, clearly has concerns about his own reputation. It is immediately after the Skipwith narrative that he confides to D'Aumont how much he values himself "upon the reputation of an impartial historian, neither blind to Rivella's weaknesses and misfortunes, as being once her lover, nor angry and severe as remembring I could never be beloved" (74). That Lovemore would have made Rivella his mistress had she agreed suggests teasing parallels between the aspiring lover and the would-be rake Skipwith, in whom Manley combines the phallogocentric desire for social recognition and linguistic mastery with the emasculating realities of unfulfilled sexual passion.[1] Powerless to make Rivella either his mistress or his wife, the "never ... beloved" Lovemore, solicitous friend and overseer, may finally be something of a poseur himself. It is, after all, expressly from Rivella, not Lovemore, that we derive her narratives of masked male social and political ambition, stories that Lovemore may well suppress not out of gallant deference to the personal testimony of female experience but because they threaten to expose his own phallogocentric ambitions to exercise ultimate mastery over his heroine's unruly world of appearances.

---

1   Also see Carol L. Barash, "Gender, Authority and the 'Life' of an Eighteenth-century Woman Writer: Delariviäre Manley's *Adventures of Rivella*." Barash argues that Manley wished to make the point in the Skipwith narrative that "she *wasn't* Skipwith's mistress, not because she didn't want to be but because he was unable. A story of women's sexual forwardness is rewritten as one of male impotence in the face of female desire" (168).

Rivella, the Albemarle Trial, and "the Law"

[A] woman's legitimacy is only tolerated when she speaks under the sign of the imaginary, when her voice is confined within the boundaries of a discourse marked as fictional, as not true.

Susan Sage Heinzelman, "Women's Petty Treason."

When a writer is seen in relation to the dominant discourses of power s/he was simultaneously inscribing and resisting, the "innocence" of autobiography as a naïve attempt to tell a universal truth is radically particularized by a specific culture's notion of what truth is, who may tell it, and who is authorized to judge it."

Leigh Gilmore, "Policing Truth."

The prolixity with which Lovemore treats the dangers of lost reputation in the Hilaria and Vainlove narratives is exceeded only by the protractedness of his account of Rivella's involvement in the famous Albemarle lawsuit. That this is the most lengthy section of the history again reflects the extent to which Rivella's history bears the ideological signature of its "impartial" historian. From the biography's outset, in fact, Lovemore interweaves amatory and juridical strains, as Rivella's adventures in love recurrently turn on questions of guilt or innocence. Rivella's covert act of filial disobedience in which she steals from her father to help Lysander, for example, becomes for Lovemore a story of the redeeming (and exculpatory) power of passion, a misdemeanour that convinces the hitherto unerring daughter, who was "perfectly just by nature, principle, and education [that] nothing but love, and that in a high degree could have made her otherwise" (56). But it is Lovemore's preoccupation with the appearance and rumour of sexual indiscretion, which forms the focus of Rivella's relationships with Hilaria and Vainlove, that most clearly signals the discursive intersections of romance and jurisprudence. Repeatedly condemning Rivella not for her liberal sexual activities but for her imprudent "hazard[ing] [of] appearances"(74), Lovemore performs less a directive than a judicial function, since it is the laws of polite society and the judgments of "the world" that largely authorize his pronounce-ments of Rivella's guilt or innocence. Indeed, it is Rivella's mandate to corroborate by means of additional "facts" D'Aumont's belief, which he has derived from the testimony of her writings, that Rivella is "entirely mistress of the art of love" (46). No more the impartial judge than the "impartial historian," Lovemore ultimately demonstrates in his lengthy account of the Albemarle lawsuit, followed by Rivella's own (mis)treatment at the hands of the law, the folly of women's intrusions in the public (masculine) domains of jurisprudence and politics. It is, paradoxically, in his detailed account of Rivella's involve-ment in the most public and protracted trial of the century that Love-more is most resolute in his judgments about women's proper sphere, for he finally recontains her within the private (feminine) realm of romance, within the only cultural space where, as a veritable *feme covert*, she has any legitimacy and authority as a speaking subject.

In view of her nominal status as a woman vis-à-vis seventeenth-century jurisprudence, Manley's detailed knowledge of the Albemarle lawsuit clearly challenges the gender-regulated epistemological bounds of law. Personalized though it is, Manley's account of the trial is fundamentally true to the facts; as Dolores Duff points out, Man-ley's version is "substantially that presented by E.F Ward" (96).[1] Long and complicated, truly "a sort of seventeenth-century Jarndyce v. Jarndyce" (Morgan, *A Woman of No Character* 102), the lawsuit between Bath and Montagu stretched out over a period of seven years, and, as Estelle Ward points out, it took a full twenty years of "lit-igation, lawyers' fees, and partial settlements" before the vast Albe-marle estate legacies were finally settled on its beneficiaries (352). As Manley's version of the lawsuit and contemporary journalized accounts of the events affirm, the trial was a drama of profound human interest. Richard Lapthorne, for example, records in his letter to Richard Coffin of 28 November 1691, the death of a witness in the courtroom: "One day this weeke there being a Tryall at the King's bench Bar between the Duke of Albemarle and the Earl of Bath in which Sir Thomas Higgins having given evidence immediately after fell down dead in Court and never revived to the astonishment of the

---

1   Cf. Estelle Frances Ward, *Christopher Monck Duke of Albemarle* (London: John Mur-ray, 1915).

Spectators" (*The Portledge Papers* 125). The following year, in a letter dated 17 September 1692, Lapthorne relates the ominous news that "[t]he Dutchess of Albemarle was marryed to the Lord Muntegue the same day the earthquake [that shook the earth "throughout all London citty and suburbs"] happened" (146-47). As Lapthorne's entries suggest, and as Manley well knew, the famous lawsuit was of interest not only because of what happened within but also, and perhaps primarily, because of what happened outside of the courtroom in the not so hermetically enclosed personal and domestic sphere.

At the root of the famous lawsuit was a will drawn up in 1675 by Christopher Monck, the second Duke of Albemarle, in which he bequeathed his vast fortune to his cousin Lord Bath and his heirs-male. In 1681, Albemarle effectively reinforced the document's validity with a Deed of Release that made Bath heir of all his possessions, and which clearly stipulated the conditions under which the will could be changed: a new will must be signed by six witnesses, of whom three were to be peers, and the old will and deed revoked only if accompanied by the exchange of sixpence. Although the deed was drafted in secret, through a conduit of gossips, Elizabeth, the Duchess of Albemarle, became apprised of the document and, in response, redoubled her efforts to pressure her husband into drawing up a new will. The Duchess had always opposed Lord Bath's interests, championing instead the cause of Colonel Thomas Monck and, after his death, that of his sons Christopher and Henry (cf. *Rivella* 77-79). Apparently succumbing to the coercive tactics of the by then insane Duchess, the Duke had a new will drawn up in the winter of 1685, which remained unsigned until July 1687, despite threats from the Duchess's physicians (and co-conspirators) that failure to comply with her demands would incite a return of her "'former malady'" (Ward 230). In the interim, in the midst of spies hired by the Duchess to listen in on their conversations, Albemarle assured Bath that he would do everything in his power to secure the validity of the first will, and Bath, who sought the additional confirmation of legal counsel, reported to Albemarle the reassuring news that the will could be revoked only in the manner prescribed in the deed. When Albemarle, then Governor of Jamaica, finally signed the second will, there were only three witnesses present (none of them peers) and no giving of sixpence. Albemarle clearly believed in the prevailing authority of the initial settlement.

Others, however, did not. The legal complications surrounding the two wills and deed only intensified with Albemarle's death in 1688. By then, Colonel Thomas Monck, primary heir to the second will, was also dead, leaving his claims to the Albemarle fortune to his fourteen-year-old son Christopher. Bath continued to claim full rights to the estate; as Narcissus Luttrell records in his entry of 1 July 1691: "A great suit in chancery is commenced between the dutchesse of Albemarle and the earl of Bath, about part of the estate of the late duke of Albemarle" (II.259). A year later, the Duchess married the unscrupulous Ralph Montagu. According to Estelle Ward, Montagu married the widow under a variety of false pretenses in order to manoeuvre his way into her inheritance as well as to contest the will of 1675. Apparently, in response to the Duchess's refusal to marry any man short of an emperor, Montagu effected the union by disguising himself as the Emperor of China, having convinced her that the reconstruction of his burned down Bloomsbury mansion was in fact the construction of the Great Wall (344). Ward goes on to speculate, and Manley's account likewise suggests, that Montagu was assisted by the Duchess's two women attendants (cf. *Rivella* 80). Two years later, in 1694, Montagu and Bath became allies against George Monck's cousins, who filed a suit claiming that Monck's marriage to Anne Clarges was not legal, and thus that their son Christopher Albemarle was not the rightful, legitimate heir to the fortune. Four years later, after resuming their feud, Bath agreed to an arrangement with Montagu and the Duchess in which he relinquished his claim to the Duchess's lifetime estates. Bath then convinced Christopher Monck to sell all his rights to the Albemarle estates in exchange for £1000 per year and the manor of Flourny (cf. *Rivella* 91), a deal that neither Monck nor Bath enjoyed for long: Monck died in July and Bath shortly after in August 1701. Eight years later, in March 1709-10, Ralph Montagu also died, only months after the Monck cousins resumed their lawsuit after a seven-year injunction that stopped the proceedings, and which was finally settled with the Lord Chancellor's dismissal of the claims with costs paid to the heirs-at-law. The Duchess, whose death Montagu had eagerly awaited, lived on until 1734, her estate of over £120,000 divided among various relatives. Whether or not Manley was as involved in this complex legal drama as *Rivella* indicates remains largely a matter of speculation. Clearly, she formed part of an important circle of players by virtue of her close relationships with two of the trial's lawyers: her estranged husband John Manley and her lover John Tilly, with whom she lived from 1697 until his mercenary marriage to Margaret Reresby in 1702. Just how amicable her relationship with John Manley was during their involvement in the lawsuit is uncertain. By the time she had begun her literary career with the production of her first two plays in London in 1696, two years had elapsed since she left her bigamous husband, who had already returned to Parliament for the second time and had been employed, for two years, as barrister and steward to the Tory Lord-Lieutenant of Devon and Cornwall, John Granville, first Earl of Bath. According to the (auto)biography, Rivella renewed friendly relations with him in order to assist "her sister authoress" (82) Calista (Catherine Trotter), whose friend's husband Cleander (John Tilly), Governor of the Prison at the Fleet, was facing charges of administrative graft. John Manley was, in fact, a member of the parliamentary committee established in December 1696 to investigate prison officials, including John Tilly, accused of accepting bribes in exchange for releasing prisoners.[1] As the account goes, Catherine Trotter evidently believed that Manley could influence her estranged husband to help free Tilly and thereby assist her ostensible object of concern, Tilly's wife. But as the narrative later reveals, Rivella's sister authoress has sexual rather than sisterly motives for seeking her assistance, for it is Cleander, not his wife, in whose interests Calista acts. As Fidelis Morgan points out, Manley's account of her renewal of relations with John Manley may also be disingenuous. After leaving Barbara Villiers in 1694, she may have gone to Cornwall, where her bigamous husband, his first wife, and (perhaps) his son John resided, before she returned to London in 1696. It is quite possible that financial necessity and concern for her son prompted Manley to maintain

---

1   According to Duff: "The whole prison system was a mass of graft and confusion.
     John Tilly typifies the easy and confused state of the prisons in his own career as warden of the Fleet" (86). For further details of Tilly's criminal activities see pp. 87-89.

contact with her cousin-husband regardless of whether the boy was in her actual care or not.[1]

Such half-truths and false pretenses form a persistent narrative thread in *Rivella*'s factually grounded lawsuit sequence, which features a full cast of dissimulators, from the highly polished Lord Crafty to the vulgar but self-important Tim Double, to the scheming retainer Old Simon. Lawyers, however, appear to be the narrative's central villains. As Lovemore suggests in reference to Crafty, those who practice law may be the greatest dissimulators: "fortune that caused him to be born the heir of a good family mistook his bent; she had done much better in making him an attorney, for there was no point how difficult or knotty soever, but what he could either untie or evade" (77). But Lovemore is himself no stranger to evasion. "Crafty" as well, from the moment Rivella becomes involved in the lawsuit in response to Calista's plea for assistance, Lovemore introduces a subplot of female deception and rivalry that strategically deflects attention from the corrupt legal system and its key players to its opportunistic pawns. If Calista's appeal to friendship is a ruse that veils her romantic interest in Cleander, Lovemore's account of women's involvement in the lawsuit is a cover for his deep-seated belief in the exclusivity and integrity of the masculine domain of law. Caught in his own knotty dilemma, Lovemore can appease his male auditor only by introducing romantic (and domestic) intrigue into the very jurisdiction that would prohibit it access.

Despite the lawsuit's rich array of devious males, including the primary claimants Lord Crafty, Baron Meanwell, and Tim Double, and the lawyer-criminals, Cleander and Oswald, it is arguably devious and / or spiteful females who provide Lovemore's primary focus, beginning with the deceptive Calista, whom he terms "the most of a *prude* in her outward professions, and the least of it in her inward practice" (83).[2] Vested with the talent of dissimulation particularly where romance is concerned, women also possess the power to destroy a rival's reputation (recall Hilaria earlier), as Lovemore cautions Rivella, who has captivated the married Cleander: "Wives were with reason

---

1   See Fidelis Morgan, *A Woman of No Character* 70-71, for a speculative discussion of Manley's whereabouts from 1694-96 before her return to London.
2   See p. 103, note 1.

so implacable, so invenomed against those who supplanted them, that they never forbore to revenge themselves at the expence of their rival's credit; for if nothing else ensued, a total deprivation of the world's esteem, was sure to be the consequence of an injured wife's resentment" (86). Lovemore concludes his account of the lawsuit with yet another "termagant"'" (86), Cleander's second wife, whom he denounces as "always speak[ing] of [Rivella] with language most unfit for a gentlewoman, and [as having] used her with the spite and ill nature of an enraged jealous wife" (106). Within the parameters of the lawsuit itself, however, the aspiring actress Bella and Rivella's servant Mrs. Flippanta figure as the heroine's greatest enemies, each duped by Crafty's pawn Old Simon, who convinces Bella that "Rivella was her mortal enemy" and persuades Mrs. Flippanta to enter into "a confederacy against her mistress" (98). Enemies of Rivella, Bella, and Flippanta are also the primary saboteurs of Rivella, Cleander, and Oswald's greedy attempts to reap financial gain from the lawsuit. Encouraged by Flippanta, Bella succeeds in seducing Tim Double, the key to John Tilly's ill-conceived money-making scheme. That the hapless aspiring actress ends up in a "poor woman's house in an obscure part of the town" is clearly fair punishment according to Lovemore, who defends Cleander's refusal to assist her: "had she not seduced Tim Double from his engagements, Cleander would have taken care of her interests so far (since her highest ambition was only to be a mistress) as that the Squire should have done something for her above that extream contempt which her vices have since brought upon her" (100). It would appear that "treacherous" Bell gets only what she deserves in a world of masculine law where it is indeed treacherous for women to hold sway.

Lovemore's plots of female betrayal and rivalry thus ultimately unmask not his heroine's enemies but his own fear of women's power to influence the public realms of law and politics. But Lovemore's fear is also his culture's, a fear that finally led to Manley's arrest for libel in October 1709. And as Lovemore himself suggests, Manley's enemies belonged to both camps, not only to the Whigs who orchestrated her arrest and under whose judgment she fell, but also to the Tories in whose service she wrote and from whom she received only nominal rewards. It is, however, through Rivella's "impartial historian," an amalgam of friend and enemy, supporter and circumscriber, that Manley most fully elaborates the gender-based politics of treachery. Like the judge(s) in front of whom Rivella, "with an air full of penitence" (110), claims inspiration as the animating purpose behind her writings, Lovemore at last exacts her admission that "politicks is not the business of a woman" (112). Reintegrating her once again into the realm of romance, Lovemore literally proffers Rivella for consumption, tantalizing D'Aumont with a vision of her table "well furnished and well served," followed by the prospect of her bed "nicely sheeted and strowed with roses, jessamins or orange-flowers" (113).

Fittingly, Rivella's consumption/consummation occurs in the realm of imagination beyond textual (and sexual) boundaries, the penetration of her (bawdy) body a perpetually deferred male fantasy. And so it is with Rivella's history, whose narrator neither makes her his mistress nor (re)forms the events of her life into a tale of pure romance. That Lovemore's heroine finally repudiates politics for "more gentle pleasing theams" (112) speaks to Manley's struggle against the pervasive cultural interdictions that would exclude women from public activities and forms of expression. But, as her subsequent political writings confirm, it does not speak to her capitulation. As her "life story," *Rivella* suggests, Manley could repudiate the business of politics only by also disavowing the inextricable demands of romance. Lovemore himself requires of Rivella what his biography of her renders impossible, for as discrete as he would wish the boundaries of masculine and feminine spheres to be, it is his own account of the "mistress of the art of love" that bears continual testimony to the indivisibility of masculine and feminine, public and private, domains. Lovemore may, in the end, invoke the law that would punish women for straying from the realm of love, but it is finally his unrepentant subject and creator who reveals that "our laws [are] defective" (111), themselves testimonials to the flawed and misguided cultural legislators who would dare pronounce judgment on her.

A Note on the Text

This text is based on the first edition, published by Edmund Curll in 1714. There were three subsequent publications of the novel: the 1715 edition entitled *The Adventures of Rivella; or, The History of the Author of the Four Volumes of the New Atalantis*; the 1717 edition entitled *Memoirs of the Life of Mrs. Manley*; and the 1725 edition bearing the title *Mrs. Manley's History of Her Own Life and Times*. With the exception of the fourth (1725) edition, which includes Curll's preface to the reader (see Appendix A.i), and minor typographical variations between the exact 1715 and 1717 keys and the 1725 key, all four editions are identical. I have included Curll's key to *Rivella* (see Appendix A.ii), which appears at the end of my 1714 copytext, and which is an exact replica of the 1725 key. My thanks to Rosalind Ballaster who explained to me that the 1714 key was obviously bound in at a later date, since revealing the actual names of the fictionalized characters, on first publication, would have undermined the purpose of the *roman à clef*.

Brief though it is, *Rivella* provides a challenging array of eighteenth-century grammatical and typographical conventions, many of which I have approached with editorial restraint. The novel's royalist flavour, for example, is compromised by the modern resistance to capitals; therefore, virtually all capitalized words that designate ranks and titles of persons, from kings down to squires, have been retained. Elsewhere, I have dispensed with most capitals. Spelling inconsistencies such as *ingage* and *engage*, *joyn* and *join*, and *forgo* and *forego* remain inconsistent in keeping with eighteenth-century practice. The clipped and colloquial *tho'* and *'em* are also preserved; however, contracted forms such as *shou'd*, *chang'd* and *sob'd* become *should*, *changed*, and *sobbed*. Obvious printing errors have been silently amended.

Punctuation remains largely untouched, although periods replace colons that previously joined breathlessly accretive independent clauses. Any additional changes in punctuation are indicated in the footnotes. Italicization has been pushed in the direction of modern practice with the disappearance of italicized proper nouns such as *Rivella* and *England*. Direct and indirect speech, also italicized in *Rivella*, has been romanized, with the exception of aphoristic phrases, such as Lovemore's pithy summary of the heroine with which he concludes his narrative. Italics disappear in the case of such anglicized words as *feint*, *foible* and *incognito*, but are retained for foreign words such as *eclaircisment* and *billet-deuxs*. As much as possible, italicization has been retained to preserve the nuances of emphasis and contrast that earmark Manley's dynamic speech. Finally, the copytext introduces quotation marks on only two occasions: in the translator's preface and in the dramatic clash between Rivella and Hilaria involving Hilaria's son. In the interests of consistency and simplicity, all quotation marks have been eliminated without imperilling the distinguishability of the speakers.

A Note on Manley's Christian Name

Following the lead of such scholars as Fidelis Morgan, Isobel Grundy, and Rosalind Ballaster, I agree that the final 'e' in *Delariviere* should be dropped in keeping with Manley's own anglicized spelling of her name. See especially Fidelis Morgan, *A Woman of No Character: An Autobiography of Mrs. Manley* (14). For other discussions of the controversy over Manley's Christian name, see Patricia Köster ("Delariviere Manley and the DNB: A Cautionary Tale about Following Black Sheep" 106-111) and Dolores Diane Clark Duff ("Materials Toward a Biography of Mary Delariviere Manley" 13).

Delarivier Manley: A Brief Chronology

1660:   Restoration of Charles II.

1663:   Delarivier Manley born.

1665:   Her father, Roger Manley, back in England after exile in Holland.

1667:   Roger Manley stationed on the island of Jersey; becomes lieutenant-governor in October.

1672:   Roger Manley and family leave Jersey.

1679:   John Manley, Delarivier Manley's cousin, marries Ann Grosse.

1680:   Manley family moves to Landguard Fort, Suffolk, where Roger Manley serves as governor.

1685:   Captain Francis Braithewaite's Twelfth, or Suffolk, Regiment comes to Landguard Fort; Delarivier falls in love with James Carlisle. James II assumes the throne.

1687:   Roger Manley dies.

1688:   Brother, Edward, dies. James II deposed; William and Mary accede to the throne.

1689:   Marries the bigamous John Manley.

1691:   Birth of her son, John.

1693:   Brother, Francis, dies.

1694:   Resides for six months with Barbara Palmer, Duchess of Cleveland. Travels throughout the West country until 1695 or 1696.

1695:   Dedicates poem to Catherine Trotter, author of *Agnes de Castro*.

1696:   Shares friendship with Skipwith. *Letters Written by Mrs. Manley*. *The Lost Lover* and *The Royal Mischief* produced.

1697:   Affair with John Tilly begins.

1700:   *The Nine Muses*, a collection of elegiac poems on the death of John Dryden, possibly organized by Manley.

1702:   Tilly, heavily in debt, marries Margaret Reresby. Anne becomes queen. Tories achieve victory in the general election.

1705:   Whigs make significant gains in the general election, sharing almost equal power in the House of Commons. *The Secret History of Queen Zarah and the Zarazians.*

1707: *Almyna* and *The Lady's Paquet Broke Open.*

1709: Possible author of *The Female Tatler. New Atalantis* (2 vols.). Arrested for libel.

1710: Case dismissed. *Memoirs of Europe* (2 vols.). Tories rise to power.

1711: *Court Intrigues* (previously published as *The Lady's Paquet Broke Open*); *The Duke of M——h's Vindication*; *A Learned Comment on Dr. Hare's Sermon*; *A True Narrative of ... the Examination of the Marquis de Guiscard*; *A True Relation ... of the Intended Riot and Tumult on Queen Elizabeth's Birthday*; and the *Examiner*, nos. 46-52.

1713: John Manley dies. *The Honour and Prerogative of the Queen's Majesty Vindicated and Defended.*

1714: Queen Anne dies; succession to throne of German-born George I. *The Adventures of Rivella* and *A Modest Enquiry.*

1717: *Lucius, the First Christian King of Britain.*

1720: *The Power of Love in Seven Novels.*

1724: Manley dies 11 July.

1725: *Bath Intrigues* and *A Stagecoach Journey to Exeter* (reissue of *Letters Written by Mrs. Manley*).

THE
ADVENTURES
OF
RIVELLA;
OR, THE
HISTORY
Of the AUTHOR of the
ATALANTIS.
WITH

Secret *Memoirs* and *Characters* of several
confiderable Perfons her *Cotemporaries.*

Deliver'd in a Converfation to the Young
Chevalier D'AUMONT in *Somerfet-Houfe*
Garden, by Sir CHARLES LOVEMORE.

Done into Englifh *from the* French.

L O N D O N:
Printed in the Year M. DCC. XIV.
Price 2 *s.* in Sheep, 2 *s.* 6 *d.* in Calf's Leather.

Frontispiece to the 1714 edition of *The Adventures of Rivella*.

THE TRANSLATOR'S PREFACE.

THE French publisher has told his reader, that the means by which he became master of the following papers, was by his being Gentleman of the Chamber to the young Chevalier D'Aumont when he was in England with the Ambassador of that name. He recounts in his preface, that after the conference in Somerset-House Garden,[1] those two persons were at supper together, where himself attended; and that the young Chevalier laid a discretion with Sir Charles Lovemore[2] (who reproached him with not being attentive to his relation) that he would recite to him upon paper most of what he had discoursed with him that evening, as a proof both of the goodness of his memory, and great attention: that soon after he, the publisher, was employed at several times, as amanuensis to the said Chevalier, by which means the papers remained in his hands at the death of young D'Aumont, which happened by a fever, soon after his return into France.

The English reader is desired to take notice that the verses are not to be found in the French copy; but to make the book more perfect, care has been taken to transcribe them with great exactness from the English printed tragedy of the same author, yet extant among us.[3]

London, June 3d, 1714.

---

1 London's riverside palace, constructed *circa* 1547, where such female royals as Catherine of Braganza (Charles II's queen) lived. George Monck's ("Old Double's") body lay in state for months at Somerset House. The building, transformed in the nineteenth century into, among other things, a repository for proved wills, also housed one of the original drafts of the 1687 will of Christopher Monck (*Rivella*'s "Merchant Double").

2 According to Curll's key and most scholars, John Tidcomb (1642-1713), appointed colonel of a regiment of foot in 1692 and made a major general in 1705. See introduction for discussion of Tidcomb.

3 The verses precede Manley's play *The Royal Mischief* (April 1696), which had a run of six nights at Lincoln's Inn Fields; it was later satirized in the anonymously-authored play *The Female Wits* (1697). See *Rivella* 68-69.

THE HISTORY OF RIVELLA

INTRODUCTION

ON one of those fine evenings that are so rarely to be found in England, the young Chevalier D'Aumont, related to the Duke of that name, was taking the air in Somerset-House Garden, and enjoying the cool breeze from the river; which after the hottest day that had been known that summer, proved very refreshing. He had made an intimacy with Sir Charles Lovemore, a person of admirable good sense and knowledge, and who was now walking in the garden with him, when D'Aumont leaning over the wall, pleased with observing the rays of the setting sun upon the Thames, changed the discourse; dear Lovemore, says the Chevalier, now the Ambassador is engaged elsewhere, what hinders me to have the entire command of this garden? If you think it a proper time to perform your promise, I will command the door-keepers, that they suffer none to enter here this evening, to disturb our conversation. Sir Charles having agreed to the proposal, and orders being accordingly given, young D'Aumont re-assumed the discourse. Condemn not my curiosity, said he, when it puts me upon enquiring after the ingenious women of your nation. Wit and sense is so powerful a charm, that I am not ashamed to tell you my heart was insensible to all the fine ladies of the Court of France, and had perhaps still remained so, if I had not been softned by the charms of Madam Dacier's[1] conversation; a woman without either youth or beauty, yet who makes a thousand conquests, and preserves them too. I have often admired her learning, answered Lovemore, and to such a degree, that if the war[2] had not prevented me, I had doubtless gone to France to have seen amongst other

---

1 Anne Dacier (c.1654-1720), renowned for her French translations of such works as the poems of Anacreon and Sappho, and especially for her translations of Homer's *Iliad* and *Odyssey*.

2 Most likely the War of the Spanish Succession (1701-13), in which the powers of France, Bavaria, and Spain fought against Britain, Austria, Prussia, Denmark, the Netherlands, and Savoy for succession to the Spanish throne following Charles II of Spain's death.

curiosities, a lady who has made her self admired by all the world. But I do not imagine my heart would have been in any danger by that visit, her qualifications are of the sort that strike the mind, in which the sense of love can have but little part. Talking to her is conversing with an admirable scholar, a judicious critick, but what has that to do with the heart? If she be as *unhandsom* as fame reports her, and as *learned*, I should never raise my thoughts higher than if I were discoursing with some person of my own sex, great and extraordinary in his way. You are, I find, a novice, answered D'Aumont, in what relates to women; there is no being pleased in their conversation without a mixture of the sex which will still be mingling it self in all we say. Some other time I will give you a proof of this, and do my self the honour to entertain you with certain memoirs relating to Madam Dacier, of the admiration and applause she has gained, and the con-quests she has made; by which you will find, that the Royal Academy[1] are not the only persons that have done her justice; for whereas they bestowed but the prize of eloquence, others have bestowed their heart. I must agree with you, that her perfections are not of the sort that inspire immediate delight, and warm the blood with pleasure, as those do who treat well of love. I have not known any of the moderns in that point come up to your famous author of the *Atalantis*. She has carried the passion farther than could be readily conceived. Her Ger-manicus on the embroidered bugle bed, naked out of the bath: – her young and innocent Charlot, transported with the powerful emotion of a just kindling flame, sinking with delight and shame upon the bosom of her lover in the gallery of books: Chevalier Tomaso dying at the feet of Madam de Bedamore, and afterwards possessing her in that sylvan scene of pleasure the garden;[2] are such representatives of nature, that must warm the coldest reader; it raises high ideas of the dignity of human kind, and informs us that we have in our composi-tion, wherewith to taste sublime and transporting joys. After perusing her inchanting descriptions, which of us have not gone in search of

---

1   The precise referent remains unclear. Dacier received accolades from members of
     L'Académie Francaise and *L'Académie Royale des Inscriptions et Médailles* (later called
     L'Académie des Inscriptions et Belles Lettres). Her father, Tanneguy Le Fèvre, was a dis-
     tinguished member of *L'Académie Royale*, so named by Louis XIII in 1611. See F.
     Farnham, *Madame Dacier* (1976).
2   Cf. *New Atalantis* Appendix B. iii.

raptures which she every where tells us, as happy mortals, we are capable of tasting. But have we found them, Chevalier, answered his friend? For my part, I believe they are to be met with no where else but in her own embraces. That is what I would experience, replied D'Aumont, if she have but half so much of the practic, as the theory, in the way of love, she must certainly be a most accomplished person. You have promised to tell me what you know of her life and conduct; I would have her mind, her person, her manner described to me; I would have you paint her with as masterly an hand, as she has painted others, that I may know her perfectly before I see her.

Is not this being a little too particular, answered Sir Charles, touching the form of a lady, who is no longer young, and was never a beauty? Not in the least, briskly replied the Chevalier, provided her mind and her passions are not in decay. What youthful charmer of the sex ever pleased to that height, as did Madam the Dutchess of Mazarin,[1] even to her death; tho' I am told she was near twice Rivella's age? Were not all eyes, all hearts, devoted to her, even to the last? One of the most lovely Princes of the Court reduced himself almost to beggary, only, to share with others, in those delights which she was capable of dispensing? Last night I heard Mr. C——[2] discoursing of her power; he was married, as you know, to a lady perfectly beautiful, of the age of sixteen, who has set a thousand hearts on fire;[3] and yet he tells you, one night with Madam Mazarin made him happier, than the whole sex could do besides; which proceeded only (as himself

---

1   Hortense Mancini (1646-1699), niece of Cardinal Mazarin; she married and later separated from Charles de la Porte, the abusive and mad former duke of Meilleraye and Mayenne, and later became a mistress to Charles II. Manley may have felt both a personal and a literary bond with the disreputable duchess, who likewise engaged in the process of self-fashioning in the autobiographical *Mémoires D'Hortense et de Marie Mancini* (1676). Manley's obvious admiration for the duchess was shared by other female literary contemporaries; Aphra Behn dedicated her novel *The History of the Nun: or, The Fair Vow-Breaker* (1689) to Mancini, and Mary Astell wrote her polemical *Some Reflections Upon Marriage* (1700) upon reading the legal briefs of the famous lawsuit that the duke brought against the duchess, in his attempts to force her to return to France from England following their separation. See Ruth Perry, *The Celebrated Mary Astell* (1986) 153-55.

2   Benedict Leonard Calvert (1679-1715), 4th Baron of Baltimore, great-grandson of George Calvert, 1st Baron of Baltimore and founder of Maryland.

3   Charlotte Lee (1678-1720), whose mother, Charlotte Fitzroy, was a child of Charles II and Barbara Cleveland.

remarks) from her being entirely mistress of the art of love; and yet she has never given the world such testimonies of it, as has Rivella, by her writings. Therefore, once more, my dearest friend, as you have, by your own confession, been long of her intimate acquaintance, oblige me with as many particulars relating to her life and behaviour as you can possibly recollect. By this time, the two cavaliers[1] were near one of the benches; upon which reposing themselves, Sir Charles Love-more, who perceived young D'Aumont was prepared with the utmost attention to hearken to what he should speak, began his discourse in this manner.

---

1   In this context, courtly, gallant gentlemen.

THE HISTORY OF RIVELLA

THERE are so many things praise, and yet blame-worthy, in Rivella's conduct, that as her friend, I know not well how with a good grace, to repeat, or as yours, to conceal, because you seem to expect from me an impartial history. Her vertues are her own, her vices occasioned by her misfortunes; and yet as I have often heard her say, if she had been a man, she had been without fault. But the charter of that sex being much more confined than ours, what is not a crime in men is scandalous and unpardonable in woman, as she her self has very well observed in divers places, throughout her own writings.

Her person is neither tall nor short; from her youth she was inclined to fat; whence I have often heard her flatterers liken her to the Grecian Venus.[1] It is certain, considering that disadvantage, she has the most easy air that one can have; her hair is of a pale ash-colour, fine, and in a large quantity. I have heard her friends lament the disaster of her having had the small-pox in such an injurious manner, being a beautiful child before that distemper; but as that disease has now left her face, she has scarce any pretence to it.[2] Few, who have only beheld her in publick, could be brought to like her; whereas none that became acquainted with her, could refrain from loving her. I have heard several wives and mistresses accuse her of fascination. They would neither trust their husbands, lovers, sons, nor brothers with her acquaintance upon terms of the greatest advantage. Speak to me of her eyes, interrupted the Chevalier, you seem to have forgot that index of the mind; is there to be found in them, store of those animating fires with which her writings are filled? Do her eyes love as well as her pen? You reprove me very justly, answered the Baronet, Rivella would have a good deal of reason to complain of me, if I should silently pass over the best feature in her face. In a word, you

---

1 Aphrodite, Greek goddess of love and beauty.
2 Smallpox often leaves indelible scarring. Manley's unlikely reversal of the ravaging effects of the disease anticipates, both by contrast and resemblance, such permanently scarred literary descendants, all testimonials to eighteenth-century English society's victimization of the "flawed" woman, as Lady Mary Wortley Montagu's Flavia in *Six Town Eclogues* (1716), Charlotte Lennox's Harriet Darnley in *Sophia* (1762), Charlotte Smith's Mrs. Manby in *The Old Manor House* (1793), and Frances Burney's Eugenia in *Camilla* (1796).

have your self described them. Nothing can be more tender, ingenious and brilliant with a mixture so languishing and sweet, when love is the subject of the discourse, that without being severe, we may very well conclude, the softer passions have their predominancy in her soul.

How are her teeth and lips, spoke the Chevalier? Forgive me, dear Lovemore, for breaking in so often upon your discourse; but kissing being the sweetest leading pleasure, 'tis impossible a woman can charm without a good mouth. Yet, answered Lovemore, I have seen very great beauties please, as the common witticism speaks, *in spight of their teeth*. I do not find but love in the general is well natured and civil, willing to compound for some defects, since he knows that 'tis very difficult and rare to find true symmetry and all perfections in one person. Red hair, out-mouth, thin and livid lips, black broken teeth, course ugly hands, long thumbs, ill formed dirty nails, flat, or very large breasts, splay feet; which together makes a frightful composition, yet divided amongst several, prove no allay to the strongest passions. But to do Rivella justice, till she grew fat, there was not I believe any defect to be found in her body: her lips admirably coloured; her teeth small and even, a breath always sweet; her complexion fair and fresh; yet with all this you must be used to her before she can be thought thoroughly agreeable. Her hands and arms have been publickly celebrated; it is certain, that I never saw any so well turned. Her neck and breasts have an established reputation for beauty and colour: her feet small and pretty. Thus I have run thro' whatever custom suffers to be visible to us; and upon my word, Chevalier, I never saw any of Rivella's hidden charms.

Pardon me this once, said D'Aumont, and I assure you, dear Sir Charles, I will not hastily interrupt you again, what humour is she of? Is her manner gay or serious? Has she wit in her conversation as well as her pen? What do you call wit, answered Lovemore. If by that word, you mean a succession of such things as can bear repetition, even down to posterity? How few are there of such persons, or rather none indeed, that can be always witty? Rivella speaks things pleasantly; her company is entertaining to the last; no woman except one's mistress wearies one so little as her self. Her knowledge is universal; she discourses well, and agreeably upon all subjects, bating a little affectation, which nevertheless becomes her admirably well; yet this thing is to be commended in her, that she rarely speaks of her own writings, unless when she would expressly ask the judgment of her friends, insomuch that I was well pleased at the character a certain person gave her (who did not mean it much to her advantage) that one might discourse seven years together with Rivella, and never find out from her self, that she was a *wit*, or an *author*.[1]

I have one pardon more to ask you, cried the Chevalier (in a manner that fully accused himself for breach of promise). Is she genteel? She is easy, answered his friend, which is as much as can be expected from the *en bonne point*.[2] Her person is always nicely clean, and her garb fashionable.

What we say in respect of the fair sex, I find goes for little, persued the Chevalier, I'll change my promise of silence with your leave, Sir Charles, into conditions of interrupting you when ever I am more than ordinarily pleased with what you say, and therefore do now begin with telling you, that I find my self resolved to be in love with Rivella. I easily forgive want of beauty in her face, to the charms you tell me are in her person. I hope there are no hideous vices in her mind, to deform the fair idea you have given me of fine hands and arms, a beautiful neck and breast, pretty feet, and, I take it for granted, limbs that make up the symmetry of the whole.

Rivella is certainly much indebted, continued Lovemore, to a liberal education, and those early precepts of vertue taught her and practised in her father's house. There was then such a foundation laid, that tho' youth, misfortunes, and love, for several years have interrupted so fair a building, yet some time since, she is returned with the greatest application to repair that loss and defect; if not with relation to this world (where women have found it impossible to be reinstated) yet of the next, which has mercifully told us, *mankind can commit no crimes but what upon conversion may be forgiven*.[3]

Rivella's natural temper is haughty, impatient of contradiction. She is nicely tenacious of the privilege of her own sex, in point of what

---

1 The unassuming writer, Rivella, contrasts sharply with the witless braggart, Marsil-ia (Manley's parodic counterpart), of *The Female Wits*.
2 A variant spelling of *embonpoint*, signifying plumpness; said especially of women.
3 Possibly an allusion to the teachings of Dr. Thomas Yalden (1670-1736), poet and divine, chaplain to Manley's patron, Henry Somerset, 2nd Duke of Beaufort. Yalden is identified in the key to *New Atalantis* as the Grand Druid. See Constance Clark, *Three Augustan Women Playwrights* (140-41).

respect ought to be paid by ours to the ladies; and as she understands good breeding to a punctuality, tho' the freedom of her humour often dispenses with *forms*, she will not easily forgive what person soever shall be wanting in that which custom has made her due. Her soul is soft and tender to the afflicted, her tears wait upon their misfortunes, and there is nothing she does not do to asswage them. You need but tell her a person is in misery to engage her concern, her purse, and her interest in their behalf. I have often heard her say, that she was an utter stranger to what is meant by hatred and revenge; nor was she ever known to persue hers upon any person, tho' often injured, excepting Mr. S——le,[1] whose notorious ingratitude and breach of friendship affected her too far, and made her think it the highest piece of justice to expose him.

Now I have done with her person, I fear you will think me too particular in my description of her mind. But Chevalier there lies the intrinsick value; 'tis that which either accomplishes or deforms a person. I will in few words conclude her character; she has loved expence, even to being extravagant, which in a woman of fortune might more justly have been termed generosity. She is grateful, un-alterable in those principles of loyalty, derived from her family: a little too vain-glorious of those perfections which have been ascribed to her; she does not however boast of what praise, or favours, persons of rank may have conferred upon her. She loves *truth*, and has too often given her self the liberty to *speak*, as well as *write* it.

She was born in Hampshire, in one of those islands, which former-ly belonged to France, where her father was governour;[2] afterwards he enjoyed the same post in other places in England. He was the second son of an ancient family;[3] the better part of the estate was

---

1   Sir Richard Steele (1672-1729), playwright, journalist, politician. Embroiled in a protracted public feud with Manley, Steele figures as Monsieur l'Ingrate in *New Atalantis* and as Isaac Bickerstaff, Stelico, and Don Phoebo in *Memoirs of Europe*. See Appendix C.

2   See introduction p. 21 for discussion of Manley's birthplace. Sir Roger Manley (1626-1687) was stationed in the Channel Islands from 1667 to 1672; on 2 Novem-ber 1667, he was made lieutenant-governor of the island of Jersey under Sir Thomas Morgan, after whose wife, Delariviere Morgan, Delarivier Manley was probably named. See Dolores Diane Clarke Duff, v and 13.

3   His father was Sir Richard Manley of Denbighshire, Wales. See Dolores Diane Clarke Duff, 9-10, who argues against a local historian's identification of Sir Roger's father with Cornelius Manley of Erbistock.

ruined in the Civil War by adhering to the Royal Family, without ever being repaired, or scarce taken notice of, at the Restoration.[1] The Governour was brave, full of honour, and a very fine gentleman. He became a scholar in the midst of a camp, having left the university at sixteen years of age, to follow the fortunes of K. Charles the First. His temper had too much of the stoick in it for the good of his family. After a life the best part spent in civil and foreign war, he began to love ease and retirement, devoting himself to his study, and the charge of his little post, without ever following the Court. His great vertue and modesty rendered him unfit for solliciting such persons, by whom preferment[2] was there to be gained; so that his deserts seemed buried and forgotten. In his solitude he wrote several tracts for his own amusement; his *Latin Commentaries* of the *Civil Wars of England*,[3] having passed through Europe, may perhaps have reached your notice, which is all that I shall mention to you of his writings,[4] because you are unacquainted with our English state of learning; and yet upon recollection, since the *Turkish-Spy* has been translated into other languages, I must likewise tell you that our Governour was the genuine author of the first volume of that admired and successful work. An ingenious physician, related to the family by marriage, had the charge of looking over his papers amongst which he found that manuscript, which he easily reserved to his proper use; and both by

1   A Royalist, Roger Manley fought in the garrison of Denbigh Castle during the First Civil War (1642-46) until its surrender to Parliament in 1645. In 1646, Manley, along with numerous other Cavaliers, escaped to Holland, where he remained until the Restoration of Charles II in 1660. His unrepaired estate may have been the result of the Act of Indemnity and Oblivion (1660). While some exiled Royalists recovered confiscated estates, many were forced to sell portions of their land because of government fines imposed for "delinquency"; others never recovered their properties. See also *New Atalantis,* in which Delia deplores her father's misfortunes following the Restoration: "[T]he suffering loyalty of our family, like virtue, met little else but it self for a reward. My father had, indeed, a military employment, which, tho' not of half the value of that paternal estate which was lavished in the Royal Service; yet upon his decease, we were sensible of the loss of it" (II.182).
2   Advancement, promotion. See introduction, p. 23.
3   The actual title is *Commentariorum de Rebellione Anglicana* (1686)[*History of the Rebellion in England, Scotland and Ireland* (1691)].
4   Roger Manley also translated into English the Dutch work by Francis Caron and Joost Schorten, *A True Description of the Mighty Kingdoms of Japan and Siam* (1663). He also wrote *A History of the late Warres in Denmark* (1670) and a continuation, covering the years 1676-86, of *The Turkish History* (1687) by Richard Knolles and Sir Paul Rycaut.

his own pen, and the assistance of some others, continued the work until the eighth volume, without ever having the justice to name the author of the first.[1]

But this is little relating to the adventures of Rivella, who had the misfortune to be born with an indifferent beauty, between two sisters perfectly handsom;[2] and yet, as I have often thought my self, and as I have heard others say, they had less power over mankind than had Rivella. Maria the eldest, was unhappily bestowed in marriage, (at her own request, by her father's fondness and assent to his daughter's choice) on a wretch every way unworthy of her,[3] of her fortune, her birth, her charms or tenderness.

My father's estate lay very near Rivella's father's government. I was then a youth, who took a great deal of delight in going to the castle, where three such fair persons were inclosed.

The eldest was now upon her marriage. Cordelia the youngest scarce yet thought of. Rivella had just reached the age of twelve, when I beheld the wonderful effects of love upon the heart of young and innocent persons. I had used to please my self in talking romantick stories to her, and with furnishing her with books of that strain. The fair Maria was six years elder, and above my hopes; I was a meer lad, as yet unfashioned; I beheld her with admiration, as we do a glorious sky; it is not yet our hemisphere, nor do we think of shining there. Rivella was nearer to my age and understanding, and tho' four

---

1   As Fidelis Morgan points out, Manley may have confused this work, generally ascribed to Giovanni Paolo Marana (1642-1693), with Roger Manley's *The Turkish History*. The "ingenious physician, related to [Manley's] family by marriage," remains unidentified.

2   Mary Elizabeth and Cornelia Manley.

3   Captain Francis Braithewaite, whose Twelfth, or Suffolk, Regiment came to Land-guard Fort, Suffolk, where Roger Manley was governor, on 11 July 1685 and returned to Yarmouth weeks later on 3 August (see Fidelis Morgan, *A Woman of No Character* 37-8). He married Mary Elizabeth Manley that year; a Catholic, Braithe-waite was disliked by the Manley children, though apparently not because of encouragement on the part of their father. Duff speculates that Roger Manley was then involved in some secret, possibly treasonable, business which linked him to Braithewaite. In the *Calendar of State Papers, Domestic* of 1681 and 1682, the names Manley and Mildmay are connected in a Royalist plot, and in a later volume, the names Braithewaite and Mildmay number among "Popish recusants" who were absolved, in 1685, from penalties previously incurred because of their faith (see "Materials Toward a Biography" 29-31).

years younger than my self, was the wittiest girl in the world. I would have kissed her, and embraced her a thousand times over, but had no opportunity. Never any young ladies had so severe an education. They had lost their mother when very young,[1] and their father, who had past many years abroad, during the exile of the Royal Family[2] had brought into England with him all the jealousy and distrust of the Spaniard and Italian. I have often heard Rivella regret her having never gone to school, as losing the innocent play and diversions of those of her own age. A severe *governante*, worse than any *duenna*,[3] forbid all approaches to the appartment of the fair; as young as I was, I could only be admitted at dinner or supper, when our family visited; but never alone. She was fond of scribling: tho' in so tender an age, she wrote verses, which considering her youth were pardonable, since they might very well be read without disgust; but there was something surprizing in her letters, so natural, so spirituous,[4] so sprightly, so well turned, that from the first to the last I must and ever will maintain, that all her other productions however successful they have been, come short of her talent in writing letters. I have had numbers of them; my servant used to wait on her as if to bring her books to read, in the cover of which I had contrived always to send her a note, which she returned in the same manner. But this was perfect fooling; I loved her, but she did not return my passion, yet without any

---

1 See introduction, pp. 21-22.
2 Charles I fled to Carisbrooke Castle on the Isle of Wight in November 1647; he was executed on 30 January 1649. The year in which Roger Manley returned to England is uncertain, but in 1665 he was living there as an ensign in the Royal Holland Regiment.
3 Governante: A governess, a female teacher.
   Duenna: A chaperon, an "old woman kept to guard a younger" (Johnson).
   According to Manley's Delia in *New Atalantis*, her father cared for and educated his nephew, Don Marcus (John Manley), as his own son. Apparently, while on his deathbed, Roger Manley entrusted him with the guardianship of Delia and her younger sister (Cornelia Manley). Marcus subsequently sent the girls "into the country, to an old out-of-fashion aunt" (see Appendix B.iv). This aunt may be the "severe governante" to whom Lovemore alludes. Patricia Köster, following the lead of Dolores Diane Clark Duff, identifies the aunt with Dorothy Manley (née Eyton) who married Roger Manley's brother, Francis, but Fidelis Morgan disproves the identification, suggesting the possibility of Sir Roger Manley's younger brother John's second wife, Mary (see *A Woman of No Character* 46).
4 Spirited, lively.

affected coyness, or personating a heroine of the many romances she daily read. Rivella would let me know in the very best language, with a bewitching air of sincerity and manners, that she was not really cruel, but insensible; that I had hitherto failed of inspiring her with new thoughts: since her young heart was not conscious of any alteration in my favour; but in return to that generous concern I expressed for her, she would instruct it as much as possible to be gratefull; 'till when my letters, and the pleasure of writing to me again, was a diversion more to her taste than any she met with besides; and therefore would not deny her self the satisfaction of hearing from, or of answering me, as often as she had an opportunity.

But all my hopes of touching her heart were suddenly blasted. To bring my self back to what I was just now telling you of the strange effects of love in youthful hearts, I must acquaint you that upon the report of an invasion from Holland,[1] a supply of forces was sent to the garrison, amongst which was a subaltern officer,[2] the most beautiful youth I remember to have ever seen, till I beheld the Chevalier D'Aumont; Monsieur D'Aumont told Sir Charles, with a smile, his compliment should not procure him a pause in his relation, and therefore conjured him to proceed.

This young fellow, pursued Lovemore, had no other pretences but those of his person, to qualify him for being my rival; neither of himself did he dream of becoming such; he durst not presume to lift up his eyes to the favourite daughter of the Governour; but alas! hers descended to fix themselves on him. I have heard her declare since, that tho' she had read so much of love, and that I had often spoke to her of it in my letters, yet she was utterly ignorant of what it was, till she felt his fatal power; nay after she had felt it, she scarce guessed at her disease, till she found her cure. Young Lysander, for so was my rival called, knew not how to receive a good fortune, which was become so obvious, that even her father and all the company perceived her distemper better than her self. Her eyes were continually fixed upon this young warrior, she could neither eat nor sleep; she became

---

1   The Duke of Monmouth invaded England from Holland in June/July 1685, approximately a month after the Duke of Argyle's expedition.
2   "A junior officer below rank of captain" (OED). James Carlisle (d. 1691) was an ensign in Braithewaite's Suffolk Regiment, as well as an actor and playwright; his play The Fortune Hunters was produced in 1689.

hectick, and had all the symptoms of a dangerous indisposition. They caused her to be let blood, which joyned to her abstinence from food, made her but the weaker, whilst her distemper grew more strong. The gentleman who had newly married her sister, was of counsel with the family how to suppress this growing misfortune; he spoke roundly to the youth, who had no thoughts of improving the opportunity, and charged him not to give in to the follies of the young girl; he told him he would shoot him thro' the head if he attempted any thing towards soothing Rivella's prepossession, or rather madness. Lysander who was passionately in love elsewhere, easily assured them he had no designs upon that very young lady, and would decline all opportunities of entertaining her; but as the Governour's hospitable table made most persons welcom, he forbore not to pursue his first invitation, and came often to dinner where the dear little creature saw him constantly, and never removed her eyes from his face. His voice was very good; the songs then in vogue amorous, and such as suited her temper of mind; she drank the poyson both at her ears and eyes, and never took care to manage, or conceal her passion; possibly what she has since told me in that point was true, that she knew not what she did, as not having freewill, or the benefit of reflection; nor could she consider any thing but Lysander, tho' amidst a croud.

The Governour was a wise man, and forbore saying any thing to the girl which might acquaint her with her own distemper, much less cause her to suspect that himself and others were acquainted with it. He caressed her more than usual, soothed and lamented her indisposition, proposed change of air to her; she fell a weeping, and begged she might not go to be sick from under his care, for that would certainly break her heart. He thought gentle methods were the best, and therefore ordered her sisters, and their governess, to do all they could to divert, but never to leave her alone with young Lysander.

In the mean time, by the interest the Governour made at Court, he procured that battalion to be recalled, and another to be deputed in place of what had given him so much uneasiness. The day before their marching orders came; he proposed playing after dinner for an hour or two at hazard;[1] most of the gentlemen present were willing

---

1 "A game at dice in which the chances are complicated by a number of arbitrary rules" (*OED*).

to entertain the Governour. Lysander excused himself, as having lost the last night, all his small stock at backgammon;[1] his little mistress heard this with a vast concern; and as she afterwards told me, could have readily bestowed upon him all she had of value in the world. Her father, who beheld her in a deep resvery,[2] with her eyes fixed intently upon Lysander, called her to him, and giving her a key where his money was kept, ordered her to fetch him a certain sum to play with; she obeyed, but no sooner beheld the glittering store, (without reflecting on what might be the consequence, or indeed any thing else but that her dear Lysander wanted money) than she dipt her little hand into an hundred pound bag full of guineas, and drew thence as much as it would hold. Upon her return she met him in the gallery; (seeing the company ingaged in play he was stolen off, possibly with an intent to follow Rivella, and have a moment to speak to her in without witnesses; for the regards he gave her from his eyes, when he durst encounter hers, spoke him willing to be grateful). She bid him hold out his hat and say nothing, then throwing in the spoil, she briskly passed on to the company, brought her father the money he wanted; returned him the key, and set her self down to overlook the gamesters.

This story I have had from her self, by which action she was since convinced of the greatness of her prepossession, being perfectly just by nature, principle, and education, nothing but love, and that in a high degree could have made her otherwise. The awe she was in of her father was so great, that upon the highest emergency she would not, durst not have wronged him of a single shilling. Whether the Governour never missed those guineas, as having always a great deal of money by him for the garrison's subsistence; or that he was too wise to speak of a thing that would have reflected upon his daughter's credit; Rivella was so happy as to hear no more of it.[3]

Mean time my affair went on but ill; she answered none of my letters, nay forgot to read them; when I came to visit her, she shewed me

---

1   A game played on a double board on which pieces are moved according to the throw of dice.
2   An obsolete form of reverie readopted in the seventeenth century from the forms *resverie* and *rêverie*.
3   The copytext contains a question mark here.

a pocket full which she had never opened; this vexed me excessively, and the more, when she suffered me with extream indifference to take them again. I would have known the reason of this alteration; she could not account for it, so that I left her with outward rage, but inwardly my heart was more her slave than before: whether it be the vile and sordid nature of the god of love[1] to make us mostly doat upon ungenerous usage, and at other times to cause us to return with equal ingratitude the kindness we meet from others.

The next day I ingaged my sister to make a visit to the castle; we took the cool of the morning, she was intimate with Maria before her marriage, and suffered her self to be persuaded to let me wait on her; we were drinking chocolate at the Governour's toilet,[2] where Rivella and her sisters attended; when the drums beat a loud alarm, we were presently told we should see a very fine sight, the new forces march in, and the old ones out, if they can properly be called so, that had not been there above eighteen days;[3] at the news my mistress, who had heard nothing of it before, began to turn pale as death; she ran to her papa, and falling upon his bosom, wept and sobbed with such vehemence, that he apprehended she was falling into hysterick fits. Her father sent for their governess to carry her to her bed-chamber, but she hung upon him in such a manner, that without doing her a great deal of violence, they could not remove her thence. I ran to her assistance with a wonder great as my concern, but she more particularly rejected my touches, and all that I could say for her consolation.

Mean time the Commander in Chief, followed by most of his officers (amongst which the lovely Lysander appeared with a languishing air full of disappointment, which yet added to his beauty) came up to the Governour, and told him his men were all under arms and ready to march forth, whenever he pleased to give the word of command. At the same time entred another gentleman equally attended, whom the Governour stept forth to welcome. He assured

---

1 Cupid. Lovemore employs the conventional rhetoric of emotional enslavement associated with the often cruel god of love.
2 Dressing room.
3 The Suffolk Regiment was stationed at Landguard Fort for twenty-four days. Given the travel time between Yarmouth and Landguard, the regiment's stay at the Fort was quite likely about eighteen days (see p. 52, note 3).

him the forces that obeyed him were all drawn up upon the counter-scarp,[1] and thought themselves happy, more particularly himself, to have the good fortune of being quartered where a person of such honour and humanity was Governour.

To conclude, poor Rivella fell from one fainting into another without the least immodest expression, glance or discovery of what had occasioned her fright. She was removed, and we had the satisfaction of seeing the military change of forces, and poor Lysander depart without ever beholding his mistress more.

Methinks, Monsieur le Chevalier, continued Lovemore, I am too fond of such particularities as made up the first scene of my unhappiness. I call it so, when I remember how dangerously ill that poor girl grew, and how my soul sickned at her danger. What avails it to renew past pains or pleasures? Rivella recovered, and begged she might be removed for some time to any other place, which would perhaps better agree with her than the air wherein I breathed. In a word, without ever having been beloved, my importunities now caused me to be for some time even hated by her.

The lady had a younger brother[2] who was pensioned at a Hugenot[3] minister's house on the other side of the sea and country, about eighteen miles farther from London, a solitude rude and barbarous. Rivella begged to be sent thither, that she might improve time,[4] and learn French. She would not have any servant with her for fear of talking English; nor would she ever speak to her brother in that language. What shall I say, so incredible was her application, tho' she had a relapse of her former distemper, that in three months time she was instructed so far as to read, speak and write French with a perfection truly wonderful; insomuch that when her father came to take her home, finding the air had very much impaired her health, the

---

1   "The outer wall or slope of the ditch, which supports the covered way" (*OED*).

2   Francis Manley, Delarivier's older brother, pursued a naval career, becoming Lieutenant of the York on 11 October 1688 and graduating to Captain of the Swan or Sun Prize in 1693. Manley died 17 June 1693, in France, as a result of wounds inflicted by the French, who took over the Swan.

3   Huguenots were adherents of the reformed faith in France; persecuted under the Catholic king, Louis XIV, many Huguenots emigrated to England and other countries in the late seventeenth century.

4   Make good use of time.

good minister, her master, who was a learned and modest person, begged the Governour to leave Mademoiselle with him, and he would engage in twelve months, counting from the time she first came, to make her mistress of those four languages of which he was master, *viz.*[1] Latin, French, Spanish and Italian.

The next day after her return, I came to pay my duty to her, and welcome her back; she was less averse, but not more tender. The respect I had for her, made me forbear to reproach her with the passion she had shewn for Lysander; my sisters tattling with her sisters, had gained the secret, and very little to my ease imparted the confidence to me. We began an habit of friendship on her side, tho' on mine it never ceased to be love. And I may very truly tell you, Chevalier, that such was the effect of that early disappointment, as has for ever hindered me from knowing the true pleasures of passion, because I have never felt a concern for any other woman, comparable to what I felt for Rivella.

After this short absence, I found my self condemned to a more lasting one. My father designed to send me abroad with an intent that I might spend some years in my travel. At the same time Rivella had the promise of the next vacancy for Maid of Honour to the Queen.[2] I congratulated her good fortune, acquainting her with my ill fortune in being condemned to separate my self from her. Tho' I was never happy in her love, yet I was jealous of losing her friendship, amidst the diversions of a Court, and the dangers of absence. Who does not know the fervency of our early passions? I begged to secure her to me, by a marriage unknown to our parents, but I could not prevail with her; she feared to displease her father, and I durst not ask the consent of mine. I had flattered my self that it was much easier to gain their pardon than procure their approbation, because we were both so young. But Rivella was immoveable, notwithstanding all I could say to her. How often for her sake, have I lamented her disdain, and little foresight, for refusing to marry me, which had she agreed to, all those misfortunes that have since attended her, in point of honour and the world's opinion, had probably been prevented, which shews there is

---

1   An abbreviated form of *videlicet*; namely, in other words.
2   Mary Beatrice of Modena (1658-1718), Italian Catholic daughter of Alphonso IV, Duke of Modena, and second wife of James II.

something in what the vulgar conceive, of *its being once in our lives in our own power to make or assist our fortune.*

I departed for Italy; the abdication immediately came on, the Queen was gone to France,[1] and Rivella thereby disappointed of going to Court. Her father was what he termed himself, truly loyal; he laid down his command and retired with his family, to a private life, and a small country-house,[2] where the misfortunes of his Royal Master sunk so deep into his thoughts, that he died soon after,[3] in mortal apprehension of what would befall his unhappy country.

Here begins Rivella's real misfortunes; it would be well for her, that I could say here she died with honour, as did her father. I must refer you to her own story, under the name of Delia, in the *Atalantis*, for the next four miserable years of her life. My self did not return from travel in three years. My father was also dead, and left me a fair estate without any incumbrance; my sister having been married some time before. I heard this news when I was upon my return, resolving to offer Rivella my whole fortune, as she was already possessed of my heart. Absence, nor the conversation of other women had not supplanted her in my esteem. When I thought of her genius and sprightly wit, comparison indeared her to me the more; but I was extreamly grieved and disappointed, when I learned her ruin. I will not tell you how much I was touched with it. I sought her out with obstinacy; but could not tell where to meet her. I was almost a year in the search, and then gave it over; till one night I happened to call in at Madam Mazarin's,[4] where I saw Rivella introduced by Hilaria, a Royal Mistress of one of our preceding Kings.[5] I shook my head in

---

1   James II was deposed in 1688. On 11 December he fled from Whitehall for France to be reunited with his wife and infant son, James Francis Edward, who had fled the palace on 9 December.

2   At Kew in Surrey.

3   See introduction, p. 23.

4   Most likely at her house on Paradise Row in Chelsea, where many of London's intellectuals and socialites gathered for such festivities as gambling and dinner parties.

5   Barbara Palmer (née Villiers, 1641–c.1707), Duchess of Cleveland, Countess of Southampton, Baroness Nonsuch, and Countess of Castlemaine; mistress to Charles II from 1660 to 1674. Manley lived with Cleveland on Arlington Street for six months, immediately upon leaving her sham marriage to John Manley in January 1694. As Rosalind Ballaster points out ("Introduction," *New Atalantis* x), Cleveland

beholding her in such company. I was so much improved by travelling, that, as she told me afterwards, she did not know me 'till I had spoken to her. I could not say the same thing of her. She was much impaired; her sprightly air, in which lay her greatest charm, was turned into a languishing melancholy; the white of her skin, degenerated into a yellowish hue, occasioned by her misfortunes, and three years solitude; tho' quickly after she recovered both her air and her complexion.

How confused and abashed she was at my addressing to her! The freedom of the place gave me opportunity to say what I pleased to her. She was not one of the gamesters, but begged me I would be pleased to retire, and spare her the shame of an *eclaircisment*[1] in a place no way proper for such an affair. I obeyed, and accepted the offer she made me of supping with her at Hilaria's house, where at present she was lodged; that lady having seldom the power of returning home from play before morning, unless upon a very ill run, when she chanced to lose her money sooner than ordinary.

Never was there a more desolate meeting than between my self and Rivella. She told me all her misfortunes with an air so perfectly ingenuous, that, if some part of the world who were not acquainted with her vertue, ridiculed her marriage, and the villany of her kinsman;[2] I, who knew her sincerity, could not help believing all she said. My tears were witnesses of my grief; it was not in my power to say any thing to lessen her's. I therefore left her abruptly, without being able to eat or drink any thing with her for that night.

Time, which allays all our passions, lessened the sorrow I felt for Rivella's ruin, and even made me an advocate to asswage hers. The diversions of the house she was in were dangerous restoratives. Her wit, and gaity of temper returned, but not her innocence.

(or perhaps John Manley) may have been the chief information source for Manley's fictionalized account of the court scandal in *New Atalantis*, in which Cleveland herself appears in the guise of Duchess de l'Inconstant.

1 A variant spelling of *éclaircissement*; revelation, explanation.

2 John Manley (1654-1713), son of Margaret Dorislaus and John Manley (Roger Manley's Puritan brother); also a Tory lawyer and Member of Parliament. He married the heiress, Ann Grosse (1655-c.1735), on 19 January 1678/9 and Delarivier Manley, bigamously, in 1689. See Appendix B.iv.

Hilaria had met with Rivella in her solitary mansion, visiting a lady who lived next door[1] to the poor recluse. She was the only person that in three years Rivella had conversed with, and that but since her husband was gone into the country. Her story was quickly known. Hilaria, passionately fond of new faces, of which sex soever, used a thousand arguments to dissuade her from wearing away her bloom in grief and solitude. She read her a learned lecture upon the ill-nature of the world, that would never restore a woman's reputation, how innocent soever she really were, if appearances proved to be against her; therefore she gave her advice, which she did not disdain to practice; the English of which was, to make her self as happy as she could without valuing or regretting those, by whom it was impossible to be valued.

The lady, at whose house Rivella first became acquainted with Hilaria, perceived her indiscretion in bringing them together. The love of novelty, as usual, so far prevailed, that herself was immediately discarded, and Rivella perswaded to take up her residence near Hilaria's; which made her so inveterate an enemy to Rivella, that the first great blow struck against her reputation, proceeded from that woman's malicious tongue. She was not contented to tell all persons, who began to know and esteem Rivella, that her marriage was a cheat, but even sent letters by the penny-post[2] to make Hilaria jealous of Rivella's youth, in respect of him who at that time happened to be her favourite.[3]

Rivella has often told me, that from Hilaria she received the first ill impressions of Count Fortunatus,[4] touching his ingratitude, immoral-

---

1   Anne Ryder (b. 1655), daughter of the scholar and diplomat Sir Richard Fanshawe, 1st Baronet, and Anne Harrison.

2   "An organization for the conveyance of letters or packets at an ordinary charge of a penny each" (*OED*).

3   Cardonell Goodman (b. 1653), actor and highwayman. He was sentenced for conspiring to have Barbara Cleveland's sons, the Dukes of Grafton and Northumberland, poisoned, but was later pardoned by James II in response to Cleveland's plea for clemency.

4   John Churchill, Duke of Marlborough (1650-1722), statesman and general; son of Sir Winston Churchill (d. 1688) and Elizabeth Drake; brother of Arabella Godfrey, and husband of Sarah Jennings (satiric target of Manley's *The Secret History of Queen Zarah*). Marlborough figures as Count Fortunatus, as well as the Marquis of Caria, in Manley's *New Atalantis*; Hippolito in *Queen Zarah*; and Stauracius the Thracian and Attilius Regulus in *Memoirs of Europe*.

ity, and avarice; being her self an eye-witness when he denied Hilaria (who had given him thousands)[1] the common civility of lending her twenty guineas at basset;[2] which, together with betraying his Master, and raising himself by his sister's dishonour,[3] she had always esteemed a just and flaming subject for satire.

Rivella had now reigned six months in Hilaria's favour, an age to one of her inconstant temper; when that lady found out a new face to whom the old must give place, and such a one, of whom she could not justly have any jealousie in point of youth or agreeableness; the person I speak of, was a kitchin-maid married to her master,[4] who had been refuged with King James in France. He died, and left her what he had, which was quickly squandered at play; but she gained experience enough by it to make gaming her livelihood, and returned into England with the monstrous affectation of calling her self a *French-woman*; her dialect being thence-forward nothing but a sort of broken *English*. This passed upon the town, because her original was so obscure, that they were unacquainted with it. She generally plied[5] at Madam Mazarin's basset-table, and was also of use to her in affairs of pleasure; but whether that lady grew weary of her impertinence, and strange ridiculous airs, or that she thought Hilaria might prove a better bubble;[6] she profited of the advances that were made her, and accepted of an invitation to come and take up her lodging at Hilaria's house, where in a few months she repaid the civility that had been shewn her, by clapping up a clandestine match between her

---

1 During Churchill's affair with Barbara Cleveland, she provided him with considerable sums. In 1672, for example, she gave him £5000 with which he purchased an annuity from George Savile, Marquis of Halifax; months later, he procured the position of captain in a foot regiment. (John Churchill's distant descendant, Sir Winston Churchill [1874-1965], refutes Manley's avaricious portrait of Marlborough in *Marlborough: His Life and Times* I:145.)

2 An obsolete card game, similar to Faro, especially popular among women in the seventeenth and eighteenth centuries.

3 Manley here alludes to John Churchill's desertion of the royal army at Salisbury in 1688 and to Arabella Godfrey's term as mistress to James II (then Duke of York), from whom she bore four children. John Churchill became a page at sixteen to the Duke; he later became Knight of the Garter and Captain-General of the Forces upon Anne's accession to the throne.

4 Identified in the key only as Madam Beauclair, pretended Frenchwoman and gamester.

5 Applied her trade, practised her craft.

6 A dupe.

patroness's eldest son,[1] a person tho' of weak intellects, yet of great consideration, and a young lady of little or no fortune.

But to return to Rivella. Hilaria was tired, and resolved to take the first opportunity to be rude to her. She knew her spirit would not easily forgive any point of incivility or disrespect.

Hilaria was *querilous, fierce, loquacious,* excessively fond, or infamously rude. When she was disgusted with any person, she never failed to reproach them with all the bitterness and wit she was mistress of, with such malice and ill-nature, that she was hated not only by all the world, but by her own children and family; not one of her servants, but what would have laughed to see her lie dead amongst them, how affecting soever such objects are in any other case. The extreams of *prodigality,* and *covetousness;* of *love* and *hatred;* of *dotage* and *aversion,* were joyned together in Hilaria's soul.

Rivella may well call it her second great misfortune to have been acquainted with that lady, who, to excuse her own inconstancy, always blasted the character of those whom she was grown weary of, as if by *slander* and *scandal,* she could take the odium from her self, and fix it upon others.

Some few days before Hilaria was resolved to part with Rivella, to make room for the person who was to succeed her; she pretended a more than ordinary passion, caused her to quit her lodgings to come and take part of her own bed. Rivella attributed this feint[2] of kindness to the lady's fears, lest she should see the man Hilaria was in love with, at more ease in her own house than when she was in hers; tho' that beloved person had always a hatred and distrust of Rivella. He kept a mistress in the next street,[3] in as much grandeur as his lady. He feared she would come to the knowledge of it by this new and young favourite, whose birth and temper put her above the hopes of bringing her into his interest, as he took care all others should be that approached Hilaria. He resolved, how dishonourable soever the procedure were, to ruin Rivella, for fear she should ruin him; and

---

1 Charles Fitzroy (1662-1730), Duke of Cumberland and Southampton, son of Charles II and Barbara Cleveland; he married Anne Pulteney (his second wife) in November 1694.

2 Pretense, display.

3 Identified in the key only as Mrs. Wilson of the Pope's Head Tavern in Cornhill.

therefore told his lady she had made advances to him, which for her ladyship's sake he had rejected; this agreed with the unknown intelligence that had been sent by the penny-post; but because she was not yet provided with any lady that would be her favourite in Rivella's place; she took no notice of her fears, but politickly chose to give her a great and lovely amusement; it was with one of her own sons, whom she caressed more than usual to draw him oftner to her house, leaving them alone together upon such plausible pretences, as seemed the effect of accident not design. What might have proceeded from so dangerous a temptation, I dare not presume to determine, because Hilaria and Rivella's friendship immediately broke off upon the assurance the former had received from the broken French-woman, that she would come and supply her place.

The last day she was at Hilaria's house, just as they sat down to dinner, Rivella was told that her sister Maria's husband was fallen into great distress, which so sensibly affected her, that she could eat nothing; she sent word to a friend, who could give her an account of the whole matter, that she would wait upon her at six a clock at night, resolving not to lose that post, if it were true that her sister was in misfortune, without sending her some relief. After dinner several ladies came in to cards; Hilaria asked Rivella to play; she begged her ladyship's excuse, because she had business at six a clock; they persuaded her to play for two hours, which accordingly she did, and then had a coach sent for and returned not till eight. She had been informed abroad that matters were very well composed touching her sister's affairs, which extreamly lightned her heart; she came back in a very good humour, and very hungry, which she told Hilaria, who, with leave of the first Dutchess in England[1] that was then at play, ordered supper to be immediately got ready, for that her dear Rivella had eat nothing all day. As soon as they were set to table, Rivella repeated those words again, that she was very hungry; Hilaria told her, she was glad of it, there were some things which got one a good stomach. Rivella asked her ladyship what those things were? Hilaria answered, Don't you know what? That which you have been doing

---

1   Mary Howard (*c.*1659-1705), Duchess of Norfolk. She married Henry (Howard) Duke of Norfolk in 1677; they were divorced in April 1700.

with my —— [and named her own son,][1] Nay, don't blush Rivella;
'twas doubtless an appointment, I saw him to day kiss you as he lead
you thro' the dark drawing-room down to dinner. Your ladyship may
have seen him attempt it, answered Rivella, [perfectly frighted with
her words,] and seen me refuse the honour. But why [replied Hilaria]
did you go out in a hackney-coach,[2] without a servant? Because [says
Rivella] my visit lay a great way off, too far for your ladyship's chair-
men to go. It rained, and does still rain extreamly; I was tender of your
ladyship's horses this cold wet night; both the footmen were gone on
errands; I asked below for one of them, I was too well mannered to
take the *black*, and leave none to attend your ladyship; especially when
my Lady Dutchess was here. Besides, your own porter paid the coachman, which was the same I carried out with me; he was forced to
wait some time at the gate, till a guinea could be changed, because I
had no silver; I beg all this good company to judge, whether any
woman would be so indiscreet, knowing very well, as I do, that I have
one friend in this house, that would not fail examining the coachman
where he had carried me, if it were but in hopes of doing me a prejudice with the world and your ladyship.

The truth is, Hilaria was always superstitious at play; she won
whilst Rivella was there, and would not have her removed from the
place she was in, thinking she brought her good luck. After she was
gone, her luck turned; so that before Rivella came back, Hilaria had
lost above two hundred guineas, which put her into a humour to
expose Rivella in the manner you have heard; who briskly rose up
from table without eating any thing, begging her ladyship's leave to
retire, whom she knew to be so great a mistress of sense, as well as of
good manners, that she would never have affronted any person at her
own table, but one whom she held unworthy of the honour of sitting
there.

Next morning she wrote a note to Hilaria's son, to desire the
favour of seeing him; he accordingly obeyed. Rivella desired him to
acquaint my lady where he was last night, from six till eight; he told
her at the play in the side box with the Duke of ——[3] whom he

---

1   Probably Charles Fitzroy, though possibly his brother George, Duke of Northum-
    berland (1665-1716).
2   A hired coach.
3   Not identified.

would bring to justify what he said. I chanced to come in to drink tea with the ladies; Rivella told me her distress; I was moved at it, and the more, because I had been my self at the play, and saw the person for whom she was accused, set the play out. In a word Rivella waited till Hilaria was visible, and then went to take her leave of her with such an air of resentment, innocence, yet good manners, as quite confounded the haughty Hilaria.

From that day forwards she never saw her more; too happy indeed if she had never seen her. All the world was fond of Rivella, and enquiring for her of Hilaria she could make no other excuse for her own abominable temper, and detestable inconstancy, but that she was run away with —— her son, and probably would not have the assurance ever to appear at her house again.

But I who knew Rivella's innocency, begged she would retire to my seat in the country, where she might be sure to command with the same power as if it were her own, as in effect it must be, since my self was so devoted to her service. I made her this offer because it could no longer do her an injury in the opinion of the world which was sufficiently prejudiced against her already; she excused her self, upon telling me she must first be in love with a man before she thought fit to reside with him; which was not my case, tho' she had never failed in respect, esteem and friendship for me. She told me her love of solitude was improved by her disgust of the world; and since it was impossible for her to be publick with reputation, she was resolved to remain in it concealed. She was sorry that the war[1] hindered her to go to France, where she had a very great inclination to pass her days; but since that could not be helped, she said her design was to waste most of her time in England in places where she was unknown.[2] To be short, she spent two years in this amusement; in all that time never making her self acquainted at any place where she lived. 'Twas in this solitude, that she composed her first tragedy,[3] which was much more famous for the language, fire and tenderness than the conduct. Mrs.

---

1 War of the Grand Alliance (also called War of the League of Augsburg, 1689-97), in which the British, under William III, joined with the Austrians, Germans, Savoyards, Dutch, and Spanish against Louis XIV.
2 In the West country (Devon and possibly Cornwall) from 1694 to 1696 (see Fidelis Morgan, *A Woman of No Character* 70-71).
3 *The Royal Mischief.*

Barry[1] distinguished her self as much as in any part that ever she played. I have since often heard Rivella laugh and wonder that a man of Mr. Betterton's[2] grave sense and judgment should think well enough of the productions of a woman of eighteen,[3] to bring it upon the stage in so handsom a manner as he did, when her self could hardly now bear the reading of it.

Behold another wrong step towards ruining Rivella's character with the world; the incense that was daily offered her upon this occasion from the men of vogue and wit. Her appartment was daily crouded with them. There is a copy of verses printed before her play, said to be writ by a great hand,[4] which they agreed to make their common topick when they would address to her. I have heard them so often recited, that I still remember them, which are thus in English. If you don't thoroughly understand it, I'll give you the words in French:

> What! all our sex in one sad hour undone?
> Lost are our arts, our learning, our renown,
> Since nature's tide of wit came roulling down:
> Keen were your eyes we knew, and sure their darts;
> Fire to our soul they send, and passion to our hearts!
> Needless was an addition to such arms,
> When all mankind were vassals to your charms:
> That hand but seen, gives wonder and desire,
> Snow to the sight, but with its touches fire!
> Who sees thy *yielding queen*, and would not be
> On any terms the blest, the happy he;
> Entranced we fancy all his extasie.

---

1 Elizabeth Barry (c.1658-1713), prominent actress whose career spanned thirty seven years. She played Homais, the leading role, in *The Royal Mischief*.

2 Thomas Betterton (c.1635-1710), actor and theatre manager. His company at Lincoln Inn Fields produced *The Royal Mischief* after Manley quarreled over its production with the Drury Lane company; Betterton played the role of Osman.

3 If the 1663 birthdate is correct (see introduction, pp. 20-21), Manley was in her early thirties at the time. Even if, as Lovemore earlier tells D'Aumont, Rivella [Delarivier] had been born during her father's term as governor of Jersey (1667-72), she would have been well into her twenties when the play was produced in 1696.

4 Possibly William Cavendish (1640-1707), Duke of Devonshire, judge, statesman, critic, and poet. See Constance Clark, 111-12, who casts doubt on Paul Bunyan Anderson's ascription of the "great hand" to Cavendish.

Quote *Ovid*[1] now no more ye amorous swains,
Delia than *Ovid* has more moving strains.
Nature in her alone exceeds all art;
And nature sure does nearest touch the heart.
Oh! might I call the bright discoverer mine,
The whole fair sex unenvied I'd resign;
Give all my *happy* hours to Delia's charms,
She who by writing thus our wishes warms,
What worlds of love must circle in her arms?

I had still so much concern for Rivella, that I pitied her conduct, which I saw must infallibly center in her ruin. There was no language approached her ear but flattery and persuasion to delight and love. The casuists[2] told her a woman of her wit had the privilege of the other sex, since all things were pardonable to a lady *who could so well give laws to others, yet was not obliged to keep them her self.* Her vanity was now at the height, so was her gaiety and good humour, especially at meat,[3] she understood good living, and indulged her self in it. Rivella never drank but at meals, but then it was no way lost upon her, for her wit was never so sparkling as when she was pleased with her wine. I could not keep away from her house, yet was stark mad to see her delighted with every fop, who flattered her vanity. I used to take the privilege of long acquaintance and esteem to correct her ill taste, and the wrong turn she gave her judgment in admitting adulation from such wretches as many of them were; tho' indeed several persons of very good sense allowed Rivella's merit, and afforded her the honour of their conversation and esteem. She looked upon all I said with an evil eye; believing there was still jealousy at the bottom. She did not think fit to correct a conduct which she called very innocent, for me whose passion she had never valued. I still preached, and she still went on in her own way, without any regard to my doctrine, till experience gave her enough of her indiscretion.

---

1   Latin poet (43 B.C.–*c.*17 A.D.), popular in Manley's day for his *Epistles*, which contain romantic letters from famous heroines of antiquity to their absent husbands or suitors.
2   Quibblers, sophists.
3   At meals.

A certain gentleman, who was a very great scholar and master of abundance of sense and judgment, at her own request, brought to her acquaintance one Sir Peter Vainlove,[1] intending to do her service as to her design of writing for the theater, that person having then interest enough to introduce upon one stage whatever pieces he pleased. This Knight had a very good face, but his body was grown fat. He was naturally short, and his legs being what they call somewhat bandy, he was advised to wear his cloaths very long, to help conceal that defect; insomuch that his dress made him look shorter than he was. He was following a handsom lady in the Mall,[2] after a world of courtship, and begging her in vain to let him know where she lived; seeing she was prepared to leave the park he renewed his efforts, offering to go down upon his knees to her, to have her grant his request; the lady turned gravely upon him, and told him she thought, he had been upon his knees all this time. The Knight conscious of his duck legs and long coat, retired in the greatest confusion, notwithstanding his natural and acquired assurance. Sir Peter was supposed to be towards fifty when he became acquainted with Rivella, and his constitution broken by those excesses, of which in his youth he had been guilty. He was married young to a lady of worth and honour,[3] who brought him a very large joynture; never any woman better deserved the character of a good wife, being universally obliging to all her husband's humours; the great love she had for him, together with her own sweetness of temper, made him infinitely easy at home; but he was detestably vain, and loved to be thought in the favour of the fair, which was indeed his only fault, for he had a great deal of wit and good nature; but sure no youth of twenty had so vast a foible for being admired. He wrote very pretty well-turned *billet-deuxs*;[4] he was not at all sparing of his letters when he met a woman that had any knack that way. Rivella was much to his taste, so that presently there grew the greatest intimacy in the world between them; but because he found she was a

---

1   Thomas Skipwith (1652-1710), 2nd Baronet of Methseringham, Lincolnshire, Member of Parliament, and part owner of the Drury Lane and Dorset Garden Theatres.
2   A fashionable promenade in London's St. James's Park.
3   Margaret Brydges, daughter of George Brydges, 6th Baron Chandos of Sudeley.
4   Love letters.

woman of fire, more than perhaps he could answer, he was resolved to destroy any hopes she might have of a nearer correspondence than would conveniently suit with his present circumstances, by telling her his heart was already prepossessed. This served him to a double purpose, *first*, to let her know that he was reciprocally admired: and *secondly*, that no great things were to be expected from a person who was engaged, or rather devoted to another. He made Rivella an entire confident of his amour, naming fine Mrs. Settee,[1] then of the city, at the head of her six tall daughters, not half so beautiful as their mother. This affair had subsisted ten years, according to the Knight's own account. The lady had begun it her self (falling in love with him at the temple-revels)[2] by letters of admiration to him; after some time, corresponding by amorous high-flown *billets*, she granted a meeting, but was three years before she would let him know who she was, tho' there were most liberties but that of the face allowed. Afterwards they met without any of that reserve. It cost the Knight according to his own report three hundred pounds a year (besides two thousand pounds worth of jewels presented at times) to see her but once a week, and give her a supper. He managed this matter so much to his own vain false reputation, that it was become a proverb amongst his friends, *Oh 'tis Friday night, you must not expect to see Sir Peter!* He put a relation of his own into a house, and maintained her there, only for the conveniency of meeting his mistress. This creature in some time proving very mercenary, and the Knight unwilling to be imposed upon, she dogged the lady home, and found out who she was; when once she had got the secret, she made Sir Peter pay what price she pleased for her keeping it; not that his *vanity* was at all displeased at the town's knowing his good fortune, for he privately boasted himself of it to his friends, but this baggage[3] threatned to send the husband and his own lady news of their amour.

Behold what a fine person Rivella chose to fool away her reputation with. I am satisfied that she was provoked at the confidence he

---

1 Identified in the key only as Mrs. Pym. A discrepancy exists between the novel and the key, the former of which refers to Settee's six daughters, and the latter of which states that she has four.
2 A festive event, such as a masque or a society ball, given by noblemen.
3 A disreputable or "immoral" woman; a prostitute.

put in her, and thought her self piqued in honour and charms to take him from his real mistress. She was continually bringing in the lady's age, in excuse of which the Knight often said, Settee was one of those lasting beauties that would have lovers at fourscore; he often admired the delicacy of her taste, upon which Rivella was ready to burst with spleen, because she would not permit her husband any favours after she was once engaged with his *Worship*, her conduct and nice reasoning forcing the *good plain man* to be contented with separate beds. Sir Peter was however exactly scrupulous in doing justice to the lady's honour; protesting that himself had never had the *last favour*, tho' she loved him to distraction, for fear of consequences; yet she never scrupled to oblige him so far, as to undress and go even into the naked bed with him once every week, where they found a way to please themselves as well as they could.

Rivella was wild at being always entertained with another woman's charms. Vainlove used to show her Mrs. Settee's letters, which were generally as long as a taylor's bill, stuffed with the *faux brillant*;[1] which yet fed the Knight's vanity, and almost intoxicated his brain. He had found an agreeable way of entertaining himself near Rivella, by talking incessantly of his mistress; he did not pass a day without visiting and showing her some of her *billet-deuxs*. Mean time he was so assiduous near Rivella, that Mrs. Settee took the alarm. He always sat behind her in the box at the play, led her to her chair, walked with her in the park, introduced her to his lady's acquaintance, and omitted no sort of opportunity to be ever in her company. Rivella put on all her arts to ingage him effectually, tho' she would never hear that she had any such design; but what else could she mean by a song which I am going to repeat to you, made upon the Knight's dropping a letter in her chamber, writ by his darling mistress, wherein she complained of his passion for Rivella? It began thus; It is in vain you tell me that I am worshipped and adored when you do things so contrary to it; Rivella immediately sent it back to him enclosed with these verses,

---

1 False brilliance.

I.

Ah dangerous swain, tell, tell me no more
Of the blest nymph you worship and adore;
When thy filled eyes are sparkling at her name
I raving wish that mine had caused the flame.

II.

If by your fire for her, you can impart
Diffusive heat to warm another's heart;
Ah dang'rous swain! what would the ruin be,
Should you but once persuade you burn for me?[1]

Tho' possibly this might be only one of the thoughtless sallies of
Rivella's wit and fire, yet it was of the last consequence to her reputation. The Knight was perfectly drunk with *vanity* and *joy*, upon
receiving such agreeable proofs of his merit. He caused the words to
be set to notes, and then sung them himself in all companies where
he came. His flatterers, who were numerous, and did not now want to
learn his weak side, gave him the title of *the dangerous swain*, which he
prided himself in; till his mistress grew down right uneasy, and would
have him visit Rivella no longer. He capitulated, as reason good, and
would be paid his price for breaking so tender a friendship, and what
so agreeably flattered his vanity, which in short was, as the scandalous
chronicle speaks, that his mistress should go to bed to him without
reserve. Either the weakness of his constitution, or the greatness of his
passion, was prejudicial to his health. He grew proud of the disorder,
and went into a publick course of physick, as if it were a worse matter; finding it extreamly for his credit, that the town should believe so
well of him (for upon report of a fair young lady whom he brought
to tread the stage, that he had passed three days and nights successive-
ly in bed with her without any consequence, he was thought rather
dangerous to a woman's reputation than her vertue) he would smile
and never disabuse his friends, when they rallied him upon his disorder. For some time poor Rivella's character suffered as the person that

---

1   Skipwith helped produce Manley's first play, *The Lost Lover*, first performed at
Drury Lane in March 1696; the song, "Ah dangerous swain," was sung in Act One,
Scene One.

had done him this injury, till seeing him equally assiduous and fond of her in all publick places, joined to what the operator[1] discovered of his pretended disease;[2] the world found out the cheat, detesting his vanity and Rivella's folly; that could suffer the conversation of a wretch so insignificant to her pleasures, and yet so dangerous to her reputation.

This short-lived report did not do Rivella any great prejudice, amongst the crowd of those who followed and flattered her with pretended adoration. She would tell me that her heart was still untouched, bating a little concern from her pride to move old Vainlove's, who so obstinately defended it for another. 'Tis true, she often hazarded appearances by indulging her natural vanity, and still continued to do so, tho' perhaps with more innocency than discretion; till the person came, who indeed fixed her heart. I am going to shew you a gentleman of undoubted merit, accomplished both from without and within. His face was beautiful, so was his shape, till he grew a little burly. He was bred to business, as being what you call in France, one of the long robe:[3] his natural parts prodigious, which were happily joined by a learned and liberal education: his taste delicate, in respect of good authors; remarkable for the sweetness of his temper, and in short, every way qualified for being beloved, where ever he should happen to love.

Valuing my self as I do upon the reputation of an impartial historian, neither blind to Rivella's weaknesses and misfortunes, as being once her lover, nor angry and severe as remembring I could never be beloved; I have joined together the just, and the tender, not expatiated with malice upon her faults, nor yet blindly overlooking them. If I have happened, by repeating her little vanities, to destroy those first inclinations you may have had to esteem what was valuable in her composition; remember how hard it is in youth, even for the stronger sex to resist *the sweet poyson of flattery, and well directed praise or admiration.*

During the short stay Rivella had made in Hilaria's family, she was become acquainted with the Lord Crafty.[4] He had been Ambassador

---

1 A doctor who performs surgical procedures.
2 Syphilis.
3 One who wears legal attire, especially lawyers.
4 Ralph Montagu (1638-1709), 1st Duke, Ambassador to Paris, and Member of Parliament. His first wife, Elizabeth Wriothesley, was the wealthy widow of Algernon

in France, where his negotiations are said to have procured as much advantage to your King,[1] as they did dishonour to his own country. He had a long head turned to deceit and over-reaching. If a thing were to be done two ways, he never loved the plain, nor valued a point if he could easily carry it. His person was not at all beholding to nature, and yet he had possessed more fine women than had the finest gentleman, not less than twice or thrice becoming his Master's rival. When Hilaria was in France he found it extreamly convenient for his affairs to be well with her,[2] as she was Mistress, and himself Ambassador. For some time 'tis supposed that he loved her out of inclination, her own charms being inevitable; but finding she was not very regular, he reproached her in such a manner, that the haughty Hilaria vowed his ruin. She would not permit a subject to take that freedom she would not allow a Monarch, which was, prescribing rules for her conduct. In short, her power was such over the King, tho' he was even then in the arms of a new and younger Mistress,[3] and Hilaria at so great a distance from him, as to yield to the plague of her importunity with which she filled her letters. He consented that Lord Crafty should be recalled, upon secret advice that she pretended to have received of his corruption and treachery. The Ambassador did not want either for friends in England, nor in Hilaria's own family, who gave him very early advice of what was designed against him. He had the dexterity to ward the intended blow, and turn it upon her that was the aggressor; Hilaria's own daughter[4] betrayed her to the Ambassador. He had corrupted not only her heart, but seduced her from her duty and integrity. Her mother was gone to take the Bourbon waters, leaving this young lady the care of her family, and more immediately of such letters as a certain person should write to her, full of amorous raptures for the favours she had bestowed. These fatal letters, at least

---

Percy, 11th Earl of Northumberland. He later married Elizabeth Cavendish, Christopher Albemarle's widow, on 8 September 1692.

1   Louis XIV.

2   Barbara Villiers lived with Montagu, as his mistress, in Paris.

3   Louise Renée de Keroualle (1649-1734), Duchess of Portsmouth and Aubigny. She met Charles II in 1670, when she accompanied the Duchess of Orleans to England to negotiate the Treaty of Dover, and became his mistress in 1671. Catholic and French, she was unpopular with Charles's subjects.

4   Köster identifies her in her index as Anne Palmer (b. 1661), Countess of Sussex, daughter of Barbara Palmer and Charles II or Philip Stanhope, 2nd Earl of Chesterfield.

several of them with answers full of tenderness under Hilaria's own hand, the Ambassador proved so lucky as to make himself master of.[1] He returned with his credentials to England to accuse Hilaria and acquit himself. The Mistress was summoned from France to justify her ill conduct. What could be said against such clear evidences of her disloyalty? 'Tis true, she had to deal with the most merciful Prince in the world, and who made the largest allowances for human frailty, which she so far improved, as to tell his Majesty, there was nothing criminal in a correspondence designed only for amusement, without presuming to aim at consequences; the very *mode* and *manner* of expression in *French* and *English*, were widely different; that which in one language carried an air of extream gallantry, meant no more than meer civility in t'other. Whether the Monarch were, or would seem persuaded, he appeared so, and ordered her to forgive the Ambassador; to whom he returned his thanks for the care he had taken of his glory, very much to Hilaria's mortification, who was not suffered to exhibit her complaint against him, which was looked upon as proceeding only from the malice and revenge of a vindictive guilty woman.

Lord Crafty made a very successful embassy touching his own interest, tho' he failed of bringing the Court altogether into those measures which the French King desired. His paternal estate was not more than five thousand pound a year, which he extreamly improved, as you may know by the rent-roll,[2] delivered in upon his son's marriage, which doubled that sum six times over, all due to his own contrivance, wherein he was assisted often by the ladies, which made him have a very great opinion of their management. This Lord used to value himself upon certain rules in policy, of trusting no person with his real designs. What part he gave any one in his confidence when they were to negotiate an affair for him, was in his own expression

---

1   Manley appears to be alluding to the events of 1678, leading up to the 'Popish Plot' to kill Charles II, when Barbara Cleveland complained to Charles II that Montagu had seduced their daughter. Montagu was dismissed from his embassy, and in retaliation revealed to the House of Commons Lord Treasurer Thomas Danby's letters to him tracing his part in the king's secret negotiations with Louis XIV, letters that led to Danby's impeachment and the dissolution of the Cavalier Parliament.

2   "A list of lands and tenements belonging to one, together with the rents paid on them" (*OED*).

but tying 'em by the leg to a table, they could not go farther than the line that held them. He was incapable of friendship but what made for his interest, or of love but for his own proper pleasures. Nature formed him a politician, and experience made him an artist in the trade of dissimulation; but the best that can be said of those great parts, which he put to so bad an use, is, that there was a wrong turn in his birth, fortune that caused him to be born the heir of a good family mistook his bent; she had done much better in making him an attorney, for there was no point how difficult or knotty soever, but what he could either untie or evade.

He was married to the relict[1] of one who had been the richest merchant in England;[2] she brought along with her not only a very large jointure, but a larger law-suit, which hit Lord Crafty's genius; he became much more in love with that than her person. Mr. Double her husband was childless, and had contracted an inviolable friendship with Baron Meanwell,[3] insomuch that they had interchangably made each other their heir by deed of gift.[4] Mr. Double's affairs called him abroad to the plantations,[5] which opportunity his wife took to

---

1   A widow, namely Elizabeth Cavendish (1654-1734), daughter of Henry, 2nd Duke of Newcastle. Her grandfather's second wife was the author Margaret Cavendish. See Appendix (H. 1).

2   Christopher Monck (1653-1688), 2nd Duke of Albemarle, son of General George Monck and Anne Clarges, appointed Governor of Jamaica in 1686; he married Elizabeth Cavendish in December, 1669. By the time of Albemarle's deed of 1681, which strengthened his will of 1675, the Duchess stood to inherit eight thousand pounds a year and the use of the manor, New Hall, for life. Elizabeth Albemarle also received, as part of her dower, an income from the rents of the manor of Grindon, as well as from such other sources as the customs collected as Searcher for the county of Kent, to which she held a patent, and a lace trade which yielded hundreds of pounds yearly. Estelle Ward points out that the Duchess died with a personal estate in excess of 120,000 pounds (352).

3   John Granville (1628-1701), 1st Earl of Bath, cousin of General George Monck and primary beneficiary of Christopher Albemarle's will of 1675.

4   "The transference of property in a thing by one person to another, voluntarily and without any valuable consideration" (OED).

5   To Jamaica, where Christopher Albemarle served as governor from 1686 to 1688. Likewise an important historical event for Manley's Tory precursor, Aphra Behn, Albemarle's Jamaican appointment inspired her commendatory poem *To the Most Illustrious Prince Christopher, Duke of Albemarle, on His Voyage to His Government of Jamaica: A Pindarick* (1687) on the occasion of Albemarle's departure for the island.

revenge her self upon the Baron, for advising her husband to pull down a very large house and to sell the ground and materials to the builders. This lady, who was remarkable for her pride, regretted so fine a seat,[1] and was resolved to punish Lord Meanwell for the loss of it. She persuaded her spouse to make a will in the Indies, whereby she relinquished one quarter part of her joynture, conditionally that Lord Meanwell's pretensions might be struck out; and young Double,[2] who had no relation to the merchant but the name, appointed heir to the estate. During King Charles the First's troubles, Merchant Double's father[3] resided at a seat he had in Essex near the sea-side,[4] he was walking one evening upon the strand, regarding several poor half naked, half starved passengers that were getting out of a ship lately come into the road; these miserable wretches were escaped from the Massacre in Ireland,[5] amongst them was a well looked woman with a boy in her hand, habited 'en peasant.[6] Mr. Double asked her several questions, which she answered to his satisfaction, amongst the rest that her name and her sons were Double, but her husband had been killed by the rebels, which affected him so much, that he ordered her home to his own house, where she remained the rest of her life. Her son was made Mr. Double's gardener; thriving under a flourishing family he

1 Possibly a reference to the events of 1682, when Albemarle, who was experiencing financial difficulties, was forced to sell his stately Albemarle house in London.
2 Christopher Monck (1674-1701), whom Christopher Albemarle adopted after the death of Christopher Monck's father, Thomas. Estelle Ward speculates that Thomas Monck may have been Christopher Albemarle's illegitimate elder brother. See *Christopher Monck* (68).
3 General George Monck (1608-1670), 1st Duke of Albemarle, Earl of Torrington, Viscount Coldstream, Baron Monck of Potheridge, Beauchamp, and Teyes. Monck held such royal and military offices as Gentleman of the Bedchamber, Knight of the Garter, Master of the Horse, Lord General of the Army, and Admiral of the Navy, and was awarded for his services to King Charles II with immense grants of Crown lands. Ward claims that Albemarle left £15,000 a year in income and £60,000 in property (*Christopher Monck* 46-7).
4 Manor of New Hall.
5 The Irish Rebellion of October-November 1641 in which the Irish Catholics, including the Anglo-Irish party and native Irish, massacred thousands of Protestants to retaliate prolonged religious persecution and social inequality. According to George Trevelyan, *England under the Stuarts*, some four to five thousand Protestants died in the uprising, not including those who perished from related causes, such as hunger (218-19).
6 In peasant's clothing.

married very well, and also left a son,[1] whom old Double put into the army, where he rose to be a lieutenant colonel; but did not die rich, leaving a widow and several children; the eldest of which, Merchant Double's lady had picked out, as an heir worthy to revenge her quarrel against the Lord Meanwell. Her husband died in the Indies not long after he had obliged his wife in a point so much to his dishonour, considering the deed he had executed in favour of the Baron. Some persons who knew the little regard he had for that worthless brood of the Doubles, thought he yielded to his lady's importunities only for a quiet life, thinking he did little more than make her an insignificant compliment, because two days before he went to the Indies, he had added a codicel which was affixed to the deed, whereby he for ever incapacitated himself to revoke the said deed, but in the presence of six witnesses; two whereof were to be Prelates of the Church of England; dying in the Indies as he did, whatever will he could make there, must be defective in that main article.[2] His lady returned with all the pomp and splendour of an eastern queen; but her pride working to an excessive height, soon turned her brain; whereby young Tim Double was deprived of a powerful patroness to carry on those pretensions she had brought over from the Indies in his favour; and Baron Meanwell in all probability likely to enjoy for himself, and his heirs for ever, the use fruit[3] of the forementioned deed of gift.

Fortune that loves to mingle her self in all events, thrust between the Baron and his great hopes the most powerful, most cunning, and most dexterous adversary that she could possibly have raised; it was the Lord Crafty, who had swallowed in his imagination all Double's estate. He knew himself blest with a purse and a capacity equal to the

---

1   Thomas Monck was introduced as an object of charity in George Monck's household by one of the Duke's sisters. He later became a captain and a colonel with the help of George Monck's military influence. In his last will of 1687, Christopher Albemarle made Colonel Monck and his heirs the chief beneficiaries of his estate, essentially leaving to them what was bequeathed to Lord Bath and his male heirs in the earlier will. The 1687 will also contained a petition to Charles II to grant Thomas Monck and his male heirs the title of Baron Monck of Potheridge. Tim Double (Thomas Monck's fictional son) later insists on being made a lord.

2   See also introduction, pp. 28-30.

3   A colourful, obsolete variation of *usufruct*; the "use, enjoyment, or profitable possession" of another's property (*OED*).

work. He therefore bought the merchant's widow of her two women,[1] his own chaplain married them together; but the lady being supposed *non compos*,[2] it is said one of her female directors was, in effect the bride,[3] lying behind the pillows, and making proper answers for the lunatick; whereby she got to her self the management of that old fox, and to the day of his death used to carry whatever point she had in hand, by only threatning to take upon her self, the title and quality of his wife.

Lord Crafty, as reason good, immediately assumed the management of his lady's affairs, and commenced a suit in young Tim's name against the Baron; the progress of that suit, would make an honest man for ever detest going to law; the point Crafty contended for, was to invalidate the codicel, which he attempted to prove spurious. How many verdicts were there given and reversed? What number of witnesses convicted of perjury? How much treasure expended in the pursuit and the defence? Our courts of judicature rung of nothing else;[4] in the mean time the cause, was a fat cause, and the lawyers contrived how to prolong it whilst none were gainers but themselves. Baron Meanwell almost beggared himself; Lord Crafty was indeed better circumstanced, but seeing the delays of the courts of justice, and the tricks of young Tim Double; he began to breathe an air of accommodation as well as the Baron. But Tim's pretensions being the difficultest point to be adjusted, they were at a loss how to find a method by which all things might be settled in that calm, which the exigency of both their affairs seemed to require.

Tim Double proved not only a sot, but the most dissolute, senseless, obstinate wretch, that a man could deal with. His education and natural parts were both mean, his temper extravagant and vain; he

---

1   Mary and Sarah Wright, Elizabeth Albemarle's servants. Apparently keeping their own interests in mind, the sisters, who were summoned in various courts about the details of the marriage, sometimes swore that the Duchess and Montagu were married and at other times that they were not.

2   Mad, insane. Elizabeth Cavendish, who came to be called the *mad Duchess*, began to show signs of mental illness in the early 1680s.

3   Unidentified.

4   The expensive lawsuit between Bath and Montagu began in 1691 and was settled in 1698, the result of a compromise, after seven years in various courts. See Narcissus Luttrell, *A Brief Historical Relation of State Affairs* for the numerous hearings.

valued himself extreamly upon his province of dissimulation, as having practised under a very great master. At the age of sixteen he was trapanned[1] when he was drunk, to marry the daughter of a poor petty-pan merchant;[2] the girl was pretty and ingenious enough; she made him a very good wife, and often by her management prevented his being undone by sharpers,[3] to whom he was naturally addicted. But he hated her, and studied nothing so much as how to get rid of her; tho' to her face he affected so prodigious a passion, that he could not breathe without mixing eyes, pressing and kissing her hands and neck; nor would he touch a bit of meat but what she cut; nay, he must sit by her at table, and often eat off of no plate but hers. This was a fulsom sight to all who knew he had brought his marriage into parliament, where it was likely to have been disannulled,[4] had not Lord Crafty by his underhand practices prevented it, least Tim, becoming a single man, some rich powerful family might espouse his cause, and by virtue of his title to so great an estate, give his Lordship an unexpected diversion, in the views he had of gaining it all to himself.

Lord Crafty had from time to time supplied him with several large sums of money, whereby he pretended to purchase his title to the whole estate; but the point being yet undecided, that was looked upon no better than champarty and maintainance.[5] Tim executed several deeds, whereby he divested himself of all pretensions to the estate, when it should be recovered; which, when he had done, Lord Crafty brought him in a bill of threescore thousand pounds; some for monies received, and the rest for vast sums expended in the law-suit. Tim entered into bonds and judgments, by which he acknowledged himself debtor to my Lord Crafty; after which, he was left at liberty to go where he pleased; his Lordship before, never suffering him to stir, but under the conduct of some person he could confide in. Tim's

---

1 Tricked.
2 A small pan.
  At the age of 14, Christopher Monck married Sarah Hungerford, daughter of Matthew Hungerford, identified in the key as a pastry cook in Limestreet.
3 Swindlers, tricksters.
4 Annulled, made null and void.
5 Champerty: "The offense of assisting a party in a suit in which one is not naturally interested with a view to receiving a share of the disputed property" (OED).
  Maintenance: "Aiding a party in litigation without lawful cause" (OED).

riots were so great, that Lord Crafty would no longer supply him with money; he ran in debt where-ever he could, till at length he was arrested and forced to surrender himself a prisoner at Westminster-Hall, before the Lord Chief Justice of the Common-Pleas.[1]

It was perfectly necessary that I should enter into this long digression, to inform you of the true state of things, before I give you knowledge of an affair, by which Rivella was presented with fresh occasion to renew the complaint she so justly had against fortune, for turning all her prospects of good into evil.

At that time Rivella lived in a pretty retirement, some few miles out of town, where she diverted her self chiefly with walking and reading. One day Calista, her sister authoress[2] (with whose story I may hereafter entertain you, as well as with the other writing ladies of our age) came, as usual, to make her a visit; she told her that Cleander,[3] a friend of hers, one of the most accomplished persons living, was in custody of a Serjeant of Arms for some misdemeanours, which were nothing in themselves, but as he had been of council on Lord Crafty's side, against Lord Meanwell, and was supposed to have had the chief conduct of the last trial, matters were like to be partially carried, because Oswald (poor Rivella's kinsman and husband, tho' she always hated his being called so) was appointed Chairman of the Committee ordered to examine Cleander;[4] and Oswald being long known a champion for Lord Meanwell, in respect of his cause, it was very justly feared, that he would joyn revenge and retaliation to his own native temper of choler and fury, by which means Cleander was to expect very severe usage, if not a worse misfortune.

---

1 Westminster Hall: A building in London where the business of Parliament was conducted and, into the nineteenth century, where the three courts of justice – the Chancery, King's Bench, and Common Pleas – were held.
Common Pleas: The court that had jurisdiction over civil suits.

2 Catherine Trotter (1679-1749), playwright and poet; she was, together with Delarivier Manley and Mary Pix, one of the three playwrights satirized in *The Female Wits*. Manley honoured Trotter with a poem celebrating the publication of her first play, *Agnes de Castro* (1696). The next season Trotter wrote a poem in praise of Manley's *The Royal Mischief* (see Appendix G.2).

3 John Tilly, Governor of Fleet Prison; Tory lawyer. In 1696, Tilly was charged by a House of Commons' committee with releasing prisoners in exchange for money.

4 John Manley, who was on the committee investigating Tilly, was also his adversary in the Albemarle case, in which Manley represented Bath, and Tilly championed Montagu.

To conclude; after Calista had raised Rivella's pity, wonder and curiosity, for the merit, beauty, and innocence of the gentleman under prosecution; she proposed a real advantage to her self, if she could influence her kinsman to stand neuter in the cause; or if that was not to be expected, that she would so far ingage him, that he should keep away on the day which was appointed for Cleander's examination.

Rivella was always inclined to assist the wretched; neither did she believe it prudence to neglect her own interest, when she found it meritorious to persue it. She told Calista, that being only her friend was enough to ingage her to endeavour at serving this Cleander whoever he were; but that since she had taken care to add interest to friendship, which were motives her circumstances were no way qualified to refuse, she was resolved upon that double consideration, to attempt doing whatever was in her power for both their services; but because she was not willing to embark without some prospect of a fortunate voyage, she desired to speak with Cleander in person, as well to inform her self of the merits of the cause, as to be acquainted with a gentleman of whom she had given so advantagious a description.

Calista blushed at the proposal, which Rivella observing, immediately asked her, if he were her lover, which would be enough to ingage her to serve him without any other motive; and thereupon said, that she would be contented to take minutes from Calista only, without concerning her self any further about being acquainted with Cleander.

Calista who was the most of a *prude* in her outward professions, and the least of it in her inward practice, unless you'll think it no *prudery* to allow freedoms with the air of restraint; asked Rivella with a scornful smile, what it was she meant? Cleander was a married man, and as such, out of any capacity to engage her secret service; her friendship was meerly with his wife, and as such if she would assist him, she should be obliged to her for her trouble. Rivella who hates dissimulation, especially amongst friends, was resolved to pique Calista for her insincerity, and therefore said, since it was so; she insisted upon seeing and informing her self from Cleander's own mouth, or else she would not ingage in the business.

The next day Cleander sent a gentleman to wait upon Rivella, and beg her interest in his service, together with the promise and assurance of a certain sum of money if she should succeed.

These preliminaries settled, the day after Cleander sent the same person (who happened to be a sort of an insignificant gentleman, acquainted long since both with Rivella and himself) in a chariot, with an unknown livery[1] to bring her to town, and even to the Serjeant at Arms's house, where Cleander was at that time confined.

Rivella had formed to her self what it was going to speak to a man of business in private, that she must at least wait till the croud were dismissed, and therefore took a book in her pocket, that she might entertain her self with reading whilst she waited for audience. She chose the Duke de Rochfoucaut's *Moral Reflections*;[2] she had not attended long, before Cleander came to wait on her, tho' but for two or three moments till he could dismiss his company, praying her to be easy till he might have the honour to return; during this short compliment, Rivella had thrown her book upon the table, Cleander whilst he was speaking took it up, as not heeding what he did, and departed the room with the book in his hand. Who that has ever dipped into those *Reflections*, does not know that there is not a line there, but what excites your curiosity, and is worth being eternally admired and remembred? Cleander had never met with it before. He formed an idea from that book of the genius of the lady, who chose it for her entertainment, and tho' he had but an indifferent opinion hitherto of woman's conversation, he believed Rivella must have a good taste from the company she kept. He found an opportunity of confirming himself, before he parted, in Rivella's sense, and capacity for business as well as pleasure; which were agreeably mingled at supper, none but those two gentlemen and Rivella being present. Behold the beginning of a friendship which endured for several years even to Cleander's death. He was married young, but as yet knew not what it was to love. His studies and application to business, together with the desire of making himself great in the world, had employed all his hours.

---

1 "Distinctive clothes worn by member of city company or person's servant" (*OED*).

2 Francis (Duke of) Rochefoucault (1613-80), statesman and writer. He achieved fame primarily for his *Moral Reflections* (*Réflexions ou Sentences et Maximes Morales*, 1665), a work that Voltaire praised for its propriety and correctness. Manley here appears to suggest Cleander's naivete and obtuseness, unable as he is to discern Rochefoucault's cynicism.

Neither did his youth and vigour stand in need of diversions to relieve his mind; he was civil to his lady,[1] meant very well for her children, and did not then dream there was any thing in her person defective to his happiness, that was in the power of any other of that sex to bestow.

Early in the morning Rivella went to Westminster-Hall, she took up her post at the booksellers-shop, by the foot of those stairs which go up to the Parliament-House. She had not waited long but she saw her kinsman; he was covered with blushes and confusion, not imagining what business she had there, unless to expose him; he had not even seen her face in some years nor she his, having sought nothing so much as to avoid one another.

Rivella advanced to speak with him, he blushed more and more, several members coming by to go to the House, and observing him with a lady in his hand, he thought it was best to take her from that publick place, and therefore led her the back way out of the Hall, called a coach put her in it, and afterwards got in himself without having power to ask her what business brought her to enquire after him in a place so improper for conversation, at the same time ordering the coachman to drive out of town.

Thus was that important affair neglected, they chose another chairman for the committee, which sat that morning. Cleander was acquitted, with the usual reprimand, and ordered to be set at liberty, very much to the regret of Oswald when he came coolly to consider how scandalously he had abandoned an affair of that importance, and which Lord Meanwell had left wholly to his management.

Before Rivella parted with her spouse, she told him, what was her designed request, and the motive. He seemed very well pleased that nothing but interest had engaged her. He bid her be sure to cultivate a friendship with Cleander, who would doubtless come to return his thanks for the service she had done him; recommending to her at the same time, *first*, not to receive the money which had been promised her, because there were better views, and which would be of more importance to her fortune; and *secondly*, to leave her house in the country for some time, to come and take lodgings in London, where

---

1 Not identified.

he would wait upon her to direct her in the management of some great affair.

Behold Rivella in a new scene, that of business; in which however Love took care to save all his own immunities. He bespoke the most considerable place for Cleander, who often visited her with a pleasure new and surprizing to his hitherto insensible breast. I was lately come to town. Rivella's conversation always made part of my pleasure, if not my happiness; so that whenever she allowed me that favour, I never omitted waiting on her. Some presentiment told me this agreeable gentleman would certainly succeed. I saw his eyes always fixed on her with unspeakable delight, whilst hers languished him some returns. He approved rather than applauded what she said, but would always shift places, till he got one next her, omitting no opportunity to touch her hand, when he could do it without any seeming design. I told her she had made a conquest, and one that she ought to value her self upon; for Cleander was assuredly a man of worth as well as beauty. She laughed, and said he was so awkward, and so unfashioned as to love; that if he did bear her any great good will, she was sure he neither durst, nor knew how to tell it her. I perceived the pleasure she took in speaking of him: wherefore I came in with my old way of caution and advice, bidding her have a care. One affair with a married man did a woman's reputation more harm than with six others.[1] Wives were with reason so implacable, so invenomed against those who supplanted them, that they never forbore to revenge themselves at the expence of their rival's credit; for if nothing else ensued, a total deprivation of the world's esteem, was sure to be the consequence of an injured wife's resentment. Cleander was too handsom a man to be lost with any patience; his wife was much older than himself, and much a termagant, therefore nothing but fire and fury could be expected from such a domestick evil: the deprivation of a charming husband's heart, being capable to rouse the most insensible. Rivella laughed, and thanked me for my advice, but how she profited by it a very little time will shew us.

Her kinsman (I chuse to call him so, rather than by that hateful name her husband) caressed her with the utmost blandishments; he

---

1   Manley did, in fact, risk her reputation, living openly with Tilly, despite his being married, from 1696 to 1702.

told her it was now in her own power to redeem all the mismanagement they had both been guilty of in respect of her fortune. Cleander was the person that could do miracles in point of accommodation between Lord Crafty and Baron Meanwell. He empowered her to make him very advantagious offers, if he would but use his interest towards composing that affair. She sounded Cleander upon that head. He answered her as a person who could refuse nothing to a woman he loved, but at the same time told her they were all mistaken; he had not any part of Lord Crafty's confidence which he was now very glad of, because he must either disoblige her, or, which was a worse evil, betray my Lord. Nay more, his Lordship had been wanting in doing him little services during his confinement, which he would nor easily forgive; that true indeed he had been of *council* for him in the last trial; but not *trusted*; tho' that very suspicion had drawn upon him Lord Meanwell's displeasure, and Oswald's persecution, notwithstanding which, Lord Crafty had failed of generosity enough to stand by him, perhaps not esteeming him of sufficient consequence to his service. Rivella reported this back to her principal; he would not believe Cleander, which made her likewise distrust his integrity; he never came to visit her, but she always teized him with these words, You can oblige me! you can retrieve my broken fortune! you can give peace to Westminster-Hall, between those mighty potentates that have so long divided it! and you refuse to do it! did I serve you with such an ill-will, or by halves? Cease professing your gratitude and friendship to me when it rises no higher than common effects; you had better never visit, than disoblige me. Cleander was quite vanquished by her reproaches and importunity; the evil was in his heart, he could not refrain seeing her, and took this opportunity to declare himself, by telling her his opinion, was, that no lover either could, or ought to refuse what was asked him by the person he loved. In short, he gave her to understand, that he had not any obligation to Lord Crafty, and he was very glad of it, but that he thought the Baron's way did not lie towards an accommodation with that Lord, but with Mr. Timothy Double, because if matters were agreed between them two, and the deed and the will joyned, what had Lord Crafty to do in it any further than to expect to find his wife's jointure well paid. Double is a prisoner, said Cleander; where I command; if you, Madam, were secured, so that our interest could become mutual, and we not make our selves the Baron's, or your kinsman's tools, I don't find there would be any great difficulty in bringing this matter to bear.

Rivella immediately gave part of her secret to her cousin, and he to the Baron; they could not help wondring at their own blindness which had till then missed so obvious a mark. The Baron admitted Cleander's genius for business, and ordered Rivella to meet his Lordship at a third place, there to take his instructions. He began with assuring her of his entire confidence in her honour and capacity, bidding her make it Cleander's interest to conclude this project of reconciliation, for which when it was accomplished they should have between them eight thousand pounds paid down upon the nail; it was her business, either to come in for half, or to make what terms she could with Cleander; that in the mean time Tim Double should be introduced to her lodgings, where they would have her entertain and caress him to all the height of his own extravagant humour. In a few days they should be able to see whether the project would bear, which if it did not, Rivella should have a present of an hundred guineas, to defray what expence she might be at, and over and above his Lordship's acknowledgment and protection as long as he lived. Cleander, to oblige Rivella, agreed to these proposals, because he could not refuse what she so earnestly insisted on; but he bid her remember it was only to please her, not thro' any great prospect he had of advantaging himself, because the persons they had to deal with, he feared, had not all the honour that was required in such an affair, where much more was to be left to the *bona fide*[1] than to any security, that could, as matters stood, be made obligatory or binding in law.

Thus was Timothy Double introduced to Rivella's appartment; but before he could make his appearance there, poor Cleander was forced to accouter him at his own cost; he was horribly out of humour because he was very much out of repair. Therefore he sent him his taylor, of whom Tim immediately bespoke two suits that came to more than sixscore pound, full of gold and silver. The perriwig-maker furnished him upon Cleander's credit, with two perriwigs upwards of

1   Good faith.

thirty guineas apiece. Lace and linnen made another improving article; so that before Cleander durst ask him a question, he was dipped above three hundred pound for his service, without putting one piece into his pocket. He would not trust him with ready money, lest he should elope, and fall again into some of the hands of his old comrades the sharpers. Cleander did not fail to hint to Rivella the expence he had been at to please her humour; at the same time making her observe Lord Meanwell's parsimony, that would venture no more than an hundred guineas, and that not paid down, to gain so vast an advantage to himself as an accommodation with Tim, asking her with a smile, how one of her great soul, could so earnestly engage her cares and interest for the service of him, who had so little a soul?

Tim stuck full of gold and silver lace, made a tolerable figure, he was neither ugly nor conceited; his habit having so much of the fine gentleman, the worst of it was, his conversation did not well agree with his dress; but he had been long enough with Lord Crafty to learn an outward civility, his behaviour was seemingly modest and full of bows; Cleander brought him to Rivella, as an injured gentleman, who had been ruined by that Lord's refinements. Tim presently recounted several pleasant acts of management, which would make no ill figure in secret history. Cleander was obliged to endure this booby for several days, to drink with him, nay, to sleep with him, till he had gotten into his confidence; in all that time never naming Lord Meanwell's name; that task was left to Rivella, of whose good sense and honour he gave Tim a very advantagious character. They used generally to dine with her, she did pennance enough, being obliged to deny her self to all other company, and to lengthen out dinner till it came to supper time, from whence Tim must always go to the tavern before he went to bed. Miserable Cleander kept him company, for fear he should get some of his old gang, who were spies gained by Lord Crafty. In conclusion he began to talk freely with Rivella by way of unlading his grievances, the wretchedness of his circumstances; great debts and incumbrance with Lord Crafty, did not make him half so uneasy as the difficulty of being rid of his wife: tho' he was sure he could still be divorced from her, if he had any friend to stand by him, who would be kind enough to assist him with his purse. This naturally introduced Lord Meanwell, of whose vertues

Rivella made a pompous dissertation, which much surprized Tim who had been used to hear the Baron treated as the greatest *fourb*[1] in nature. The first thing instilled into him was the forgery of the clause, which had been annexed to old Double's deed. Rivella endeavoured to set him right as to that suspicious circumstance, and with much more ease and justice displayed Lord Crafty in his political capacity; Tim could help her in her task, and did not scruple to give her many instances relating to himself, particularly one night when Lord Crafty got Tim behind a table with deeds and conveyances before him, to which end he had kept him close up for several days, Tim's nose fell a bleeding, he rose to fetch a handkerchief, my Lord would not let him go but presented him his own, which being quickly wet, the lawyer and his witnesses supplied him with theirs; in conclusion they would have suffered him to bleed to death, rather than stir till he had signed and sealed, according to his Lordship's own heart's desire.

By these practices Tim was ruined to all intents and purposes and condemned to perish in prison, without he could relieve himself by some other method than had yet been taken. He had cost Cleander just five hundred pound when Rivella proposed to him an accommodation with Lord Meanwell, in which the young man was at first very sincere. But here the parcimony of that Lord, or the folly of his manager Oswald spoiled all; Rivella was of Tim's side, and, reason good, strove to make as advantagious a bargain for him as she could; nothing would serve Tim but to be made a lord, he had all the time of Crafty's management been flattered with a much greater title when the estate should be once recovered. That which stuck hardest with Tim, was a point which Lord Meanwell strenuously insisted upon, nay, would do nothing without, *viz.* parting with the superbious[2] chief seat of the Doubles, which the Baron wanted to settle upon his second son[3] whom he loved extreamly. Tim was told that as matters stood, it was

---

1 An impostor, a cheat.

2 Grand, stately. Manley here refers to New Hall in Essex, which George Monck acquired in 1660 and which became his most treasured property. In a letter of 14 December 1684 to Christopher Albemarle, the Duke of Newcastle called the manor "the best House, the best Seate ... of any subject's House in the Kingdom" (*Christopher Monck* 98).

3 John Granville (1665-1707), Tory Member of Parliament, created Baron Granville of Potheridge in 1703.

infinitely too large for any expence he could ever hope to make, but in exchange he should have the Lord Meanwell's own house,[1] with all the furniture, which was a much more modern structure, and where he constantly resided when he was in town, and with it, the house-keeper's place belonging to one of the King's palaces where Tim would have occasion to commence Courtier, a province he excessively longed for, besides frequent opportunities to oblige the Maids of Honour in the choice of their lodging, which weighed very much with Tim's amorous temper. He desired to view the inside of the house, to know whether it was a habitation fit for a man of so great a soul; this was a difficult point, which yet he insisted on so far, that he would treat no further unless he liked the house, that which he was to resign in lieu of it, being the idol of his fancy, tho' no way suitable to any but an overgrown estate. The Baron very well knew Lord Crafty had spies in his family who would soon carry the report to him of Tim Double's being to visit his house, which must certainly ruin the whole treaty; they were at their wits end to get him to pass over that circumstance, but Tim was obstinate and would not be persuaded; at length, women being good at invention, Rivella found a method how to gratify Tim's curiosity, and in a way which hit his vein, having a great inclination to be dabling with politicks and intrigues; the next Sunday the Baron and all his family were purposely to dine abroad, leave should be given to the servants to do what they would with themselves, which, if not given them, they are apt enough to take when their attendance is not required at home. His chaplain he could so far confide in, as to tell him two clergymen from the university had a curiosity to see the house incognito, which for certain reasons he desired him to show. A servant whom the Baron had long trusted was to let in the Oxonians, and introduce them to the chaplain.

Two clergymen's habits were sent to Rivella's lodgings, where the pious gentlemen were to take orders; she had sent the landlady and all the family to divert themselves at her country house, and left no soul with her self but an under servant, whom she dispatched to church. It

---

1 The Manor of Flourny, which Lord Bath convinced Christopher Monck to accept, in addition to one thousand pounds a year, in exchange for all rights to the Albe-marle estates.

fell a raining with great violence for the rest of the day; the sparks came after dinner, and were soon metamorphosed into spruce *clergy-men*. Tim had a French brocade vest under his habit which nevertheless durst not appear; the difficulty of getting a coach on Sundays, and especially in rainy weather, made them keep theirs. Tim had contracted such an ill habit of swearing, that he could neither leave it off nor knew when he did it; Rivella called the coachman in, and told him the persons he brought thither had sent him his money, having no occasion to go farther. But there were two ministers above that wanted a coach, the fellow brushed up his seats, and in they got, Cleander gave him directions where to go, which he not taking readily, Tim fell a swearing at him for a blockhead and a dunce; the man stared, got up nimbly into his coach-box, snapt his whip, and swore as loud as Tim had done, that he never saw such *pasons*[1] in his life.

All things were displayed to the best advantage at Lord Meanwell's; Tim liked it well enough when his thoughts had no return of that glorious seat in the country, which often cost him many a pang to forgo; but to comfort himself, he would needs see the cellars, the chaplain waited on him down, and civilly offered him his choice, either of champaign or burgundy; Tim liked both, and in he sat for it, Cleander winked at him in vain, jogged his knee, no notice took honest Tim, the glass went about, the chaplain was disposed to stare, seeing him swallow down the liquor so greedily; at length, Cleander told Tim in his ear, it was necessary they should be gone before church was done. Tim answered aloud, that might be, but where was there so good burgundy to be had after church? Cleander was at his wits end at the incivility of the brute; Tim laid about him, as if all the wine in the cellar was his own, because the house and furniture were to be so if he pleased. Cleander grew wild to get him away, and told him, with that reverend gentleman's leave, they would take some bottles with them in the coach to drink when they came home. The chaplain's commission did not extend so far, his lord was a good husband of his wines, and yet he knew not how to refuse; in short, he yielded that they should have half a dozen bottles. But when they came to the gate the coachman was gone unpaid; probably the fellow

---

1 Colloquial for *parsons*.

knew they were the same persons he had carried before in a lay-habit, and did not know what to make of them, yet not daring to mutter, seeing them go into such a house. Tim was half bouzy, and without any respect to his cloth, with a bottle in each hand, stood in the street calling coach! coach! The rain still continuing no coach came; the chaplain and Cleander, likewise with each their two bottles in hand, were something abashed, and did not call coach! coach! so loud as did *pot valiant* Tim;[1] at length, the expedient was found of sending the Baron's servant for two chairs. Tim would have all the six bottles along with him in his own chair, they were carried back again to Rivella's, where they unrobed and ended this troublesom adventure.

Tim having at length agreed to an exchange of houses, being persuaded to allow in point of grandeur for the difference of town and country, the treaty went on; he was promised to be relieved from all his ingagements to Lord Crafty. He demanded two thousand pounds a year to be settled upon him and his heirs for ever; to be assisted in his divorce, and if that could be effected, that he might have leave to court one of the Baron's daughters; to receive ten thousand pounds in ready money, and be made a lord; this last article was readily complied with, a patent for a barony valued at ten thousand pound being found in the family, granted by the late King for services done,[2] the other two articles they thought too large, and therefore offered but one thousand pound a year, and six in money.

Lord Meanwell's oversight lay in not fixing Tim's inconstant temper whilst he might have done it; the Squire quickly wanted a change of place, circumstances and diversion. The Baron ought to have closed with Tim's terms, when he could have had them, and not lost irrecoverable time in striving to beat down the market, tho' he confessed it was cheap, and what he would gladly give rather than go without. Besides, his worthless plenipo,[3] Oswald, who pretended to

---

1   Tim is valiant because he is drunk.

2   Quite likely an allusion to the petition to Charles II in Christopher Albemarle's will of 1687 to grant Colonel Thomas Monck the title of Baron Monck of Potheridge (see *Christopher Monck* 342).

3   An abbreviated form of *plenipotentiary*, someone invested with full power and authority.

his Lordship that he served for nought, when he saw matters were just beginning to bear, told Rivella that he understood Cleander had consented that she should divide with him the eight thousand pound, which himself very unworthily expected to divide with her. He would have two thousand for his own use, and the other two thousand settled after her death, upon a son[1] which had been the product of their marriage.

Rivella answered him, that provided the Baron were acquainted with these conditions, she would agree with them, how remote soever from what had been first promised her; but if otherwise, she would not be any longer imposed upon by Oswald's pretences. This caused bad blood between them; he began to be jealous of Tim, without suspecting Cleander. He put himself into passions and disgusts, and wore out the time in complaints and expostulations, yet took part of all those fine dinners that were every day seen at Rivella's; for which, when she desired him to represent to the Baron the expence she was unavoidably put to, he once brought her the paultry sum of three pound, which, as she said, would not furnish one *desert*;[2] and this was all the money ever tendered her from the Baron in that affair, tho' she reasonably presumed his Lordship, according to his own proposal, had trusted larger sums for her use into the hands of his treasurer Oswald.

But whilst Oswald was contriving how to reduce Tim's demands, secure two thousand pound to himself without the Baron's knowledge, and get the other two thousand pound settled in reversion upon his son, an unforeseen, and as one should think an inconsiderable accident, let all of them see the vanity of pretending to divide the spoil before the prey was secured.

There was a girl about seventeen or eighteen, named Bella,[3] who sometimes frequented the play-house, but as yet could get no salary;

---

1   John Manley, born on 24 June 1691. Details about John Manley, and his primary caregiver(s), remain sketchy. See Dolores Duff, 70–73 and Fidelis Morgan, *A Woman of No Character* 79 for brief (and somewhat speculative) discussions. See also introduction pp. 31–32 and Appendix B.iv.

2   Dessert.

3   Katherine Baker (d. 1729), actress. There were two Mrs. Bakers, Frances and Katherine, in the King's Company in 1677, sometimes confused in the cast lists. Katherine, the younger and possibly Frances's daughter, was active in the theatre from 1699 onward.

for a year or two together she used to come to Rivella's when she was in town, to beg her to speak to the managers, that she might be received into pay. She was a poor woman's daughter in the neighbourhood, which ingaged Rivella to promise her what little interest she had. Bella used sometimes to come to dinner there, as she did at other places, offering her service in making up heads,[1] and those little offices wherein the girl was tolerably handy. When there was no company, Rivella had sometimes the goodness to make her sit down at the table with her, otherwise she used to be glad to get a meals meat with Mrs. Flippanta,[2] Rivella's woman. That wench, was perfectly *mercurial*, and had the greatest propensity to intrigue, and bringing people together; tho' her lady was not then acquainted with her talent, no more than her other qualification of dissimulation; for she was perfectly demure before her mistress. Bell was greatly in her favour, because she used at spare times to entertain her with scraps of plays and amorous speeches in heroicks. The landlady and another woman who lodged in the house where Rivella lodged, were fond of the same amusement. Bell was much oftner there than Rivella knew, and when she was abroad, the wench was always repeating in a theatrical tone and manner.

Lord Meanwell's phlegm, or irresolution, made the treaty hang long, together with Oswald's very ill humour about the four thousand pounds, which he had swallowed in his imaginations, joyned to his pretended jealousy of Tim, so that Rivella was grown weary, and glad to go abroad for a little relief, leaving the house to Tim and Oswald to drink in; as for Cleander, I presume he was but seldom there; when Rivella was not, Mrs. Flippanta made a figure in her lady's absence, and Bella by this means came to be seen by Tim; he fell in love with her according to his way of loving. The girl had a round face, not well made, large dull eyes, but she was young, and well enough complexioned, tho' she wanted air, and had a defect in her speech, which were two things they objected against as to her coming into the playhouse. Tim bribed Flippanta to get the girl's company in her lady's absence, as he would have done for any girl that came in his way.

---

1 Hair-dressing.
2 Identified in the key only as Rivella's servant.

They were grown very well acquainted, before Tim told the news of his growing flame to Cleander; which he spoke of as a thing indispensibly necessary to his happiness. Tim fancied himself some mighty considerable person, he had three very great affairs upon his hands, to end with my Lord Meanwell, get rid of his wife, and possess himself of Bell's favours. Cleander told Rivella what a scrape they were brought into, and conjured her not to oppose him; for if Tim was crossed in his humour, all was at an end. He was already dipped several hundred pounds; for that fine 'Squire, 'tis supposed, could not be kept all this time without money in his pocket, and a great deal too. The affair had been so long depending, that his wife found out his haunt at Rivella's, of which she immediately gave notice to Lord Crafty. She was fixed immoveably to his Lordship's service, notwithstanding her husband's interest, which Tim had honestly told Cleander in the beginning, and therefore begged he might remain concealed from his wife till all was concluded with the Baron. Lord Crafty knew so much of Rivella's temper, that she would not have endured such a booby as Tim, and have made great expence upon him without better views. He heard of Tim's bravery, and what airs he gave himself. Lord Crafty had never been so defective in any point of policy as in abandoning of Tim; it must cost him considerable to retrieve that false step. It was no hard matter to find his lodging by dogging him from Rivella's house, which when once done, he sent a person to him, called old Simon,[1] who had long been Lord Crafty's creature, and by humouring Tim in his vices and vanities, had gained an absolute ascendant over him; but when Tim grew poor and no longer of consequence to Lord Crafty, Mr. Simon forsook him with the rest, yet soon regained his former station by flattery; and finding the place of a favourite vacant, he reassumed it as formerly. Tim asked Cleander to intercede with Rivella that Mr. Simon might be permitted to make one of the company. Rivella told them they were undone from that minute, he was a creature of my Lord Crafty's and the whole design would certainly come to nothing. Tim assured Cleander that Simon was a convert and hated my Lord's ill usage of him as

---

1   Identified in the key only as Mr. Simpson, retainer (servant, attendant) to Ralph Montagu.

much as they did. Rivella knew Tim's tallent at dissembling, which he openly valued himself upon, and therefore did not much regard what he said; she sent to the Baron to give him notice of this accident. Then his Lordship and Oswald began to put themselves upon the frett; Tim had sometime since sunk his pretensions, of two thousand to fifteen hundred pounds a year, and was come to close with their own offer of six thousand pound in money, which these shallow, or greedy politicians finding, thought to sink him further, and in that view kept the affair so long in hand that it got wind; but then Lord Meanwell began to bestir himself too late, he ordered Rivella to tell the Squire, that he did agree to all his demands, and was accordingly seeing the writings perfected; in the mean time, the articles were drawing up for Tim to sign, upon which, he was to receive eight hundred pound overplus for his present necessities. Simon had leave given to make one at Rivella's, and she had orders to assure him of a present of five hundred pound for his own occasions.

Mean time, Tim's flame for Bella daily increased, Rivella called her to her, and bid her keep away from her house; for she would not charge her self with the consequences, Squire Tim being a married man. The girl did not scruple to tell her, that her design of going to the play-house was in hopes of finding some body to keep her, she had often seen in the dressing room, what great respect Mrs. Barry and the rest, used to pay to Mrs. Alyse[1] when she used to come thither, and how fine they all lived, which she was sure they could not do upon their pay. Rivella was amazed at her confidence, which she thought no way suitable to a maid. She then spoke to Tim to give over the pursuit, since that girl could not possibly be of any consequence to a man like him, and to ruin her, would be an eternal reproach to the whole company; Tim swore he would marry her to morrow, or as soon as he was divorced, and old Simon thought this a very good handle, he made his court in the Squire's name more artfully to the girl. He assured her that Rivella was her mortal enemy, and envied her least she should come to be greater than herself. For Tim had indeed told Rivella, as I said before, that if he could be

---

1 Mrs. Ayliff (or Ayloffe), singer and actress, whose career flourished between 1690 and 1697. Her mother, Elizabeth Price, was also an actress and, for a time, Cardonell Goodman's mistress.

divorced he would marry Bella; this gained his point with the girl. She assumed very haughty airs towards Rivella, and very tender ones towards Tim. Old Simon had likewise succeeded his court to Flippanta, by making believe he was smitten with her beauty. Poor decayed Flip was proud of a conquest, and readily entered into a confederacy against her mistress. To conclude, Bella was become the head of the company, neither durst Rivella contradict her. She thought some small time longer would put an end to her suffering, and betrayed as little uneasiness as possible. Simon persuaded Tim that he had no other way to preserve Bella's favour, but by breaking that dishonourable treaty he had been drawn into with the Lord Meanwell; Bella assured him of the same thing. Simon told him, that Lord Crafty heartily repented the neglect had been shown whilst his Lordship was in the country, and to make appear that he was sincere, offered to give him up all his ingagements, and to prosecute the suit against the Baron, till he had put him in possession of the whole estate. Tim did not know which part to chuse, when he was with Bell and Sim, he was theirs, when he was with Cleander and Rivella he was for them; at length, the long looked for hour came, when he was to sign the articles and receive his eight hundred pounds bounty money. The Baron would needs have him come alone to the tavern where they were to meet, that so the act might look voluntary; but, the difficulty was how to get him there; they durst not so much as tell him, least he should give part of the intelligence to Mr. Simon; in short, it was left to Rivella's management, she took him out in a coach with her to the appointed place, upon pretence of meeting a gentleman who had a mind to part with a diamond buckle for his hat, and if Tim liked it, he might become a proprietor in the buckle, and have six month's credit given him; this was something that hit the Squire's vanity; but as they were going thither, Rivella told him the real design; but that since the utmost secresy was necessary, she had used that artifice to prevent Mr. Simon, and consequently Lord Crafty from knowing his good fortune till it was beyond their power to prevent. She said, that faithful Cleander attended with the Lord Meanwell's lawyer, who for his own honour, as well as out of respect and friendship for Tim, would take care to have all possible justice done him in an affair that was going to make such a noise in the world. To be short, Rivella fortified him so well that he promised to go in and perform what he had covenanted; she set him down two doors, short of the tavern, he kissed her hand with an air entirely satisfied, and told her she should always command that fortune, which she had been so good to procure for him; and that the next day at dinner, he would do himself the honour to wait upon her to pay his acknowledgments more at large. Thus was that great affair dispatched; and the eighth day after appointed for executing the deeds, and putting the Squire in possession of what estate and money had been stipulated for him.

Old Simon revelled with the money Tim brought home, who had never the honesty to repay Cleander the least part of what he had borrowed of him; as to Rivella's expences, they were come to a sum so much beyond what the Baron had promised her, in case that affair did not succeed, that she never demanded any money from him; throwing *at all*,[1] as in a desperate game; where nothing less can repair the former loss.

The eighth day did come; the Lord and his agent, the deeds and the lawyers were ready; but not the Squire. Old Simon and Mr. Timothy, Madam Bell and Mademoiselle Flippanta silently dislodged without beat of drum, and left Cleander and Rivella to repent of their grand expensive negotiation; by which in the end, no persons happened to be gainers, but the Lord Crafty and Mr. Simon.

I will not tire you with many more particulars. Tim was infatuated by Bell's persuasions who now lodged with him as his lady, but incog, for fear of the Baron and Cleander. Lord Crafty let them spend together the money Tim had so basely acquired, and then sent him away to Flanders under Sim's conduct, who took care to confine him to a house they had taken, not suffering him to converse with any company, but three or four rakes that they had gotten purposely to drink with him from morning till night, keeping him perpetually flustered, least his cooler sense should make him consider what he had done, and put him upon stealing away from them to return back into England, there to perform articles with the Lord Meanwell. Treacherous Bell was likewise over-reached, she was put for sometime to pension by a feigned name at a poor woman's house in an obscure

---

1   Altogether, wholly (*OED*).

part of the town, with daily promises of being sent into Flanders to her beloved, who had stipulated with Lord Crafty's agent that she should follow him; telling Rivella and others that he was married to her, which whether true or false signified little, since Bell very well knew, unless he could make his former marriage null, Tim was in no capacity to marry again.

Here that insignificant treacherous creature grew poor and was forgotten; for when Bell no longer served their ends, Lord Crafty and his managers remembred her no more than if she never had been born; a very quick return for her perfidy, folly and ingratitude; had she not seduced Tim Double from his engagements, Cleander would have taken care of her interests so far (since her highest ambition was only to be a mistress) as that the Squire should have done something for her above that extream contempt which her vices have since brought upon her; whence most who have heard even her own pretences, have been uncharitable enough to conclude, that so vile a nature as hers could hardly ever have been otherwise; since extream corruption does not all at once, but rather gradually seize upon such who have any degree of vertue in their composition.

Soon after these disappointments, Rivella received an anonymous letter by the penny-post, to beg her to be next day at twelve a clock, all alone, in a hackney-coach, in the upper Hyde-Park near the lodge. She asked Cleander's opinion; he assured her it was the hand-writing of Lord Crafty, which was so particular that no body could be mistaken that had once seen it; he advised her to go to the appointment, for that Lord had too much respect for the fair sex to do an outrage to any lady; accordingly she went and found that very person alone in another hackney-coach; he alighted and came into hers. After the first forms were over, he did not scruple to value himself upon defeating their well laid design. He assured her they should never recover Tim again, and therefore advised her, since she understood so much of this matter, to make up her disappointments by indeavouring an accommodation between the Baron and himself, to which end, his Lordship gave her power to a certain point, how to proceed.

The Baron approved of the project, he gave Rivella leave to treat with the Lord Crafty, with an assurance of two thousand pound for her self if they should, by her means, agree; and to shew his Lordship that Cleander and her self were *trustworthy*, and very well deserved his favour, she brought Tim's only brother, the next heir in case Tim should have no sons, to his Lordship; this poor young man wanted food, raiment and education, his parts and honesty much exceeded the Squires; he sold his reversion to the Baron for an annuity of an hundred and fifty pounds a year; and thought himself very happy to be able to secure a present maintenance out of his imaginary future hopes.[1]

This was a circumstance Lord Crafty could hardly forgive himself; looking upon Tim or his lady to be fruitful persons, tho' the males all died, he never once considered his brother might prove of consequence. In short, his Lordship and Rivella often met, he did all that was in his power to shake her fidelity to the Baron; told her he laid eighteen thousand pound a year at her feet, all his good fortune had come by ladies, but he had never found any of so great ability as her self. He endeavoured to make it her interest to corrupt Oswald to incline the Baron to easier terms of accommodation; when he saw she was not to be shaken, he consented to treat with the Lord Meanwell in person, a circumstance he had hitherto refused her whenever she proposed it. They accordingly met where Lord Crafty extolled Rivella in such an artful manner, that made the Baron suspect she was in his interest, telling him he was so well satisfied in her honour and capacity, (for no lawyer they had ever employed knew the cause so well) that he would refer the whole matter to the decision, and peremptorily offered to put it upon that very issue. The Baron at that touch shrank himself all in a heap, like the sensible plant;[2] he told Oswald, that that very artful Lord had corrupted Rivella's truth, else how was it possible he durst leave a matter of such vast consequence to her decision. Oswald had a better opinion of her, and begged his Lordship, as a proof that he would but seem to agree to Crafty's proposal, and then he would quickly find that what he said was nothing but pretence and artifice. The Baron was not of his opinion, believing himself wiser than all the world, and perhaps willing to save the

---

1 Henry Monck apparently preferred obscurity over wealth, never making claim to Christopher's estates.

2 A highly sensitive shrub whose leaflets fold together at the slightest touch; also called a sensitive plant.

money he had promised Rivella, tho' it cost him much more the other way; he clapt up an hasty agreement with Crafty, without any farther consulting Oswald in the matter, by which, out of old Double's estate, he gave that Lord threescore and twelve thousand pound, and yet still remained liable to perform conditions with Tim, when ever he should think fit to force him to it; but very much to his mortification on one side, and joy on the other, he heard that Tim was killed with drinking,[1] a just and miserable return for his debauchery, folly and villany. If the Baron had known of his death before the agreement, it would have saved him several thousand pounds; but since the agreement was made, he was very glad 'twas now become out of Tim's power to call his Lordship to an account for that which he had made with him.

Thus my dear D'Aumont, continued Sir Charles, I have finished the secret history of that tedious law suit, which I justly fear has likewise tired your patience. My business was to give you Rivella's history on those occasions that have to her prejudice, made most noise in the world; since she has writ for the Tories, the Whigs have heightened this story, and too severely reflected upon her for Bella's misfortunes, tho' they were all occasioned by her own viciousness, forwardness and treachery, in which Rivella had not any part. Rivella never saw nor applied her self to the Baron any more, nor conversed with Oswald. If that Lord ever made her an acknowledgment, it was directed to miscarry, as coming thro' Oswald's hands, and she with reason, reckons that family to be much her debtors. Poor Cleander was a great deal of money out of pocket, but he loved Rivella too well to reproach her with it.

During their mutual intelligence and friendship, Calista, after a long disuse, came to visit Rivella; Cleander was then in the room, they both looked so amazed and confounded, that Rivella took the first occasion to withdraw, to permit them an opportunity to recover their concern. If you remember Chevalier, Calista was the lady who first ingaged Rivella to serve Cleander, tho' she excused her self upon being his wife's acquaintance, and not Cleander's. When she had ended her visit, Rivella would know what had occasioned their mutual confusion; he laughed and defended himself a long time; at

---

1   Christopher Monck, who had indeed taken to drink, died 4 July 1701.

length, he confessed Calista was the first lady that had ever made him unfaithful to his wife.[1] Her mother being in misfortunes and indebted to him, she had offered her daughter's security, he took it, and moreover the blessing of one night's lodging, which he never paid her back again. Rivella laughed in her turn, because Calista had given her self airs of not visiting Rivella, now she was made the town talk by her scandalous intriegue with Cleander; Rivella desired him to give her the bond, which he promised and performed.

Much about that time, George Prince of Hess Darmstad,[2] came the second time into England; he had been Vice-Roy of Catalonia, towards the latter end of Charles the Third's reign.[3] The inclination his Highness had of returning into Spain, his adorations for the Dowager,[4] his relation being no secret, made him keep up his correspondence with the Catalans; principally with the inhabitants of Barcelona, who continually sollicited him to aid them with forces, whereby they might be enabled to declare themselves against Philip of Bourbon,[5] whom they unwillingly obeyed. The Prince of Hess represented this to the Court of England, as a matter of very great importance; he produced several letters from the chief persons of Catalonia. His Highness was recommended to a merchant in the city, whom he prayed to introduce him into the acquaintance of some of the most ingenious ladies of the English nation; this merchant was

---

1   Whether Catherine Trotter and John Tilly had a sexual relationship remains debatable. The fact that Trotter had written verses to the Duke of Marlborough, celebrating his victory at Blenheim, and, according to rumour, had had an affair with him, undoubtedly contributed to Manley's unflattering portraits of her, not only in *Rivella*, but earlier, as Daphne, in *New Atalantis* (II.52-57, 266) and as Lais in *Memoirs of Europe* (I.289). See Morgan's *A Woman of No Character* 103 and Clark's *Women Playwrights* 40-44 for discussions of the possible motives behind Manley's resentment of Trotter.

2   George von Hesse-Darmstadt (1669-1705), son of Ludwig, 2nd Landgrave of the German territory of Hesse-Darmstadt. The Prince visited England from July to November 1703.

3   Actually, towards the end of the reign of the Spanish monarch Charles II. After Charles's death, the Prince served the Austrian archduke 'Charles III,' Habsburg pretender to the Spanish throne, in the War of the Spanish Succession.

4   Maria Anna of Pfalz-Neuburg (1667-1740), widowed queen of Charles II of Spain, cousin of George, Hesse.

5   Philip V, first Bourbon king of Spain (r. 1700-46), successor to Charles II, grandson of Louis XIV, the latter of whom regarded Catalonia as French territory. The Catalans rejected Philip as king in favour of 'Charles III.'

acquainted with a gentlewoman that was newly set up to sell milliner's ware to the ladies and gentlemen; she was well born, and incouraged by several persons who laid out their money with her in consideration of her misfortunes. The merchant desired she would speak to the lady Rivella, who was her customer, and two ladies more, to come one evening to cards at her house, where himself would introduce the Prince incog. His Highness understood nothing of loo,[1] which was the game they played at; he could not speak a word of English, nor the other ladies a word of French. They knew his quality, tho' they were to take no notice of it, and thought to win his money, which is all that most ladies care for at play. Rivella sat next the Prince, and for the honour of the English women would not let him be cheated, she assisted him in his game, and in conjunction with his good luck, ordered the matter so well, that his Highness was the only person who rose a winner. From that time he conceived the greatest esteem for Rivella, the Prince presented her with his picture at length, and continued a correspondence with her till the day before his death. Cleander did not believe there was any mixture of love in it, because it was well known, the Prince had engaged his heart in Spain, and his person in England, by way of amusement to a certain celebrated lady, who had made a great figure in Flanders, and was more known by the name of the Electress of Bavaria, than her own.[2]

Rivella tasted some years the pleasure of retirement, in the conversation of the person beloved; but a tedious and an unhappy law-suit straitned Cleander's circumstances and put him under several difficulties. In the mean time his wife died; Rivella was complimented upon her loss even by Cleander himself, for all the world thought he loved her so well as to marry her; she received his address with such confusion and regret, that he knew not what to make of her disorder, till at length bursting forth into tears, she cried I am undone from this moment! I have lost the only person, who secured to me the possession of your heart! Cleander was struck with her words, I came into the room, and Rivella withdrew to hide her concern. Cleander felt himself so wounded by what she had spoken, that I shall never forget

---

1 A round card game in which penalties are paid to the pool.
2 Köster cross-references the English mistress with "a reputed daughter of the Duke of Monmouth" in Manley's *Court Intrigues*.

it; he confessed her to be the greatest mistress of nature that ever was born; she knew, he said, the hidden springs and defects of humankind; self-love was indeed such an inherent evil in all the world, that he was afraid Rivella had spoken something that looked too like truth; but what ever happened he should never be acquainted with a woman of her worth, neither could any thing but extream necessity, force him to abandon her innocence and tenderness.

Not long after Cleander was cast at law,[1] and condemned in a great sum to be paid by the next term; he concealed his misfortunes from Rivella, but she learned them from other persons. One must be a woman of an exalted soul to take the part she did. The troubles of the mind cast her into a fit of sickness; Cleander guessed at the cause, and endeavoured to restore her at any price, having assured her of it; she asked him if he would marry her; he immediately answered he would, tho' he were ruined by it; she told him that was a very hard sentence, she could not consent to his ruin with half so much ease as to her own; then enquired if there was any way to save him? He explained to her his circumstances, and the proposals that had been made to him of courting a rich young widow,[2] but that he could not think of it. Rivella paused a long time, at length pulling up her spirits, and fixing her resolution, she told him it should be so; he should not be undone for her sake; she had received many obligations from him, and he had suffered several inconveniences on her account; particularly in the affair of Mr. Timothy Double. She was proud it was now in her power to repay part of the debt she owed; therefore she conjured him to make his addresses to the lady, for tho' he might be so far influenced by his bride as afterwards to become ingrateful, she would much rather that should happen, than to see him poor and miserable, an object of perpetual reproach to her heart and eyes; for having preferred the reparation of her own honour, to the preservation of his.

I should move you too far, generous D'Aumont, in relating half that tenderness and reluctance, with which it was concluded they

---

1 Ruled against, defeated in court. On 2 March 1702, the King's Bench Court ordered Tilly to pay Thomas Richardson £1000 (see Fidelis Morgan, *A Woman of No Character* 102).

2 Margaret Smith, daughter of Sir John Reresby, 2nd Baronet, and widow of George Smith of Doctors' Commons. Tilly married her on 12 December 1702.

should part. I was the confident between them; but tho' I had esteem and friendship for Cleander, there was something touched my soul more nearly for Rivella's interest; therefore I would have disswaded her from that romantick bravery of mind, by advising her to marry her lover, who was so bright a man, that he could never prove long unhappy, his own capacity being sufficient to extricate him; but as she had never taken my advice in any thing, she did not begin now; there was a pleasure she said in becoming miserable, when it was to make a person happy, by whom she had been so very much obliged, and so long and faithfully beloved!

Cleander's handsom person immediately made way to the widow's heart; it is not my business to speak much of her, tho' the theam be very ample; I have heard him say, that he might have succeeded to his wish, if he could have had the confidence to believe a woman could have been won so quickly. Her relations got notice of the courtship, and represented the disadvantage of the match, which occasioned settlements and security of her own fortune to her own use. Cleander trusted to the power he hoped to gain over her heart; thinking when once they were married, she might be brought to recede, but he was mistaken. The woing lasted but a month; with all the obstacles her friends could raise, which perhaps was a fortnight longer than the date of her passion afterwards. Fears and jealousies ensued; they passed many uneasy hours of wedlock together. He teized the lady about cards, and she him for Rivella who seldom saw him; for she led her life mostly in the country, and never appeared in publick after Cleander's marriage; which with four years uneasiness concluded in the loss of his senses, and in three more of his life;[1] whether the want of Rivella's conversation, which he had so long been used to contributed, or the uneasiness of his circumstances; for his marriage had not answered the fancied end, or something else, which I am not willing to say, where very much may be said; tho' as Rivella's friend, I have no reason to spare Cleander's lady, because she always speaks of her with language most unfit for a gentlewoman, and on all occasions, has used her with the spite and ill nature of an enraged jealous wife.

---

1 According to Fidelis Morgan (*A Woman of No Character* 103), Tilly died in 1705; however, Dolores Diane Clarke Duff's source indicates that he was still alive in 1707 (see "Materials toward a Biography" 48).

After that time, I know nothing memorable of Rivella, but that she seemed to bury all thoughts of gallantry in Cleander's tomb; and unless she had her self published such melting scenes of love, I should by her regularity and good behaviour have thought she had lost the memory of that passion. I was in the country when the two first volumes of the *Atalantis* were published, and did not know who was the author, but came to town just as the Lord S———d[1] had granted a warrant against the printer and publisher.[2] I went as usual, to wait upon Rivella, whom I found in one of her heroick strains; she said she was glad I was come, to advise her in a business of very great importance; she had as yet consulted with but one friend, whose counsel had not pleased her; no more would mine, I thought, but did not interrupt her; in conclusion she told me that her self was author of the *Atalantis*, for which three innocent persons were taken up and would be ruined with their families; that she was resolved to surrender her self into the messenger's hands, whom she heard had the Secretary of State's warrant against her, so to discharge those honest people from their imprisonment. I stared upon her and thought her directly mad; I began with railing at her books; the barbarous design of exposing people that never had done her any injury; she answered me she was become *misanthrope*, a perfect *Timon*,[3] or *man-hater*, all the world was out of humour with her, and she with all the world, more particularly a *faction* who were busy to

---

1   Charles Spencer, 3rd Earl of Sunderland (1674-1722). He married Arabella Cavendish (1673-98), Elizabeth Albemarle's (née Cavendish) sister, in January 1694/95; in September 1699, a widower, he married the Duke and Duchess of Marlborough's daughter, Anne Churchill, and served, largely through Marlborough's influence, as Secretary of State from 1706 to 1710. Sunderland also headed the Attorney-General's committee, which discharged Manley at the Queen's Bench Court on either 13 or 14 February 1709/10.

2   Manley was arrested, along with her publishers, John Morphew and J. Woodward, and her printer, John Barber, on 29(?) October 1709, nine days after the publication of the second volume of *New Atalantis* (Paul Bunyan Anderson, "Mistress Delariviere Manley's Biography" 274, gives the above date, inconsistent with Dolores Diane Clarke Duff's date of October 20th). The men were released on November 1st; Manley was admitted to bail on November 5th (Anderson cites November 5th as the date of Manley's release on bail ["Mistress Delariviere Manley's Biography" 274], whereas Fidelis Morgan cites November 7th in her *A Woman of No Character* 151).

3   A noted Athenian misanthrope; later the misanthropic hero of Shakespeare's *Timon of Athens*.

enslave their sovereign,[1] and overturn the constitution; that she was proud of having more courage than had any of our sex, and of throwing the first stone, which might give a hint for other persons of more capacity to examine the defects, and vices of some men who took a delight to impose upon the world, by the pretence of publick good, whilst their true design was only to gratify and advance themselves. As to exposing those who had never injured her, she said she did no more by others, than others had done by her (i.e.) tattle of frailties; the town had never shewn her any indulgence, but on the contrary reported ten fold against her in matters of which she was wholly innocent, whereas she did but take up old stories that all the world had long since reported, having ever been careful of glancing against such persons who were truly vertuous, and who had not been very careless of their own actions.

Rivella grew warm in her defence, and obstinate in her design of surrendring her self a prisoner. I asked her how she would like going to Newgate?[2] She answered me very well; since it was to discharge her conscience; I told her all this sounded great, and was very heroick; but there was a vast difference between real and imaginary sufferings. She had chose to declare her self of a party most supine, and forgetful of such who served them; that she would certainly be abandoned by them, and left to perish and starve in prison. The most severe criticks upon Tory writings, were Tories themselves, who never considering the design or honest intention of the author, would examine the performance only, and that too with as much severity as they would an enemy's, and at the same time value themselves upon their being impartial, tho' against their friends. Then as to gratitude or generosity, the Tories did not come up to the Whigs, who never suffered any man to want incouragement and rewards if he were never so dull, vicious or insignificant, provided he declared himself to be for them; whereas the Tories had no general interest, and consequently no particular, each person refusing to contribute towards the benefit of the whole;

---

1 Manley here condemns the Whig junta (which included Sunderland), whose power was buttressed by Captain-General Marlborough and 1st Earl Godolphin, Lord Treasurer from 1702 to 1710, both of whom controlled Queen Anne's domestic and foreign policy until the summer of 1710 and the fall of the Whigs.
2 A famous London prison.

and when it should come to pass (as certainly it would) that she perished thro' want in a goal,[1] they would sooner condemn her folly, than pity her sufferings; and cry, she may take it for her pains. Who bid her write? What good did she do? Could not she sit quiet as well as her neighbours, and not meddle her self about what did not concern her?[2]

Rivella was startled at these truths, and asked me, what then would I have her do? I answered that I was still at her service, as well as my fortune. I would wait upon her out of England, and then find some means to get her safe into France, where the Queen, that was once to have been her Mistress, would doubtless take her into her own protection; she said the project was a vain one, that lady being the greatest bigot in nature to the Roman Church, and she was, and ever would be, a Protestant, a name sufficient to destroy the greatest merit in that Court. I told her I would carry her into Switzerland, or any country that was but a place of safety, and leave her there if she commanded me; she asked me in a hasty manner, as if she demanded pardon for hesitating upon the point, what then would become of the poor printer, and those two other persons concerned, the publishers, who with their families all would be undone by her flight? That the misery I had threatened her with, was a less evil than doing a dishonourable thing. I asked her if she had promised those persons to be answerable for the event? She said no, she had only given them leave to say, if they were questioned, they had received the copy from her hand! I used several arguments to satisfy her conscience that she was under no farther obligation, especially since the profit had been theirs; she answered it might be so, but she could not bear to live and reproach her self with the misery that might happen to those unfortunate people. Finding her obstinate, I left her with an angry threat, of never beholding her in that wretched state, into which she was going to plunge her self.

---

1 An early variant of *gaol* (jail).
2 Lovemore, here arguably Manley's mouthpiece, accurately represents Manley's neglect at the hands of the Tory establishment. The only financial reward she appears to have received for her literary contributions to the Tory cause was fifty pounds sent her, clandestinely, by Robert Harley (Earl of Oxford, Prime Minister 1710-14) in June 1714, two months before the death of Queen Anne and the end of Tory rule. See Gwendolyn Needham, "Mary de la Rivière Manley, Tory Defender" 282-84.

Rivella remained immovable in a point which she thought her duty, and accordingly surrendered her self, and was examined in the Secretary's[1] office. They used several arguments to make her discover who were the persons concerned with her in writing her books; or at least from whom she had received information of some special facts, which they thought were above her own intelligence. Her defence was with much humility and sorrow, for having offended, at the same time denying that any persons were concerned with her, or that she had a farther design than writing for her own amusement and diversion in the country; without intending particular reflections or characters. When this was not believed, and the contrary urged very home to her by several circumstances and likenesses; she said then it must be *inspiration*, because knowing her own innocence she could account for it no other way. The Secretary replied upon her, that *inspiration* used to be upon a good account, and her writings were stark naught; she told him, with an air full of penitence, that might be true, but it was as true, that there were evil angels as well as good; so that nevertheless what she had wrote might still be by *inspiration*.

Not to detain you longer, dear attentive D'Aumont, the gathering clouds beginning to bring night upon us, this poor lady was close shut up in the messenger's hands from seeing or speaking to any person, without being allowed pen, ink and paper; where she was most tyranically and barbarously insulted by the fellow and his wife who had her in keeping, tho' doubtless without the knowledge of their superiors; for when Rivella was examined, they asked her if she was civilly used? She thought it below her to complain of such little people, who when they stretched authority a little too far, thought perhaps that they served the intention and resentments, tho' not the commands of their masters; and accordingly chose to be inhuman, rather than just and civil.

Rivella's council sued out her *habeas corpus*[2] at the Queen's Bench-Bar in Westminster-Hall; and she was admitted to bail. Whether the

1   John Hopkins, Under-secretary of State, 1706-10. According to Narcissus Luttrell (*A Brief Historical Relation of State Affairs* VI.112), on 3 December 1706 the Earl of Sunderland took over Sir Charles Hedges's office as Secretary of State, appointing Hopkins and Joseph Addison as his under-secretaries. Hopkins was also godfather, together with Charles Montagu, 1st Earl of Halifax, to Richard Steele's son, Richard.

2   Writ requiring a person's body to be brought before a judge or into court.

persons in power were ashamed to bring a woman to her trial for writing a few amorous trifles purely for her own amusement, or that our laws were defective, as most persons conceived, because she had served her self with romantick names, and a feigned scene of action? But after several times exposing her in person to walk cross the court before the bench of judges, with her three attendants, the printer and both the publishers; the Attorny General at the end of three or four terms dropt the prosecution, tho' not without a very great expence to the defendants, who were however glad to compound with their purses for their heinious offence, and the notorious indiscretion of which they had been guilty.

There happened not long after a total change in the ministry,[1] the persons whom Rivella had disobliged being removed, and consequently her fears dissipated; upon which that native gaiety and good humour so sparkling and conspicuous in her, returned; I had the hardest part to act, because I could not easily forego her friendship and acquaintance, yet knew not very well how to pretend to the continuance of either, considering what I had said to her upon our last seperation the night before her imprisonment. Finding I did not return to wish her joy with the rest of her friends upon her inlargement, she did me the favour to write to me, assuring me that she very well distinguished that which a friend out of the greatness of his friendship did advise, and what a man of honour could be supposed to endure, by giving advice wherein his friend or himself must suffer, and that since I had so generously endeavoured her safety at the expence of my own character, she would always look upon me as a person whom nothing could taint but my friendship for her. I was ashamed of the delicacy of her argument, by which since I was proved guilty, tho' the motives were never so prevalent, still my honour was found defective, how perfect soever my friendship might appear.

Rivella had always the better of me at this argument, and when she would insult me, never failed to serve her self with that false one, *success*, in return, I brought her to be ashamed of her writings, saving that part by which she pretended to serve her country, and the ancient Constitution; (there she is a perfect bigot from a long untaint-

---

1   The Tories rose to power in the summer of 1710 after Queen Anne's dismissal of Godolphin and the Whigs.

ed descent of loyal ancestors, and consequently immoveable) but when I would argue with her the folly of a woman's disobliging any one party, by a pen equally qualified to divert all, she agreed my reflection was just, and promised not to repeat her fault, provided the world would have the goodness to forget those she had already committed, and that hence-forward her business should be to write of pleasure and entertainment only, wherein *party* should no longer mingle; but that the Whigs were so unforgiving they would not advance one step towards a coalition with any muse that had once been so indiscreet to declare against them. She now agrees with me, that politicks is not the business of a woman, especially of one that can so well delight and entertain her readers with more gentle pleasing theams, and has accordingly set her self again to write a tragedy for the stage.[1] If you stay in England, dear Chevalier, till next winter, we may hope to entertain you from thence, with what ever Rivella is capable of performing in the dramatick art.

But has she still a taste for love, interrupted young Monsieur D'Aumont? Doubtless, answered Sir Charles, or whence is it that she daily writes of him with such fire and force? But whether she does love, is a question.[2] I often hear her express a jealousy of appearing fond at her time of day, and full of rallery[3] against those ladies, who sue when they are no longer sued unto. She converses now with our sex in a manner that is very delicate, sensible, and agreeable; which is to say, knowing her self to be no longer young, she does not seem to expect the praise and flattery that attend the youthful. The greatest genius's of the age, give her daily proofs of their esteem and friendship; only one excepted, who yet I find was more in her favour than any other of the wits pretend to have been, since he in print has very lately told the world, 'twas his own fault he was not happy, for which omission he has publickly and gravely asked her pardon.[4] Whether this proceeding was so Chevalier as is ought, I will no more deter-

---

1   *Lucius, the First Christian King of Britain*, which was first performed at Drury Lane in May 1717.
2   The copytext contains a question mark here.
3   Raillery.
4   Richard Steele wrote the prologue to *Lucius*, and Manley, who likewise acknowledged her part in the rift, dedicated the play to Steele (see Appendix C. 4).

mine against him, than believe him against her; but since the charitable custom of the world gives the lie to that person, whosoever he be, that boasts of having received a lady's favour, because it is an action unworthy of credit, and of a man of honour; may not he by the same rule be disbelieved, who says he might and would not receive favours; especially from a sweet, clean, witty, friendly, serviceable and young woman, as Rivella was, when this gentleman pretends to have been *cruel*; considering that in the choice of his other amours, he has given no such proof of his delicacy, or the niceness of his taste? But what shall we say, the prejudice of *party* runs so high in England, that the best natured persons, and those of the greatest integrity, scruple not to say false and malicious things of those who differ from them in principles, in any case but love; scandal between Whig and Tory, goes for nothing; but who is there besides my self, that thinks it an impossible thing a Tory lady should prove frail, especially when a person (tho' never so much a Whig) reports her to be so, upon his own knowledge.

Thus generous D'Aumont, I have endeavoured to obey your commands, in giving you that part of Rivella's history, which has made the most noise against her; I confess, had I shown only the bright part of her adventures; I might have entertained you much more agreeably, but that requires much longer time; together with the songs, letters and adorations, innumerable from those who never could be happy. Then to have raised your passions in her favour; I should have brought you to her table well furnished and well served; have shown you her sparkling wit and easy gaiety, when at meat with persons of conversation and humour. From thence carried you (in the heat of summer after dinner) within the nymphs alcove, to a bed nicely sheeted and strowed with *roses, jessamins* or *orange-flowers*, suited to the variety of the season; her pillows neatly trimmed with lace or muslin, stuck round with *junquils*,[1] or other natural garden sweets, for she uses no perfumes, and there have given you leave to fancy your self the happy man, with whom she chose to repose her self, during the heat of the day, in a state of sweetness and tranquility. From thence con-

---

1 "A species of Narcissus, having long linear leaves and spikes of fragrant white and yellow flowers; the rush-leaved Daffodil" (*OED*).

ducted you towards the cool of the evening, either upon the water, or to the park for air, with a conversation always new, and which never cloys; *Allon's* let us go my dear Lovemore, interrupted young D'Aumont, let us not lose a moment before we are acquainted with the only person of her sex that knows how to *live*, and of whom we may say, in relation to love, since she has so peculiar a genius for, and has made such noble discoveries in that passion, that it would have been a *fault in her, not to have been faulty.*

FINIS.

Appendix A: Edmund Curll's[1] Preface and Key to the Fourth (1725) Edition of Rivella

1. Preface to *Mrs. Manley's History of her Own Life and Times*

To the Reader.

It must be confessed, that these *Memoirs* have been written above ten years; and, likewise, that they have been published as long, though under a different title.[2] The reason of which, as well as to prove them genuine, I shall lay before the reader with as much brevity, as the fact will admit of.

In the year 1714, Mr. Gildon,[3] upon a pique, the cause of which I cannot assign, wrote some account of Mrs. Manley's life, under the title of, *The History of Rivella, Author of the Atalantis*. Of this piece, two sheets only were printed, when Mrs. Manley hearing it was in the press, and suspecting it to be, what it really was, a severe invective upon some part of her conduct, she sent me the following letter;

Sir,
As I have never, personally, disobliged, I have no reason to fear your being inexorable as to any point of friendship, or civility, which I shall require of you, provided I make it your own interest to oblige me. If the pamphlet you have advertised be not already published, I beg the favour of you to defer it 'till I have spoken to you. Please to send me word, what hour after four o'clock, this day, you will be at home, and I will call at your house. If you should not be at home when this note comes, pray send me a line or two when I shall wait on you, which will very much oblige,

---

1 Edmund Curll (1675? 1683?-1747), publisher/bookseller; notorious for pirating and other dubious business practices, he made enemies of Swift and Pope, the latter of whom attacked him in *The Dunciad*, as well as in various political pamphlets.
2 For *Rivella's* various titles, see my note on the text.
3 Charles Gildon (1665-1724), dramatic and miscellaneous hack writer, denounced in Pope's *The Dunciad*.

Sir,

Tues. Mar. 1714.   Your humble servant,

past 12 a clock.   D. Manley.

Direct for me, at Mr. Barber's[1] on Lambeth-Hill.

I returned for answer to this letter, that I should be proud of such a visitant. Accordingly, Mrs. Manley, and her sister,[2] came to my house in Fleet-Street, whom, before that time, I had never seen, and requested a sight of Mr. Gildon's papers. Such a request, I told her, I could not, by any means, grant, without asking Mr. Gildon's consent; but, upon hearing her own story, which no pen, but her own, can relate in the agreeable manner wherein she delivered it, I promised to write to Mr. Gildon the next day; and not only obtained his consent to let Mrs. Manley see what sheets were printed, but also brought them to an interview, by which means, all resentments between them were thoroughly reconciled. Mr. Gildon was, likewise, so generous, as to order a total suppression of all his papers; and Mrs. Manley, as generously resolved to write the history of her own life, and times, under the same title which Mr. Gildon had made choice of. The truth of which will appear by this letter.

Sir,

I am to thank you for your very honourable treatment, which I shall never forget. In two or three days, I hope to begin the work.

I like your design of continuing the same name and title. I am resolved to have it out as soon as possible. I believe you will agree to print it as it is writ. When you have a mind to see me, send me word, and I will come to your house; for if you come upon this hill, B. will find it out; for God's sake let us try if this affair can be kept a secret.[3] I am, with all respects,

---

1   See Appendix E.
2   Cornelia Markendale.
3   Manley appears to have feared offending Curll's rival printer/publisher, John Bar-
    ber, with whom she was living. Years later, in his biography of Barber, Curll would
    present him as a greedy, profit-driven opportunist, who acquired vast sums from
    Manley's writings (see *An Impartial History of the Life, Character, Amours, Travels, and
    Transactions of Mr. John Barber* ..., especially xxvii, note, and 35-36). Also see Appen-
    dix E.

	Sir,
Wednesday noon	Your most obliged humble
15 Mar.	servant,
	D. Manley.

P.S. I have company, and time to tell you only, that your services are such to me, that can never be enough valued. My pen, my purse, my interest, are all at your service. I shall never be easy, 'till I am grateful.

About a week after, I received the greatest part of the manuscript, with the following letter.

Sir,

Judge that I have not been idle, when I have sent you so much copy. How can I deserve all this friendship from you? I must ask you to pity me; for I am plagued to death for want of time, and forced to write by stealth. I beg the printer may not have any other to interfere with him, especially because I shall want time to finish it with that *eclat* I intend. I dread the noise 'twill make when it comes out; it concerns us all to keep the secret. I design to wait on you, to tell you part of that extream acknowledgment, which, my heart tells me, is due to so sincere a friend.

Yours, & c.

D.M.

While these *Memoirs* were in the press, I had the favour of several other obliging letters from Mrs. Manley, in one of which she says, "though the world may like what I write of others, they despise whatever an author is thought to say of themselves."

   This being the sole reason of her throwing it into the disguise of a translation, and insisting, that it should be kept a secret during her life-time; I hope what is now produced, will be allowed to be a sufficient proof of her being the genuine author.

29 Sept. 1724.

E. Curll.

2. Key to *Rivella*

A Key to the Adventures of Rivella

Rivella,	Author of the *Atalantis*.
Sir Charles Lovemore,	Lieuten. Gen. Tidcomb.
Mr. C.	Mr. Calvert, son to the Lord Baltimore.
Mr. S—le,	Mr. Steele.
Lysander,	Mr. Carlisle.
Hilaria,	Late Dutchess of Cleveland.
A lady next door to the poor recluse,	Nominal Mrs. Rider, Sir Richard Fanshaw's daughter, sister to Mrs. Blount, house keeper to the Lord S——rs.
Count Fortunatus,	Duke of M——gh.
Kitchin-maid married to her master,	Pretended Madam Beauclair.
Her patroness's eldest son,	Duke of C——nd and S—ton.
Young lady of little or no fortune,	Late Lady Poultney's daughter, Dutchess to Ditto.
The man Hilaria was in love with,	Mr. Goodman, the player.

He kept a mistress in the next street,	Mrs. Wilson, of the Pope's-Head Tavern in Cornhill.
The First Dutchess in England,	Late Dutchess of Norfolk.
Sir Peter Vainlove,	Sir Thomas Skipwith.
Mrs. Settee,	Mrs. Pym. She has 4 daughters.
Lord Crafty,	Late Duke of M—ue.
Merchant Double,	Late Duke of A—marle.
Baron Meanwell,	Late Earl of Bath.
Old Double,	General Monk.
Two prelates of the Church of England,	i.e. Two peers.
Bought the merchant's widow of her two women,	The two Mrs. Wrights, in Bloomsbury-Square.
Tim. Double,	Christopher Monk, son to Colonel Monk.
Petty-pan merchant,	Mr. Hungerford, a pastry-cook in Limestreet.
Calista,	Mrs. Trother.
Cleander,	Mr. Tilly.
Oswald,	The late John Manley, Esq; Member of Parliament, and Surveyor-General.

The chief seat of the Doubles,	New-Hall in Essex.
Bella,	Kitty Baker, an actress.
Flippanta,	Servant to Rivella.
Old Simon,	Mr. Simpson, retainer to the Duke of M—gue.
A rich young widow,	Mr. Geo. Smith's widow of Doctors-Commons, now Mrs. Tilly.
Secretary, who examined Rivella,	John Hopkins, Esq;
The person, who publickly and gravely asked Rivella's pardon	Richard Steele, Esq;

F I N I S.

Appendix B: Excerpts from New Atalantis(1709)

i. New Atalantis: I.33-34

[Count Fortunatus (Marlborough), devises a scheme in order to dupe his mistress, the duchess (Barbara Cleveland), who expects to find him "lain down upon a day-bed." Instead, she discovers the amorous Germanicus (Henry Jermyn, Baron of Dover), who arouses her passion with his beauty. Following this scene, Fortunatus bursts in, feigns anger, and declares that he will marry Jeanatine (Sarah Jennings).]

... [T]he servants were all out of the way as usual, only one gentleman, that told her, his Lord was lain down upon a day-bed that joined the bathing-room, and he believed, was fallen a sleep since he came out of the bath; the Dutchess softly entered that little chamber of repose, the weather violently hot the umbrelloes[1] were let down from behind the windows, the sashes open, and the jessamine that covered 'em blew in with a gentle fragrancy; tuberoses set in pretty gilt and china posts, were placed advantageously upon stands, the curtains of the bed drawn back to the canopy, made of yellow velvet embroidered with white bugles, the panels of the chamber looking-glass, upon the bed were strowed with a lavish profuseness, plenty of orange and lemon flowers, and to compleat the scene, the young Germanicus in a dress and posture not very decent to describe; it was he that was newly risen from the bath, and in a lose gown of carnation taffety, stained with Indian figures, his beautiful long, flowing hair, for then 'twas the custom to wear their own tied back with a ribbon of the same colour, he had thrown himself upon the bed, pretending to sleep, with nothing on but his shirt and night-gown, which he had so indecently disposed, that slumbring as he appeared, his whole person stood confessed to the eyes of the amorous Dutchess, his limbs were exactly formed, his skin shiningly white, and the pleasure the ladies graceful entrance gave him, diffused joy and desire throughout all his form; his lovely eyes seemed to be closed, his face turned on one side

---

1   An obsolete variant of *umbrellas*.

(to favour the deceit) was obscured by the lace depending from the pillows on which he rested; the Dutchess, who had about her all those desires, she expected to employ in the embraces of the Count, was so blinded by 'em, that at first she did not perceive the mistake, so that giving her eyes, time to wander over beauties so inviting, and which encreased her flame; with an amorous sigh, she gently threw her self on the bed close to the desiring youth; the ribbon of his shirt-neck not tied, the bosom (adorned with the finest lace) was open, upon which she fixed her charming mouth, impatient and finding that he did not awake, she raised her head, and laid her lips to that part of his face that was revealed. The burning lover thought it was now time to put an end to his pretended sleep, he clasped her in his arms, grasped her to his bosom, her own desires helped the deceit; she shut her eyes with a languishing sweetness, calling him by intervals, her dear Count, her only lover, taking and giving a thousand kisses, he got the possession of her person, with so much transport, that she owned all her former enjoyments were imperfect to the pleasure of this.

ii. *New Atalantis*: I.63–65

[Manley's unregenerate Duke (William Bentinck, Earl of Portland) begins his seduction of his innocent ward, Charlot (Stuarta Howard) by means of art, introducing her to a poem by Ovid, specifically, to the passionate love between a daughter and father.]

He observed formerly, that she was a great lover of poetry, especially when 'twas forbid her; he took down an *Ovid*, and opening it just at the love of Myrra for her father, conscious red overspread his face; he gave it her to read, she obeyed him with a visible delight.... She took the book, and placed herself by the Duke, his eyes feasted themselves upon her face, thence wandered over her snowy bosom, and saw the young swelling breasts just begining to distinguish themselves, and which were gently heaved at the impression Myrra's sufferings made upon her heart, by this dangerous reading, he pretended to shew her, that there were pleasures her sex were born for, and which she might consequently long to taste! Curiosity is an early and dangerous enemy to virtue, the young Charlot, who had by a noble inclination of gratitude a strong propension of affection for the Duke, whom she called and estemed her papa, being a girl of wonderful reflection, and consequently application, wrought her imagination up to such a lively heighth at the fathers anger after the possession of his daughter, which she judged highly unkind and unnatural, that she dropped her book, tears filled her eyes, sobs rose to oppress her, and she pulled out her handkerchief to cover the disorder.... [T]he Duke's pursuing kisses overcame the very thoughts of any thing, but that new and lazy poison stealing to her heart, and spreading swiftly and imperceptibly thro' all her veins, she closed her eyes with languishing delight! delivered up the possession of her lips and breath to the amorous invader; returned his eager grasps, and, in a word, gave her whole person into his arms, in meltings full of delight!

iii. *New Atalantis*: II.227-28

[Don Tomasio Roderiguez (Thomas, 1st Earl of Coningsby) follows Diana de Bedamore (Frances Scudamore), who is staying at his country estate with her husband, into the garden where he finds her sleeping; Tomasio's seduction of Diana provides a gender-inverted counterpoint to the earlier seduction scene involving the duchess and Germanicus, who feigns sleep.]

[T]he beautiful Diana ... passed down into the gardens; she had nothing on but her night-dress, one petticoat, and a rich silver stuff nightgown that hung carelessly about her. It was the evening of an excessive hot day, she got into a shade of orange flowers and jessamine, the blossoms that were fallen covered all beneath with a profusion of sweets. A canal run by, which made that retreat *delightful* as 'twas *fragrant*. Diana, full of the uneasiness of mind that love occasioned, threw her self under the pleasing canopy, apprehensive of no Acteon[1] to invade with forbidden curiosity, her as *numerous perfect beauties*, as had the goddess. Supinely laid on that repose of sweets, the dazling lustre of her bosom stood revealed, her polished limbs all

---

1   A mythological hunter who was turned into a stag by the Roman goddess Diana (in Greek myth, Artemis), patroness of virginity and hunting, as punishment for watching her bathe.

careless and extended, showed the *artful* work of *nature*. Roderiguez (who only pretended to depart, and had watched her every motion) with softly treading steps, stole close to the *unthinking* fair, and throwing him at his length beside her, fixed his lips to hers, with so happy a *celerity*, that his arm was round her to prevent her rising, and himself in possession of her lovely mouth, before she either saw or heard his approach. Her surprise caused her to shriek aloud, but there was none in hearing; he presently appeased her, and with all the artful address of powerful love, conjured her not to remove from him that *enchanting prospect* of her beauties! He vowed he would not make himself possessor of *one* charm without her willing leave; he *sighed*, he looked with *dying! wishing! soft-regards!* The lovely *she* grew *calm* and *tender!* The *rhetorick* of one beloved, his *strange bewitching* force; she suffered all the *glowing* pressures of his *roving* hand, that hand, which with a luxury of joy, wandered through all the rich *meanders* of her bosom; she suffered him to *drink* her dazling naked beauties at his eyes! to *gaze!* to *burn!* to press her with *unbounded rapture!* taking by intervals a thousand *eager short-breathed* kisses. Whilst Diana, lulled by the enchanting poison love had diffused throughout her form, lay *still*, and *charmed* as he! — — she *thought* no more! —— she *could not* think! —— let *love* and *nature* plead the weighty cause! —— let *them* excuse the beauteous frailty! —— obedient to the dictates of the goddess!——

iv. *New Atalantis*: II.183-91

[Delia relates, to the Grand Druid, the events surrounding her bigamous marriage to her cousin, Don Marcus (John Manley).]

To him [Don Marcus] it was, that, upon his dying bed, he [Delia's father] left the care of my youngest sister and my self.... He [Don Marcus] had always had an obliging fondness, that was wonderfully taking with girls; we loved him as much as possible. He sent us into the country, to an old out-of-fashion aunt,[1] full of the *heroick stiffness* of her own times; would read books of *chivalry* and *romances* with her spectacles. This sort of conversation infected me, and made me fancy

---

1 See *Rivella*, p. 53, note 3.

every stranger that I saw ... some disguised *prince* or *lover*. It was not long before my aunt died, and left us at large, without any controul. This immediately reached Don Marcus's notice: he took post, and came down to fetch us to Angela. He was in deep mourning, and, as he told us, for his wife.... My cosin guardian immediately declared himself my lover, with such an eagerness, that none can guess at who are not acquainted with the violence of his temper. I was no otherwise pleased with it, than as he answered something to the character I had found in those books, that had poysoned and deluded my dawning reason. However, I had the *honour* and *cruelty* of a true *heroin*, and would not permit my adorer so much as a kiss from my hand.... I fell ill of a violent fever, where my life was despaired of. Don Marcus and my sister never quitted the chamber in sixteen nights.... In short, having ever had a gratitude in my nature, and a tender sense of benefits; upon my recovery I promised to marry him. ˎTwas fatally for me performed in the presence of my sister, one maid-servant, and a gentleman who had married a relation of ours. I was then wanting of fourteen, without any *deceit* or *guess* of it in others....

I was uneasy at being kept a prisoner, but my husband's fondness and jealousy was the pretence.... Soon after I proved with child, and so perpetually ill, that I implored Don Marcus to let me have the company of my sister and my friends. When he could have no relief from my importunity (being assured, that in seeing my relations, I should learn the more than barbarous deceit he had used to betray me) he thought that it was best for himself to discover it: after having first tried all the arguments he could invent, then the authority of a husband, but in vain, for I was fixt to my point, and would have my sister's company: he fell upon his knees before me, that I was at a loss to know what could work him to such a pitch. At length, with a thousand interrupting tears and sobs, he stabbed me with the wounding relation of his wife's being still alive! conjured me to have some mercy upon a lost man as he was, in an obstinate, inveterate passion, that had no alternative but death or possession; could he have supported the pain of living without me, he would never have made himself so great a *villain*....

My fortune was in his hands, or worse, already lavished away in those excesses of drinking and play, that he could not abstain from, tho' he had lately married me, a wife, whom he pretended to be fond of; I was young, unacquainted with the world, had never seen the necessities of it, knew no arts, had not been exposed to any hardships....What could I do? forlorn! distressed! beggard! to whom could I run for refuge, even from want and misery, but to the very traitor that had undone me? I was acquainted with none that would espouse my cause, a *helpless, useless* load of grief and melancholly! with child! disgraced! my own relations, either impotent of power or will to relieve me!

Thus was I detained by my unhappy circumstances, and his prevailing arts, to wear away three wretched years in his guilty house....

When by degrees I began to look abroad in the world, I found the reputation I had lost, (by living in such a clandestine manner with Don Marcus) had destroyed all the esteem that my truth and conversation might have else procured me. O nice unrelenting glory! is it impossible to retrieve thee? impossible to bend thee! wilt thou for ever be *inexorable* and *ingrateful* to my caresses? is there no retrieve for honour lost? the gracious gods more merciful to the sins of mortals, accept repentance, tho' the nobler part, the soul, be there concerned, and suffer our sins to be washed away by tears of penitence. But the world, truly inexorable, is never reconciled! unequal distribution! Why are your sex so partially distinguished? Why is it in your powers, after accumulated crimes, to regain opinion? When ours, tho' oftentimes guilty, but in appearance, are irretrievably lost?

Appendix C: Delarivier Manley and Richard Steele[1]

1. Selections from letters from *The Lady's Paquet Broke Open* (1707)

i. *The Lady's Paquet*: Letter XII

There is nothing in all my late follies and disappointments that afflicts me so much as disobliging you; to injure you, is to lose the favour of a muse. Yet, madam, I hope you will still be so good as to do me the honour you designed me on Friday evening; where you will inspire me with your presence; for to you absent I can say nothing; to you present, 'tis not excellence to be eloquent, for you are not only author of all the elegant things yourself speak, but of all that others say to you.

ii. *The Lady's Paquet*: Letter XV

...You never tell me any news. I have none but love-toys; my mistress again flies me, but I will understand no other but that 'tis to be pursued; for I make love as I would lay a siege; 'tis not my business to consider whether I shall win the town or not; but I know it's my duty to lay my bones there, or do it. I do not know what to talk to you longer, but know, I can't end till the end of the paper. Let me hear how love thrives in town, and also how you are now employed, as to business.

---

1   According to Paul Bunyan Anderson, Manley and Steele had become acquainted while Manley was living with John Tilly, became friends, and carried on an affectionate correspondence while Steele was stationed as a soldier in the Isle of Wight (1697-99). Anderson points out that letters XII-XXIV and XXXIV-XXXVII from Manley's *The Lady's Paquet Broke Open* (1707), reissued as *Court Intrigues* (1711), are "either the actual texts of Steele's correspondence with Mrs. Manley or fictionized adaptations of an actual correspondence" (see "Mistress Delariviere Manley's Biography," 271, note 37).

iii. *The Lady's Paquet*: Letter XVII

... I see you, Madam, I see *Venus* as busie in the coals, as ever *Vulcan*[1] was, and riches affixed at last to a beauteous form and engaging mien. I wish, Madam, the charms of your person as immortal as those of your wit.

iv. *The Lady's Paquet*: Letter XX

My having been a day or two out of this island,[2] prevented the receipt of yours till today; wherein you give me the exalted station of lying at your feet. Believe hereafter the call for letters to be my passing-bell, if you neglect writing. I cannot blame you, tho' I hate those that interrupt you. For, who would not engross you? The verses, I will immediately fall upon, and send you. Pray tell me seriously whether you are perfectly assured in your secret. I can depend upon what you approve. For tho' you have a great deal of will there's no deceiving you. I can't tell what my Lord's[3] intentions for me are, but am sure he has exceeded my desert already. I know not but I may be hereafter in a capacity to receive you here, and see this the fortunate island. For if you do not redress, you make us forget our misfortunes; and methinks I could ever thus delude the misery of your absence by writing to you, but that I prefer your satisfaction to my own, and return you to the company that envy me a line from you, to bribe 'em to give you leisure sometimes for a charity to, Madam,

Your most obedient,
most humble servant.

---

1   Roman god of fire and metalworking; later identified with the Greek god Hephaestus, son of Zeus and Hera.
2   Probably the Isle of Wight (see Rae Blanchard, *The Correspondence of Richard Steele*, 432, note 1).
3   Steele's patron, Colonel John Lord Cutts, Governor of the Isle of Wight from 1693 to 1707.

2. New Atalantis

i. Dedication[1]

Were not the scene of these memoirs in an island with which those of ours are but little acquainted, I should, my Lord, say something in the defence of them, as they seem guilty of particular reflections,[2] defending the author, by the president[3] of our great fore-fathers in satire, who not only flew against the general reigning vices, but pointed at individual persons, as may be seen in Ennius, Varro, Lucian, Horace, Juvenal, Persius, & c. What would have become of the immortality they have derived from their works, if their contemporaries had been of the Tatler's opinion?[4] Who tho' he allows ingratitude, avarice, and those other vices, which the law does not reach, to be the business of satire;[5] yet in another place he says, these are his words, *that where crimes are enormous, the delinquent deserves little pity, but the reporter less.*[6] At this rate vice may stalk at noon secure from

---

1   Manley dedicated both volumes of *New Atalantis* to Henry Somerset, 2nd Duke of Beaufort (1684-1714).
2   Copytext reads *reflection*.
3   Precedent.
4   In April 1709, Steele, a Whig propagandist, became, along with Joseph Addison, author of the thrice-weekly paper the *Tatler*. Manley and Steele engaged in a vitriolic feud that lasted from 1709 until 1717, probably sparked by Steele's refusal to lend her money following her separation from John Tilly in 1702; Manley needed the money in order to pay her fare into the country, where she planned to spend some time with friends. Personal differences subsequently assumed public dimensions, as the former friends sparred within the literary arena, throughout Manley's novels and political pamphlets, as well as in the journalistic domain of the *Tatler*, *Examiner*, and *Guardian* (see, for example, *Tatler*, nos. 63, 92, and 177 [Saturday, 3 September, 1709; Thursday, 10 November, 1709; and Saturday, 27 May, 1710, respectively]; *Examiner*, nos. 46-52 [June and July 1711]; and *Guardian*, nos. 53 and 63 [12 and 23 May 1713, respectively]).
5   See *Tatler*, no. 61 (Tuesday, 30 August, 1709), in which Steele writes: "The greatest evils in human society are such as no law can come at; as in the case of ingratitude, where the manner of obliging very often leaves the benefactor without means of demanding justice, tho' that very circumstance should be the more binding to the person who has received the benefit.... We shall therefore take it for a very moral action to find a good appellation for offenders, and to turn 'em into ridicule under feigned names."
6   See *Tatler*, no. 74 (Thursday, 29 September, 1709), in which Steele includes a letter to Bickerstaff, whose author accuses him of injuring a man through satire, despite

reproach, and the reformer skulk as if he were performing an inglorious as well as ingrateful office. Ingrateful only to the vicious. Whoever is with-held by the consideration of fear, danger, spiteful abuses, recriminations, or the mean hopes of missing pity, has views too dastardly and mercenary for lofty, stedfast souls, who can be only agitated by true greatness, by the love of virtue, and the love of glory!

ii. *New Atalantis*: 187–93

O let me ease my spleen! I shall burst with laughter; these are prosperous times for vice; d'ye see that black beau, (stuck up in a pert chariot) thick-set, his eyes lost in his head, hanging eye-brows, broad face, and tallow complexion, I long to inform my self if it be his own, he cannot yet sure pretend to that. He's called Monsieur LeIngrate; he shapes his manners to his name....

I remember him almost t'other day, but a wretched common trooper; he had the luck to write a small poem, and dedicates it to a person whom he never saw ... he encouraged his performance, took him into his family, and gave him a standard in his regiment;[1] the gentile company that he was let into, assisted by his own genius, wiped off the rust of education; he began to polish his manners, to refine his conversation, and in short, to fit himself for something better than what he had been used; his morals were loose; his principles nothing but pretence, and a firm resolution of making his fortune, at what rate soever, but because he was far from being at ease that way, he covered all by a most profound dissimulation, not in his practice, but in his words, not in his actions, but his pen, where he affected to be extreme religious,[2] at the same time when he had two different creatures lying-in of base children by him....[3]

The lady who had served him, lost her husband, and fell into a

---

Bickerstaff's lofty claims of championing satire's true spirit: "for as you well observe, *there is something very terrible in unjustly attacking men in a way that may prejudice their honour or fortune;* and indeed, where crimes are enormous, the delinquent deserves little pity, yet the reporter may deserve less."

1 Colonel John Lord Cutts.

2 Manley here refers to Steele's treatise *The Christian Hero* (1701), which he dedicated to Lord Cutts.

3 See *Memoirs of Europe* (II, 309), in which Manley refers to the two mothers of Steele's allegedly illegitimate children as "a little mechanick in a shop, and the other

great deal of trouble; after she had long suffered, she attempted his gratitude by the demand of a small favour, which he gave her assurances of serving her in;[1] the demand was not above ten pieces, to carry her from all her troubles to a safe sanctuary, to her friends, a considerable distance in the country; they were willing to receive her if she came, but not to furnish her with money for the journey. He kept her a long time (more than a year) in suspense, and then refused her in two lines, by pretence of incapacity; nay, refused a second time to oblige her with but two pieces upon an extraordinary exigency, to help her out of some new trouble she was involved with.

It is not only to her, but to all that have ever served him he has shewed himself so ingrateful, the very midwife was forced to sue him; in short he pays nor obliges no body, but when he can't help it.

3. *Memoirs of Europe* (1710)

i. Dedication

To
Isaac Bickerstaff, esq;[2]
Sir,
As a dedication is of necessity towards the ornament of a work of this kind, I could not hesitate upon my choice, because experience (and the example of the Indians, who in the worship of their *demons*, consult only fear, which seems to be their strongest passion) has taught me to secure any one that might have been my hero, from the well-bred, further reflections, of so polite a pen as yours. Tho' your Worship, in the Tatler of November the tenth, has been pleased to call a

---

... [a] bright cook-maid." According to Rosalind Ballaster (*New Atalantis* 284, note no. 245), the "little mechanick" was Elizabeth Tonson, niece of Jacob Tonson, the bookseller. Elizabeth gave birth to Elizabeth Ousley in 1699 or 1700; she was educated by Steele. The "bright cook-maid" remains unidentified, although Paul Bunyan Anderson suggests that the epithet is an allusion to Richard Steele's lines in Act Four, Scene Two of *The Lying Lover* (1703): "Ah! culinary fair, compose thy rage; thou whose more skilful hand is still employed in offices for the support of nature, descend not from thyself, thou bright cookmaid" ("Mistress Delariviere Manley's Biography," 265, note 19).

1   Manley recounts her request for money from Steele in 1702 after she and John Tilly separated.
2   Richard Steele (alias Isaac Bickerstaff in the *Tatler*).

patron the filthiest creature in the street,[1] & c. yet I cannot but observe, in innumerable instances, you are so delighted with such addresses, as even to make 'em to your self. I hope therefore, a corroborating evidence of your perfections, may not be unacceptable.

I have learnt from your Worship's lucubrations, to have all the moral virtues in esteem; and therefore take this opportunity of doing justice, and asking a certain worthy gentleman, one Capt. Steele, pardon; for ever mistaking him for your Worship; for if I persevered in that accusation, I must believe him not in earnest, when he makes me these following assurances in a letter, which according to your example, Sir, who seem prodigiously fond of such insertions, I venture to transcribe *verbatim*.[2]

To Mrs Manley.

Madam,

I have received a letter from you, wherein you tax me as if I were Bickerstaff, with falling upon you as author of the *Atalantis*, and the

---

1   Manley alludes to Steele's discussion of libel, libellers, and satirists, in *Tatler* 92 (10 November 1709), in which he writes: "[A]ll the pasquils, lampoons and libels, we meet with now a days, are a sort of playing with the four and twenty letters, and throwing them into names and characters, without sense, truth or wit. In this case, I am in great perplexity to know whom they mean, and should be in distress for those they abuse, if I did not see their judgment and ingenuity in those they commend. This is the true way of examining a libel; and when men consider, that no one man living thinks the better of their heroes and patrons for the panegyrick given 'em, none can think themselves lessened by their invective. The heroe or patron in a libel, is but a scavenger to carry off the dirt, and by that very employment is the filthiest creature in the street."

2   Steele's biographer, George A. Aitken, argues that *Tatler* no. 63 (3 September 1709) was written by Swift and that Manley was mistaken in attributing the scathing portrait of herself to Steele. In the lampoon, the author refers to Manley as "Epicene, the writer of *Memoirs from the Mediterranean*, who, by the help of some artificial poisons conveyed by smells, has within these few weeks brought many persons of both sexes to an untimely fate; and ... with the same odors, revived others who had long since been drowned in the whirlpools of Lethe." Aitken contends that Manley then wrote to Steele accusing him of its authorship. Steele responded on September 6th with a letter of authorial disavowal, which Manley claims to have transcribed *verbatim*. According to the undated original, however, as printed by John Nichols in 1787 (*The Epistolary Correspondence of Sir Richard Steele*), Manley judiciously omitted sentences in her version (see Aitken, *The Life of Richard Steele* 261-63). More recently, Rae Blanchard suggests that it is "quite as likely that Steele altered his draft in writing the letter finally sent" (*The Correspondence of Richard Steele* 31, note 2). I have indicated sentences omitted from Manley's version of the letter in square brackets.

person who honoured me with a character in that celebrated piece. [What has happened formerly between us can be of no use to either to repeat.] I solemnly assure you, you wrong me in this, as much as you know you do in all else you have been pleased to say of me. [I had not money when you did me the favour to ask a loan of a trifling sum of me.] I had the greatest sense imaginable of the kind notice you gave me when I was going on to my ruin, and am so far from retaining an inclination to revenge the inhumanity with which you have treated me, that I give my self a satisfaction in that you have cancelled, with injuries, a friendship I should never have been able to return.

This will convince you how little I am an *ingrate*; for I believe you will allow no one that is so mean as to be forgetful of services,[1] ever fails in returning injuries.

As for the verses you quote of mine, they are still my opinion, i.e.

Against a woman's wit 'tis full as low,
Your malice, as your bravery to show.[2]

and your sex, as well as your quality of a gentlewoman (a justice you would not do my birth and education) shall always preserve you against the pen of your provoked

Sept. 6, 1709   Most humble servant,
                                                   Rich. Steele.

Soon after, two most mighty Tatlers came out,[3] levelled directly at humble *me*; but *that* I could have forgiven, had they not aimed to asperse one *too great to name*. Vain! ridiculous endeavour! as well the sun may be covered with a hand, as such merit sullied by the attempts of the most malicious, most witty pen.

Since Mr. Steele's reconciled friendship (promised after my appli-

---

1   *Kindnesses* in the draft of Steele's letter.
2   The verses are not included in the draft version.
3   Manley here refers to *Tatler*, no. 92 of November 10th, which she mentions earlier in the dedication; the other "mighty" *Tatler* appears to be no. 63 of September 3rd, published three days before, rather than "soon after," the September 6th date in Manley's transcript of Steele's letter.

cation to him when under confinement)[1] could never be guilty of so barbarous a breach, since he could not commit the treacherousest! the basest! the most abject thing upon earth! so contrary to his assurances! It must be you, Sir, to whom my thanks are due; making me a person of such consideration, as to be worthy your important war. A weak unlearned woman's writings, to employ so great a pen! Heavens! how valuable am I? How fond of that *immortality*, even of *infamy*, that you have promised! I am ravished at the thoughts of *living a thousand years hence* in your indelible lines, tho' to *give offence*....

As to the following work (for which I humbly implore your Worship's all-sufficient protection) I refer you to it self and the preface. But could I have found you in your Sheer-lane,[2] in which attempt I have wandered many hours in vain, I should have submitted it, with that humility due to so omnipotent a censor. Receive then, Sir, with your usual goodness, with the same intent with which it is directed, this address of,

Sir,
Your most obliged
Most humble servant,
D.M.

4. *Lucius, the First Christian King of Britain* (1717)

i. Dedication[3]

To
Sir Richard Steele.
When men cast their eyes upon epistles of this kind, from the name of the person who makes the address, and of him who receives it, they

---

1 When Manley was arrested for libel by the Whig government in October 1709, she requested and received assistance from Steele; a month later, the Manley-bashing *Tatler*, no. 92 appeared.

2 Home of Isaac Bickerstaff. Sheer-lane (Shire Lane) was also home to the Kit-Cat Club, a political and literary-minded society of Whigs, which included such members as the publisher, Jacob Tonson, and writers Richard Steele and Joseph Addison (see George A. Aitken, *The Life of Richard Steele* 96-101).

3 At last reconciled with Steele, Manley dedicated *Lucius* to him, while Steele not only contributed a prologue but also helped to produce the play, as well as to promote its revival three years later in the journal *The Theatre*, nos. 10 and 26 (2 Febru-

usually have reason to expect applauses improper either to be given or accepted by the parties concerned. I fear it will, at first sight, be much more so in this address, than any other which has at any time appeared; but while common dedications are stuffed with painful panegyricks, the plain and honest business of this, is, only to do an act of justice, and to end a former misunderstanding between the author, and him, whom she, here, makes her patron. In consideration that one knows not how far what we have said of each other, may affect our character in the world, I take it for an act of honour to declare, on my part, that I have not known a greater mortification than when I have reflected upon the severities which have flowed from a pen, which is now, you see, disposed as much to celebrate and commend you. On your part, your sincere endeavour to promote the reputation and success of this tragedy, are infallible testimonies of the candour and friendship you retain for me. I rejoice in this publick retribution, and with pleasure acknowledge, that I find by experience, that some useful notices which I had the good fortune to give you for your conduct in former life, with some hazard to my self, were not to be blotted out of your memory by any hardships that followed them.

I know you so well, that I am assured you already think I have, on this subject, said too much; and I am confident you believe of me, that did I not conceal much more, I should not say so much. Be then the very memory of disagreeable things forgotten for ever, and give me leave to thank you for your kindness to this play, and in return, to shew towards your merit the same good-will. But when my heart is full, and my pen ready to express the kindest sentiments to your advantage, I reflect upon what I have formerly heard you say, that the fame of a gentleman, like the credit of a merchant, must flow from his own intrinsick value; and that all means to enlarge it, which do not arise naturally from that real worth, instead of promoting the character of either, did but lessen and render it suspicious. I leave you therefore, to the great opportunities, which are daily in your power, of bestowing on your self, what no body else can give you; and wishing you health and prosperity, I omit to dwell upon some very late actions of yours in publick, which unhappy prejudices made, as little

---

ary and 29 March 1720); no. 10 contains Steele's original prologue with additional lines. See also *The Life and Character of John Barber* (T. Cooper) 13-15, for a discussion of the circumstances surrounding the writing of the play.

expected from you, as the zeal and sollicitude which you shewed for my private interests in the success of this play. I shall say no more, trusting to the gallantry of your temper for further proofs of friendship; and allowing you, like a true woman, all the good qualities in the world now I am pleased with you, as well as I gave you all the ill one's when I was angry with you. I remain with the greatest truth,

Sir,

Your most humble,

most faithful, and

most obliged servant,

De la Rivier Manley.

ii. Prologue
By Sir Richard Steele.

> Nat Lee,[1] for buskins famed, would often say,
> To stage-success he had a certain way;
> Something for all the people must be done,
> And with some circumstance each order won;
> This he thought easy, as to make a treat,
> And, for a tragedy, gave this receipt.
> Take me, said he, a princess young and fair,
> Then take a blooming victor flushed with war;
> Let him not owe, to vain report, renown,
> But in the ladies sight cut squadrons down;
> Let him, whom they themselves saw win the field,
> Him to whose sword they saw whole armies yield,
> Approach the heroin with dread surprise,
> And own no valour proof against bright eyes:
> The boxes are your own — the thing is hit,
> And ladies, as they near each other sit,
> Cry, oh! How movingly that scene is writ![2]

---

1 Nathaniel Lee (c.1653-1692), playwright and actor. Like Manley, Lee was the target of governmental retaliation when his antimonarchical play *Lucius Junius Brutus* (1680) was banned during its first run (see Robert Hume, *The Rakish Stage* 116-17).

2 Copytext contains a question mark here.

For all the rest, with ease, delights you'll shape,
Write for the heroes in the pit, a rape:
Give the first gallery a ghost; on th' upper,
Bestow, tho' at that distance, a good supper.
Thus all their fancies, working their own way,
They're pleased, and think they owe it to the play.
But the ambitious author of these scenes,
With no low arts, to court your favour means;
With her success, and disappointment, move,
On the just laws of empire, and of love!

Appendix D: Delarivier Manley and Jonathan Swift

1. Selections from Swift's *Journal to Stella*

i. *Journal to Stella* (1710-13): Letter XXI, 16 April 1711, 244

I went with Ford[1] into the city to-day, and dined with Stratford,[2] and drank Tockay, and then we went to the auction; but I did not lay out above twelve shillings. My head is a little out of order to-night, though no formal fit. My lord keeper[3] has sent to invite me to dinner to-morrow, and you'll dine better with the Dean, and God bless you. I forgot to tell you that yesterday was sent me *A Narrative* printed, with all the circumstances of Mr. Harley's stabbing.[4] I had not time to do it myself; so I sent my hints to the author of the *Atalantis*, and she has cooked[5] it into a six-penny pamphlet, in her own style, only the first page is left as I was beginning it. But I was afraid of disobliging Mr. Harley or Mr. St. John[6] in one critical point about it, and so would not do it myself.

---

1 Charles Ford (1682-c.1741), son of Edward Ford, or Forth; an Irish absentee landlord who spent most of his later years in London, he was a close friend of Swift, frequently mentioned in his *Journal to Stella*.

2 Francis Stratford, one of Swift's schoolmates at Kilkenny Grammar School, and one of the directors (recommended by Swift) of the South Sea Company, established in 1711 by Robert Harley, in which Swift also invested.

3 Sir Simon Harcourt, Baron and 1st Viscount, Tory lawyer, Attorney-General (1707-8), became Lord Chancellor in 1713.

4 Swift here refers to Manley's *A True Narrative of ... the Examination of the Marquis de Guiscard* (1711), which gives her account of Antoine de Guiscard's stabbing of Robert Harley, Chancellor of the Exchequer and Tory party leader. Guiscard (who had worked for the Godolphin ministry during the War of the Spanish Succession, and whose government pension Harley had reduced) made the assassination attempt on 8 March 1711 at Whitehall, where he was brought before the Committee of the Privy Council upon charges of treasonable activities with France.

5 Harold Williams's edition of *Journal to Stella*, which provides my copytext, retains the original spelling *cook'd*.

6 Henry St. John (1678-1751), 1st Viscount Bolingbroke, political writer, Tory ally and later rival of Robert Harley; appointed Secretary of War in 1704.

ii. *Journal to Stella*: Letter XXVI, 3 July 1711, 306

Lord Peterborow desired to see me this morning at nine; I had not seen him before since he came home.[1] I met Mrs. Manley there, who was soliciting him to get some pension or reward for her service in the cause, by writing her *Atalantis*, and prosecution, & c. upon it. I seconded her, and hope they will do something for the poor woman.[2]

iii. *Journal to Stella*: Letter XXXII, 22 October 1711, 390-91

I dined in the city to-day with Dr. Freind,[3] at one of my printers;[4] I enquired for Leigh,[5] but could not find him: I have forgot what sort of apron you want. I must rout among your letters, a needle in a bot-

---

1 Charles Mordaunt (1658-1735), 3rd Earl of Peterborough, general, diplomat, and patron of the arts to whom Swift dedicated several poems. Swift here alludes to Peterborough's return from a diplomatic errand in Vienna in June.

2 In her anti-Whig *New Atalantis*, Manley exalts Peterborough as a General, "who at the head of only six thousand men, ill paid, and worse provided for, subdued three kingdoms as large as Atalantis" (II.144); the three kingdoms to which Manley refers are France, Spain, and Italy. Manley's praise of Peterborough is consistent with her Tory loyalties, as he had received support from the Tories in January 1707-8 in the face of a Whig enquiry into his failure to march on Madrid because of insufficient reinforcements. Swift, who had shifted his political allegiances from the Whigs to the Tories in 1710, was a potentially influential advocate for Manley, not only by virtue of his relationship with Peterborough but also because of his friendship with Harley and St. John, who may be implied in the "they" to whom Swift refers. Years later, in her will of 6 October 1723, Manley acknowledges Swift's potential influence in her request to him to assist her executors in obtaining money owed her by the bookseller and printer, Benjamin Tooke (see Appendix F for a copy of Manley's will).

3 Dr. John Freind (1675-1728), physician, author, and politician; Freind served in Spain under Peterborough in 1705-7.

4 Probably at John Barber's. Barber became Printer to the City of London in 1710; Swift assisted Barber by obtaining the patronage of the ministry, and Barber became printer of *The London Gazette*, *The Examiner*, and *The Mercator*. Swift later helped Barber to become, along with Benjamin Tooke, Stationer to the Ordnance. See *An Impartial History of the Life ... of Mr. John Barber*, especially 1-8, in which Edmund Curll enumerates instances of Swift's assistance to Barber and alleges his ingratitude. See also Appendix E.

5 James (Jemmy) Leigh, a largely absentee Irish landowner, who enjoyed London society; a friend of both Swift and Stella.

tle of hay. I gave Sterne[1] directions, but where to find him Lord knows. I have bespoken the spectacles; got a set of *Examiners*, and five pamphlets, which I have either written or contributed to, except the best, which is the *Vindication of the duke of Marlborough*; and is entirely of the author of the *Atalantis*.

iv. *Journal to Stella*: Letter XXXIII, 3 November 1711, 402

... I have sent to Leigh the set of *Examiners*; the first thirteen were written by several hands, some good, some bad; the next three and thirty were all by one hand, that makes forty six: then that author, whoever he was, laid it down on purpose to confound guessers; and the last six were written by a woman. Then there is an account of Guiscard by the same woman, but the facts sent by Presto.[2] Then *An Answer to the Letter to the lords about Greg,* by Presto; *Prior's journey,* by Presto; *Vindication of the duke of Marlborough,* entirely by the same woman. *Comment on Hare's Sermon,* by the same woman, only hints sent to the printer from Presto to give her.

v. *Journal to Stella*: Letter XL, 28 January 1711-12, 474

Poor Mrs. Manley the author is very ill of a dropsy and sore leg; the printer tells me he is afraid she cannot live long. I am heartily sorry for her; she has very generous principles for one of her sort; and a great deal of good sense and invention: she is about forty, very homely and very fat.

2. *Corinna* (1727)[3]

This day (the year I dare not tell)
Apollo played the midwife's part;

---

1   Enoch Stearne (or Sterne), Collector of Wicklow and Clerk to the Irish House of Lords, cousin of John Stearne who preceded Swift as Dean of St. Patrick's.

2   Swift was called Dr. Presto (Italian for *swift*) by the Duchess of Shrewsbury, a nickname which is used throughout the *Journal*. See Harold Williams's introduction, lviii, to his edition of the *Journal*.

3   The year in which Swift wrote *Corinna* remains in dispute (see, for example, Pat Rogers' headnote to the poem in *Jonathan Swift: The Complete Poems* 650, who

Into the world Corinna fell,
And he endowed her with his art.

But Cupid with a satyr comes;
Both softly to the cradle creep:
Both stroke her hands, and rub her gums,
While the poor child lay fast asleep.

Then Cupid thus: "This little maid
Of love shall always speak and write";
"And I pronounce," the satyr said,
"The world shall feel her scratch and bite."

Her talent she displayed betimes;
For in a few revolving moons,
She seemed to laugh and squall in rhymes,
And all her gestures were lampoons.

At six years old, the subtle jade
Stole to the pantry-door, and found
The butler with my Lady's maid;
And you may swear the tale went round.

She made a song, how little Miss
Was kissed and slobbered by a lad:
And how, when Master went to piss,
Miss came, and peeped at all he had.

At twelve, a poet, and coquette;
Marries for love, half whore, half wife;

---

argues for 1712, and Constance Clark in *Three Augustan Women Playwrights*, who maintains that it was written after 1714, "for 'Curll,' who published ... *Rivella*, had not met her before they embarked on the project" [132]). For possible alternatives to Manley as the poem's satiric object, see, for example, John R. Elwood, *Notes and Queries* 529-30, who suggests that Swift's reference to the *New Utopia* is to Eliza Haywood's *Memoirs of a Certain Island Adjacent to the Kingdom of Utopia* (1724-5), and M. Heinemann, *Notes and Queries* 218-21, who proposes that Corinna incorporates a number of Curll's women authors, including Manley.

Cuckolds, elopes, and runs in debt;
   Turns authoress, and is Curll's for life.

Her commonplace book all gallant is,
   Of scandal now a cornucopia;
She pours it out in an *Atlantis*,
   Or *Memoirs of the New Utopia*.

Appendix E: Delarivier Manley and John Barber[1]

i. *The Life and Character of John Barber*: 10-16[2]

A gentleman, one of the brightest parts in Britain, paid Mr. Barber a visit, which was succeeded by another from a lady of distinguished merit; whose works will be prized, whilst eloquence, wit and good sense are in esteem among mankind. The former was the late Lord Bolingbroke;[3] but it seems almost needless to mention the lady's name; not one of the fair sex being at that time so much in vogue for these, as Mrs. Manley, to whom we are indebted for the *Atalantis; Lucius, first Christian King of Britain,* and a *Miscellany,*[4] not yet collected, of valuable pieces in verse and prose.

The effects of these interviews proved very fortunate and happy to our alderman; from hence a friendship and intimacy commenced, which raised him in time, to be above wanting the friendships of any other persons but themselves, and of those they led him to an acquaintance with....

These were friends, but we must not forget a favourite. The transition from friendship to affection, is very easy, and often made, when the most amiable part of the species is concerned. Mrs. Manley had not conversed many months with Mr. Barber, but she began to view him in a different light from the rest; she found, that what had pleased

---

1 John Barber (1675-1741), son of a barber, began his career as a printer's apprentice, becoming Printer to the City of London in 1710; he was later elected Alderman (1722), Sheriff (1730), and Lord Mayor of London (1732). Manley lived with Barber from 1714 to the time of her death in 1724 (see Melinda Rabb, "The Manl(e)y Style" 128-31 and 151-52 for a brief discussion of Manley's arguably nonsexual relationship with the printer).

2 In the preface to the considerably less flattering biography of Barber, *An Impartial History of the Life ... of Mr. John Barber,* signed Philalethes, the author (Edmund Curll?) identifies Norton de Foe (son of Daniel Defoe) as the author of this biography, a "twelve-penny romance, published by T. Cooper in Paternoster-Row, for his reputable employer W. Rayner" (iv).

3 See Appendix D, p. 138, note 6.

4 In *An Impartial History of the Life ... of Mr. John Barber,* Curll mentions "pieces of hers [Manley's] I have by me, together with her three [sic] plays, [which] may probably see a new edition this ensuing winter" 47. This collection (which never materialized) may be the *Miscellany* to which the biographer refers.

her ear, had touched her heart; and she soon found, that his person, good sense, and address, had made a captive of her, when she only meant a courtesy. He was too discovering, not to be sensible of the impression he had made; and judged too well of the consequences, not to know, that his interest was too greatly concerned in improving the success his applications had already met with, for him to give over those applications, till the possession of the wished for prize crowned his attempt....

... Mr. Barber was now sure of a set of friends, whom he was determined to oblige at all events; his inclination and interest, in this, suited exactly; they were persons after his own heart ... and 'tis certain, that the great regard Mr. St. John upon all occasions shewed for him, and the *peculiar attachment* of Mrs. Manley to him, were incidents to which he was now indebted for the prosperity thro' every future year of business after his acquaintance with them which attended him, than to all the other fortunate accidents, which conspired, either to advance his fortune, or render him popular....

He had been acquainted with Mrs. Manley some years before this more than ordinary intimacy commenced; but then 'twas only a slight acquaintance, such as arises between an author and a printer; the employer and the employed; but when they came to an ecclarissement, they came to a much more intimate correspondence; and for the sake, *only,* of being near the press and more at hand, to see her own work done *correctly*, and better attended to than it had been; she had an apartment fitted up for her, at the house of Mr. Barber, with whom she resided, to the day of her death....

This lady's conversation and residence with Mr. Barber, continued the same for some years; and her capacity and conduct were equally concerned in rendering her person and parts subservient both to his pleasure and profit at home, and in promoting his interest abroad. Every valuable friend she had in the world, she made a friend to him; and perhaps, there was not any person to whom he was more obliged for an extensive acquaintance among the gay and the great, than to Mrs. Manley, except Mr. St. John.

He continued her favourite, and she is, in particular, all the time of Lord Oxford's ministry;[1] and was in those memorable years highly

---

1   See *Rivella*, p. 109, note 2.

serviceable to the cause Mr. Barber was, as deeply as his station would admit of engaged in. She was naturally attached to the interest of Monarchy, and therefore heartily espoused the side which she fancied inclined to the same way of thinking with herself. Several political pieces of that day, which common fame ascribed to other pens, came wholly from her own; and she often shined in the *Examiner,* without the world's knowing that she had any hand in it. 'Twas indeed by that canal[1] that she chiefly conveyed her thoughts on state affairs to the town; and for several months together she wrote the *Examiner,* without any other person's being concerned in it, but herself. And to the day of her death Mr. Barber had the advantages of her conversation, and the benefit of her pension.[2]

ii. *An Impartial History of the Life of Mr. John Barber.* 22-36[3]

...When he [Barber] arrived at Rome, and had sufficiently viewed the buildings and other curiosities of that vast city; his principles, or his vanity prompted him to desire an interview with the Chevalier....

About twelve o'clock at night, two persons came to him where he waited ... and having conducted him through several obscure passages, brought him to the Royal Apartment where that Prince, attended but by one gentleman, waited his coming. He was received with great civility, and had many questions asked him concerning his friends, the Jacobites in England. The Alderman gave the best account he could; and after a conference of about half an hour, he retired, as happy in his own opinion, as if he had gained a new addition to his fortune. But, instead of that, he was in reality a sufferer by this visit; for he not only made a considerable present on this occasion, but he engaged himself to pay an annuity during life; which he remitted

---

1 Medium, agency.

2 See *An Impartial History of the Life ... of Mr. John Barber* xxvii, note, in which the editor writes that Barber got "many thousand pounds ... and interest" by Manley's writings.

3 Attributed to Edmund Curll, who provided the introduction; purportedly written "by several hands." See Ralph Straus's *The Unspeakable Curll,* which includes a discussion of and extracts from Letitia Pilkington's *Memoirs,* in which she mentions being petitioned, unsuccessfully, by Curll to provide him with some of Swift's letters, "which may embellish the work; and also a true character of the Alderman, written by his chaplain" (191).

with the greatest regret every year after. But he was presented with a ring off the Chevalier's finger.

This affair, tho' very secretly transacted, was known in London long before his return.

Here opens a scene of the blackest ingratitude to his best friend Mrs. Manley, through whose interest all those persons who contributed to make his fortune were owing; besides the large sums he acquired from her writings: the *Atalantis*, her *Novels*,[1] play of *Lucius*, with many political pamphlets. When he heard that his correspondence with the Chevalier was known, he was very cautious in what manner to get safe home. His sole confidence for this purpose, was placed in one of his adorable modern spinsters; an ignorant and insolent country-wench, of as mean an extraction as his own. This creature he hired in the country, and brought her up to town to attend Mrs. Manley in the lowest degree of servitude, a common housemaid, at the wages of four pounds a year. His behaviour to this *dulcinea* soon broke Mrs. Manley's heart, who died before he came out of Italy....

The latter part of his life was no way remarkable. His female intimates were the same, who had ingrossed him ever since the death of the ingenious Mrs. Manley.... [A]s I have observed, he acted a most ungenerous as well as a most ungrateful part to the sister of his best benefactress Mrs. Manley. For though he derived a great part of his wealth from the writings, and interest, of that celebrated *genius*; yet, he never considered the debt he owed her.[2] Nor has he remembered those in his will, who had the *best* and *honestest* claim to his substance.

iii. *An Impartial History of the Life of Mr. John Barber.* 44–46[3]

Mrs. Manley was a gentlewoman both by birth and education. All

---

1   *The Power of Love in Seven Novels.*

2   Barber bequeathed Manley's widowed sister, Mistress Markendale (Cornelia Manley; in *Rivella*, "Cordelia"), fifty pounds "to be paid her at such times, and at such proportions as my executors shall think proper." A copy of Barber's will, dated 21 May 1741, in fact follows Curll's introduction to *An Impartial History of the Life ... of Mr. John Barber.* See, in particular, xxvii–xxviii.

3   The following first two paragraphs are enclosed by double quotation marks in the text, apparently the words of "Civis," a contributor to the biography, who provided Curll with some "facts relating to Mr. Alderman Barber, together with Mrs. Manley's character, monumental inscription, & c." (41).

who had the happiness of her conversation, were soon convinced how free she was from the general vain frailties of her sex; what a nobleness and generosity of temper she was possessed of; how distant her views from the least appearance of self-interest, or mean design; how often have I heard her compassionately regretting the miseries of mankind, but never her own, unless they prevented her benevolence to the afflicted!

Never was she vindictive against the most inveterate enemy. The innate softness of her soul rendered her deportment equally obliging to all beholders; never did she resent but with the strictest justice; and, with equal humanity, forgave the offender.

At length a most violent fit of the cholic, which kept her upon the rack no less than five days, carried her off with its exquisite torture.

She died at Barber's printing-house, on Lambeth-Hill. Her corps was very decently interred in the middle isle of the church of St. Bennet Paul's-Wharf, where, on a marble grave-stone, is the following inscription to her deserving memory, *viz*.

Here lieth the body of
Mrs. Delarivier Manley,
Daughter of Sir Roger Manley, Knight
Who, suitable to her birth and education,
Was acquainted with several parts of
Knowledge.
And with the most polite writers, both in
The French and English tongue.
This accomplishment,
Together with a greater natural stock of
Wit, made her conversation agreeable to
All who knew her, and her writings to be
universally read with pleasure.
She died July the 11th, 1724.

Appendix F: Delarivier Manley's Will[1]

I commit my body to the earth to be as decently and obscurely interred as consists with the circumstances of my birth and present manner of living and if I dye at Beckley[2] my desire is that I may be buried in the body of the said church[3] with a plaine white marble stone bearing a short inscription to be laid over me.... But if it be the will of God that I should dye at London or elsewhere my request is that I may be buried in the churchyard belonging to the same parish in which I shall happen to dye with the same covering stone of white marble only with this addition that my grave may be fenced in with iron rails to preserve it from being disturbed.[4]... Item. fifty pounds a year from off the profits of patent for Kings printer granted by Queen Anne to Ben. Took bookseller[5] and John Barber printer my salary of fifty per annum to commence when they shall receive any profit of the said patent and to continue for the same number of years as their grant shall be in force to which end I humbly beg my much honoured friend the Dean of St. Patrick Dr. Swift as he was privy to the promise that was made me of the said fifty pound a year to be received from the said patent that he will aid and assist my executors[6]

---

1 Taken from Daniel Hipwell's copy of Manley's will (*Notes and Queries*, 7th series, 8 (1889), 156–57. Signed Delarivier Manley, of Beckley, co. Oxford, it was dated 6 October 1723 and was proved 28 September 1724.

2 Manley had a house, where she spent her summers from 1714 to 1724, in Beckley, Oxfordshire. She died, however, at John Barber's house, Lambeth Hill, where she spent her winters.

3 She was buried in the middle aisle of Saint Benet's Church, Paul's Wharf.

4 According to Fidelis Morgan, "Unfortunately, the number of burials in the Wren-designed church during the following two centuries seriously undermined the foundations of the building and led to parts of the floor ominously rising. As a result the entire floor had to be excavated and layers of bones were skimmed off and (in some confusion) reburied elsewhere" (*A Woman of No Character* 160).

5 Benjamin Tooke (d. 1716), London bookseller and, previously, a Dublin printer; also a friend of Jonathan Swift whose influence led to his appointment as printer of the *Gazette*. See also Appendix D, p. 139, note 4.

6 Daniel Hipwell states that Manley appointed "sisters Cornelia Markendale and Henrietta Essex Manley, late of Covent Garden, child's coat maker, but then in the Barbadoes, joint executors of this her will." I have been unable to determine the identity of Henrietta Essex Manley; Delarivier's elder sister was Mary Elizabeth Braithewaite. Henrietta may have been Delarivier's sister-in-law.

in getting the same or having it secured to them especially the moyety from Mr. Tooks executor acknowledging to have received twenty pound of the said Mr. Took when living upon the motive of that claime for which I then gave him my note but could never get him to anything decisive notwithstanding the Deans letters and Alderman Barbers solicitations from whom I acknowledge to have received so many favours that I cannot with any assurance make my claime from him of the half of the fiftie pound a year from the patent only beging he may out of his usuall goodness assist my executors in their lawfull claime upon Mr. Benjamin Tooks share my collection of books one tragedy called the Duke of Somerset and one comedy named the double mistress[1] which may perhaps turn to some account all my other manuscripts[2] what ever I desire may be destroyed that none ghost like may walk after my decease nor any friends letters to me nor copies of mine to them or in a word nor the least from my papers be published but the said tra and com.

---

1 Neither play has been found.
2 In Langbaine and Gildon's *The Lives and Characters of the English Dramatic Poets*, Charles Gildon mentions "several other Books, which have not her [Manley's] name to 'em, and which, for that reason, I shall forbear to mention their titles." Some possibilities, as suggested by Paul Bunyan Anderson ("Mary de la Rivière Manley" 107), are: *Vertue Rewarded* (1693); *The Adventures of the Helvetian Lover* (1693); *The Rival Mother* (1694); and *The Unhappy Lovers* (1694). Robert Adams Day (*Told in Letters* 141) suggests Manley's authorship of the novel *Love Upon a Tick* (1724), whose plot resembles Manley's *Lady's Paquet of Letters* (*The Lady's Paquet Broke Open*). And Constance Clark (*Three Augustan Women Playwrights* 181-82) points to Manley's possible authorship of a ballad opera *The Court Legacy* (1733) and the play *The Unnatural Mother* (1698). The dubious Edmund Curll not only referred to "pieces of hers," which he planned to publish with her three plays (see Appendix F and note) but also tried to persuade Robert Walpole that Manley was, in 1724, working on a fifth volume of *New Atalantis* (see Ralph Straus, *The Unspeakable Curll* 94-95). Manley herself proposed a project to Harley in August 1714, in which she would detail the political changes made just before the death of Queen Anne (see Anderson, "Mistress Delariviere Manley's Biography" 275), a project which, perhaps along with the reportedly forthcoming *Atalantis* volume, may never have been undertaken or may have been destroyed as per her instructions in her will.

Appendix G: Delarivier Manley and her Female Literary Contemporaries

1. Manley's poem "To the Author of *Agnes de Castro*"[1]

Orinda[2] and the fair Astrea[3] gone,
Not one was found to fill the vacant throne:
Aspiring man had quite regained the sway,
Again had taught us humbly to obey;
Till you (natures third start, in favour of our kind)
With stronger arms, their empire have disjoyned,
And snatched a lawrel which they thought their prize,
Thus conqueror, with your wit, as with your eyes.
Fired by the bold example, I would try
To turn our sexes weaker destiny.
Oh! how I long, in the poetic race,
To loose the reins, and give their glory chase;
For, thus encouraged, and thus led by you,
Methinks we might more crowns than theirs subdue.

2. "To Mrs. Manley, by the Author of *Agnes de Castro*"[4]

Th' attempt was brave, how happy your success,
The men with shame our sex with pride confest,
For us you've vanquisht, though the toyl was yours,

---

1 Catherine (Cockburn) Trotter, whose play was based on Aphra Behn's novel, *Agnes de Castro, or The Force of Generous Love* (1688); the play was produced at Drury Lane Theatre in late December 1695 or January 1696.

2 Katherine Philips (1631-1664), poet, translator, and playwright; also called both the *matchless* and the *chaste* Orinda. She was the first English woman to publish a volume of poetry and to have a play produced by a professional London theatre company.

3 Aphra Behn (c.1640-1688), poet, novelist, playwright; possibly the first English woman to earn her living by her writing. See also Appendix H.2.

4 Manley's *The Royal Mischief*, produced in the spring of 1696, inspired Catherine Trotter's poetic tribute. In December of that same year, Trotter called on Manley to assist John Tilly (via John Manley), who was under parliamentary investigation for his activities as Deputy Warden of the Fleet prison.

You were our champion, and the glory ours.
Well you've maintained our equal right in fame,
To which vain man had quite engrost the claim:
I knew my force too weak, and but assayed
The borders of their empire to invade,
I incite a greater genius to my aid:
The war begun you generously pursued,
With double arms you every way subdued;
Our title cleared, nor can a doubt remain,
Unless in which you'll greater conquest gain,
The comick, or the loftier tragick strain.
The men always o'ercome will quit the field,
Where they have lost their hearts, the laurel yield.

3. **"To Mrs. Manley, upon her tragedy called** *The Royal Mischief*"[1]

As when some mighty hero first appears,
And in each act excells his wanting years;
All eyes are fixt on him, each busy tongue
Is employed in the triumphant song:
Even pale envy hangs her dusky wings,
Or joins with brighter fame, and hoarsly sings;
So you the unequalled wonder of the age,
Pride of our sex, and glory of the stage;
Have charmed our hearts with your immortal lays,
And tuned us all with everlasting praise.
You snatch lawrels with undisputed right,
And conquer when you but begin to fight;
Your infant strokes have such Herculean force,
Your self must strive to keep the rapid course;
Like Sappho[2] charming, like Afra[3] eloquent,
Like chast Orinda, sweetly innocent:

---

1 Written by Mary Pix (1666-1709), playwright, novelist, translator; Manley may
   have later satirized her in *New Atalantis* as "a certain poet, who had formerly wrote
   some things with success, but either shrunk in his genius, or grown very lazy"
   (I.90). See Paul Bunyan Anderson (*Philological Quarterly* 170), who connects the lazy
   poet with Pix.
2 Greek lyric poet (7th century B.C.) from the island of Lesbos.
3 Aphra Behn.

But no more, to stop the reader were a sin,
Whilst trifles keep from the rich store within.

4. *The Lover's Week*(1718), by Mary Hearne[1]

i. Dedication

To
Mrs. Manley.

Madam,

YOUR NAME prefixed to any thing of LOVE, who have carried that passion to the most elegant heighth in your own writings, is enough to protect any author who attempts to follow in that mysterious path. I hope it can be no injury in one unknown to you, to ask the patronage of your name: I am sure it is a sufficient recommendation to have it. Writers deal like strangers in these cases, who when they are to try their fortune in a new country, contrive to fix upon a standard name and reputation to assist their hopes at their first appearance.

You, Madam, may lend a portion of your light to cast a lustre over these pages without suffering any diminution, like a rich person, who may support many without feeling the least decrease of his own fortune. Should the obscurity of my writings be never so great, your NAME, like a *diamond* in the dark, will still be but the more eminently conspicuous.

In short, if this trifle has the good fortune to amuse you but one hour, it has gained the end of my ambition. The world must think the better of it; for envy itself dares not dispute when Mrs. MANLEY is the judge, and in that hope I am easy, and continue with as much passion as one of your own sex can be,

Your most obedient
humble servant,
M.H.

May 29.

1718

---

1 The dates of Hearne's birth and death remain unknown; it is possible that "Mary Hearne" is a collective pseudonym for hack writers in the employ of Edmund Curll. A novelist, her(?) works include *The Lover's Week, The Female Deserters* 1719 (a sequel to *The Lover's Week*), and *Honour the Victory and Love the Prize, Illustrated in Ten*

ii. "To the Fair and Ingenious Author of *The Lover's Week*"[1]

In the same mould when sense and beauty meet,
In her full charms the woman shines compleat;
Each might alone a thousand faults supply,
And recommend her to the lover's eye;
But she is doubly fair, in whom we find
The form of Venus and Minerva's[2] mind.

Thy pleasing week in all the force is writ
Of female softness, more than female wit;
In which conspire, my ravished soul to please,
The strength of Addison and Manley's ease;
Thro' each new scene what various charms arise?
Thy paintings please, thy incidents surprize:
Stript of her coying arts and peevish fears
Thy Amaryllis her Philander hears;
In moving words he pleads his wasteful flame,
And shews his bosom to the pitying dame;
The pitying dame is racked with equal pain,
And meets inamoured her inamoured swain.

. . . .

This praise, O! fairest, is sincerely thine,
My judgment dictates each impartial line;
Of flattery I disdain the venal art,
Nor is my tongue a traytor to my heart;

Novels (1720). *The Feminist Companion to Literature in English*, eds. Blain, Clements, and Grundy, also attributes *The German Atalantis* (1715) to Hearne. Hearne's *Lover's Week* may have been partly inspired by the story of Elonora and Don Antonio in *New Atalantis* II.60-109.

1   The poem is signed by the invented "Joseph Gay," who, like Manley's (Rivella's) lovelorn biographer and his captivated listener, D'Aumont, is enraptured by Hearne's power to arouse desire in the male observer/reader. According to Ralph Straus (*The Unspeakable Curll* 78), the actual writer of the poem was John Durant Breval.

2   Ancient Roman goddess of wisdom, invention, and military and technical skill; the Greek goddess, Athena.

By such mean frauds let servile courtiers rise,
And sooth their levees with preferment — lies;
Mine be the praise, to mean and speak the truth,
An honest, open, tho' unhappy, youth.

Nor let, to rob us of another tale,
Thy native envious modesty prevail.
(O! rigid virtue! that no praise would boast,
And then most blushes, when it merits most!)
But still go on, my rapture to improve,
And raise my soul to all the joys of love;
Still in my breast preserve that sacred rage,
And shine the Sappho of the present age;
Still keep thy pen unsheathed in beauty's cause,
And rival our Orinda in applause;
Let Behn and Manley not eclipse thy name,
And whom in beauty you outvy, outvy in fame.

iii. *The Lover's Week*, "The Third Day": 25-31

[Philander persuades Amaryllis to meet him in Covent Garden (unbenownst to Amaryllis, at a bagnio), where she ends up staying until the next morning.]

... I yielded myself entirely to his protection for that night; and received a thousand vows from him, that I should be as safe with him as if I were at home in my aunt's house. He added, to make me the more easy, this friendly advice, saying, had you not better return to morrow morning, when you may have forty excuses for your stay, as that you were at play or dancing all night? and not to go home at this unseasonable hour, without any body to wait on you, it being altogether improper for me to go along with you....

I was presently conducted by Philander up stairs ... into a very neat bed-chamber.... When the maid came up, she asked me, if I pleased to bathe? By this I found I was at a *bagnio*, which I was before ignorant of. I seemed, notwithstanding the many assurances I had received from Philander of my safety, to retain a fresh uneasiness: which he perceiving, said, fear nothing, my angel, you are as safe as if you were in the Royal Palace of St. James's.... Being pretty well satisfied, I then ordered the maid to prepare a bath....

When I returned from bathing, Philander met me on the top of the stairs, and led me into the room where I was to lodge that night ... after imprinting ten thousand kisses on my hand, he took his leave of me, as I thought, for that night. When he quitted the room, he gave such a sigh as if not only his heart, but life remained with me....

I had not been in bed above three quarters of an hour, before I heard my chamber-door open; however, a little recovering myself from my surprize, I turned to see what should be the reason of it: when, to my great astonishment, I saw Philander standing close by the bed-side.... I asked him, what was the occasion of his coming into my chamber at that unseasonable hour? but could get no answer from him; so that I began to be more surprized than before, believing it to be a spirit that stood before me, not that I am very apt to be frighted. However, again importuning him to tell me what was the occasion of his being there, and not yet obtaining any answer, I screamed out, and had certainly alarmed the whole house, had not Philander thrown himself on the bed; and after having pressed my hand, spoke. What he said, was with the greatest fear of disobliging me that could be; when getting off the bed, he kneeled by the side of it, and begged me I would pardon a presumption which nothing but his violent passion could have made him guilty of, it being impossible for him to leave the place where I was, therefore intreated me that I would at least suffer him to sit in my room till morning, not daring to leave so sacred a treasure unguarded. With these and the like expressions of love, he at length talked me to sleep. As soon as he found I was fast, he came to bed, where he lay till morning.

You'll[1] say perhaps, that Philander broke his word, and you'll wonder how I could forgive him. Indeed, I own it was a little hard for me to do so; but when I considered it was love, which generally hurries us on without consideration, that made him guilty of it, I at length excused him, though not without sufficiently upbraiding him of ungenerously betraying me into a fault which my innocence and too good opinion of him, had led me into.

---

1   Amaryllis relates the details of her seduction in the form of a letter to her friend, Emilia.

iv. *The Lover's Week*, "The Fourth Day": 36-43

[Amaryllis determines not to return home because of her aunt's gossip and its consequences to her reputation. Instead, she goes to Colonel P——'s lodging with Philander.]

Whatever inclinations I had before to return home, they immediately vanished on my hearing that my stay abroad for one night, had, thro' my aunt's indiscretion, been so blazed abroad, that should I again appear in publick, there would not be wanting a few of the ill-natured part of the world, who would be throwing reflections....

The Colonel perceiving we were both uneasy till we were fixed in a lodging, therefore proposed a place where, he said, he was sure I might be as private as I could wish....

When we came there, every thing was in very decent order, and the woman of the house seemed very assiduous to oblige us. The Colonel staid with us, and drank a bottle ... but it being twelve a-clock, he took his leave, with a promise to come and drink tea with us the next morning: upon which I ordered the maid to get the equipage ready, and call us by ten a-clock.

v. *The Lover's Week*, "The Fifth Day": 47

[Amaryllis agrees to go with Philander, here renamed Philemon, to his country estate, a pastoral retreat, away from the fashionable world of gossip and censure.]

Philemon interrupted Philander ... saying, Madam, the place which Philander talks of retiring to, believe me, is no remote desart, but an agreeable retreat for lovers; it is placed on a rising hill, though not high enough to make it bleak, nor so low but you may see beneath it a pleasant vale, enameled o'er with various flowers of nature's planting, which make a sweet and agreeable prospect; nor is it so lonely, to make it melancholy, it being within a mile and a half of a market-town, that in a quarter of an hour's driving you may be as publick as you can wish; and, in short, is the most commodiously situated that can be imagined, having gardens, orchards and fish-ponds, with every thing that can conduce to make a seat agreeable....

vi. *The Lover's Week,* "The Sixth Day": 51-54

[The narrative concludes with Amaryllis affirming her choice of Philander over the Duke of A———.]

... Philander took up my hand, and kissing it, said, now, my dear
Amaryllis, I esteem myself the happiest man living, having in my possession the only woman on earth that could make me compleatly
blessed, and that in so quiet and private a retreat, that I may uninter-
rupted enjoy the blessing without the busy prying or malicious censures of the world. As for the house, I could wish it was better for the
entertainment of my angel; but for my own part, since she is pleased
to grace it with her presence, I prefer this small cottage before the
glittering Court, and must say with the philosopher, this place, this
spot of earth whereon you stand, is more to me than the vast plains of
my great fathers ancestors.

   After he had said this, he pressed me to tell him how I liked the
place.... When he had made an end of talking, I ... said to him, Philander, that you are the most agreeable person in the world to me, I
believe I need not now tell you; my indiscreet leaving all things in this
world that ought to be esteemed valuable, and exposing myself to the
malicious censures of the intermedling part of my sex, have, I believe,
sufficiently convinced you of the truth of it; therefore as to my being
contented with the place, there is no room for my finding fault with
it.... But were it as mean as those rural cottages inhabited by the
meanest shepherd, yet, blest with my dear Philander's company, I
should esteem myself more happy than in the greatest splendor that
could be invented.

   Philander having received this assurance of my love from me....
retired to his closet ... and by his retiring, gave me an opportunity of
sending you this exact account of my six days adventures, which will,
I doubt not, meet with your severe censure: for I fancy I already hear
you blaming my folly, and too ready compliance.

   Thus, my dear Emilia, I have, without reserve, made you acquainted with every thing just as it hapned, without adding any thing to

make my story more diverting to you, or concealing any thing that may deserve your blame; therefore I beg you'll use the indulgence of a friend in this case, and consider that I have acted the most prudent, as well as generous part in what I have done; for though I have exposed myself to the censure of the world, I have this satisfaction, that it is for the man I like; and on the other hand, had I taken my aunt's advice, and married the Duke of A——, whom I could never have loved, I had not only made myself unhappy, but by my indifference to him, should have given him, and all the world, reason to have been very free with my character, and should have undergone the scandal without having the satisfaction.

Appendix H: Delarivier Manley's Female Literary Precursors

1. Margaret Cavendish (Duchess of Newcastle)[1]

i. *A True Relation of my Birth, Breeding, and Life* (1656):[2] 265-310

My father was a gentleman, which title is grounded and given by merit, not by princes; and 'tis the act of time, not favour. And though my father was not a peer of the realm, yet there were few peers who had much greater estates, or lived more noble therewith. Yet at that time great titles were to be sold,[3] and not at so high rates, but that his estate might have easily purchased, and was prest for to take; but my father did not esteem titles, unless they were gained by heroick actions; and the kingdome being in a happy peace with all other nations, and in itself being governed by a wise King, King James, there was no employments for heroick spirits; and towards the latter end of Queen Elizabeths reign[4] ... he ... killed one Mr. Brooks in a single duel; for my father by the laws of honour could do no less then call him to the field, to question him for an injury he did him, where their swords were to dispute, and one or both of their lives to decide the argument, wherein my father had the better; and though my father by honour challenged him, with valour fought him, and in justice killed him, yet he suffered more than any person of quality usually doth in cases of honour; for though the laws be rigorous, yet the present Princes most commonly are gratious in those misfortunes,

---

1 Margaret Lucas Cavendish (c.1623-1673), poet, playwright, fiction writer, philosopher, biographer, autobiographer; controversial in her behaviour as well as dress, she was styled "mad Madge" by contemporaries. See also *Rivella*, p. 77, note 1.

2 Cavendish's autobiography was not, originally, published on its own; instead, it formed part of a volume of stories entitled *Natures Pictures drawn by Fancies Pencil to the Life* (1656). In 1814, Sir Egerton Brydges printed the autobiography as a brochure, in which he included a "critical preface." The work appears, along with Cavendish's biography of her husband, in an edition by Mark Antony Lower (London: John Russell Smith, 1872), which provides my copytext.

3 During the reign of King James I (1603-25).

4 Elizabeth I reigned from 1558 to 1603.

especially to the injured. But my father found it not, for his exile was from the time of his misfortunes to Queen Elizabeths death, for the Lord Cobham[1] being then a great man with Queen Elizabeth, and this gentleman, Mr. Brooks, a kind of a favourite, and as I take it brother to the then L. Cobham, which made Queen Elizabeth so severe, not to pardon him. But King James of blessed memory graciously gave him his pardon, and leave to return home to his native country, wherein he lived happily, and died peaceably, leaving a wife and eight children ... I being the youngest child he had, and an infant when he died.

As for my breeding, it was according to my birth, and the nature of my sex; for my birth was not lost in my breeding, for as my sisters was or had been bred, so was I in plenty, or rather with superfluity; likewise we were bred virtuously, modestly, civilly, honourably, and on honest principles....

... [W]e were bred tenderly, for my mother naturally did strive, to please and delight her children, not to cross or torment them, terrifying them with threats, or lashing them with slavish whips, but instead of threats, reason was used to persuade us.... [L]ikewise she never suffered the vulgar servingmen to be in the nursery among the nursemaids, lest their rude love-making might do unseemly actions, or speak unhandsome words in the presence of her children....

...When the Queen[2] was in Oxford, I had a great desire to be one of her maids of honour, hearing the Queen had not the same number she was used to have, whereupon I wooed and won my mother to let me go; for my mother, being fond of all her children, was desirous to please them.... But my brothers and sisters seemed not very well pleased, by reason I had never been from home, nor seldome out of their sight; for though they knew I would not behave my self to their, or my own dishonour, yet they thought I might to my disadvantage, being unexperienced in the world, which indeed I did, for I was so bashfull when I was out of my mother's, brothers, and sisters sight ... that I knew not how to behave myself. Besides, I had heard that the

---

1   According to Sir Egerton Brydges's note, Lord Cobham, who suffered "subsequent misfortunes, condemnation, loss of estate, long imprisonment, and death in miserable poverty, [was] a principal in what is called *Raleigh's Plot.*"
2   Henrietta Maria, wife of Charles I.

world was apt to lay aspersions even on the innocent, for which I durst neither look up with my eyes, nor speak, nor be any way sociable, insomuch as I was thought a natural fool ... and, indeed, I was so afraid to dishonour my friends and family by my indiscreet actions, that I rather chose to be accounted a fool, then to be thought rude or wanton.... [M]y mother said, it would be a disgrace for me to return out of the Court so soon after I was placed; so I continued almost two years, until such time as I was married from thence; for my Lord the Marquis of Newcastle did approve of those bashful fears which many condemned ... and though I did dread marriage, and shunned mens companies as much as I could, yet I could not ... refuse him, by reason my affections were fixed on him, and he was the onely person I ever was in love with. Neither was I ashamed to own it ... for it was not amorous love ... but my love was honest and honourable.... [M]y mother ... having lived a widow many years, for she never forgot my father so as to marry again; indeed, he remained so lively in her memory, and her grief was so lasting ... she made her house her cloyster, inclosing herself ... for she seldom went abroad, unless to church; but these unhappy wars[1] forced her out, by reason she and her children were loyall to the King; for which they plundered her and my brothers of all their goods ... but in such misfortunes my mother was of an heroick spirit.... She was of a grave behaviour, and had such a majestic grandeur, as it were continually hung about her, that it would strike a kind of an awe to the beholders.... Also her beauty was beyond the ruin of time, for she had a well favoured loveliness in her face, a pleasing sweetness in her countenance, and a well-tempered complexion ... even to her dying hour....

... I hearing my Lord's estate, amongst the rest of many more estates, was to be sold, and that the wives of the owners should have an allowance therefrom, it gave me hopes I should receive a benefit thereby; so being accompanied with my Lords only brother ... who was commanded to return [to England after years of exile on the continent] ... I found their hearts as hard as my fortunes ... for they sold all my Lords estate ... and gave me not any part thereof ... indeed, I did not stand as a beggar at the Parliament doore, for I never was at

---

1   The English Civil Wars.

the Parliament House ... neither did I haunt the committees, for I never was at any, as a petitioner, but one in my life, which was called Gold-smith's-Hall.... But I whisperingly spoke to my brother to conduct me out of that ungentlemanly place, so without speaking to them one word good or bad, I returned to my lodgings.... [O]ur sex doth nothing but justle for the preheminence of words, I mean not for speaking well, but speaking much, as they do for the preheminence of place, words rushing against words, thwarting and crossing each other ... but if our sex would but well consider ... they will perceive and finde, that it is neither words nor place that can advance them, but worth and merit. Nor can words or place disgrace them, but inconstancy and boldness. For an honest heart, a noble soul, a chaste life, and a true speaking tongue, is the throne, sceptre, crown, and footstoole, that advances them to an honourable renown....

But now I have declared to my readers, my birth, breeding, and actions ... I think it fit, I should speak something of my humour.... I was from my childhood given to contemplation ... but when I was in the company of my naturall friends, I was very attentive of what they said or did.... [A]lso I never took delight in closets, or cabinets of toys, but in the variety of fine clothes, and such toys as onely were to adorn my person. Likewise I had a naturall stupidity towards the learning of any other language than my native tongue, for I could sooner ... understand the sense, then remember the words, and ... want of such memory makes me so unlearned in foreign languages.... I chose rather to read, than to imploy my time in any other work ... and when I read what I understood not, I would ask my brother ... he being learned, the sense or meaning thereof, but my serious study could not be much, by reason I took great delight in attiring, fine dressing, and fashions, especially such fashions as I did invent myself ... for I always took delight in a singularity, even in accoutrements of habits.... I fear my ambition inclines to vain-glory, for I am very ambitious; yet 'tis neither for beauty, wit, titles, wealth, or power, but as they are steps to raise me to fames tower, which is to live by remembrance in after-ages.... [T]hough I desire to appear to the best advantage, whilest I live in the view of the public world, yet I could most willingly exclude myself, so as never to see the face of any creature, but my Lord, as long as I live.... But I hope my readers will not think me vain for writing my life.... I verily believe some censuring readers will scornfully say, why hath this lady writ her own life? Since none cares to know whose daughter she was, or whose wife she is.... I answer that it is true, that 'tis to no purpose to the readers, but it is to the authoress, because I write it for my own sake, not theirs; neither did I intend this piece for to delight, but to divulge; not to please the fancy, but to tell the truth, lest after-ages should mistake, in not knowing I was daughter to one Master Lucas of St. Johns, near Colchester, in Essex, second wife to the Lord Marquis of Newcastle; for my Lord having had two wives, I might easily have been mistaken, especially if I should dye and my Lord marry again.

ii. *The Life of the Thrice Noble, High, and Puissant Prince William Cavendishe* (1667) [from the Preface][1]

When I first intended to write this history, knowing my self to be no scholar, and as ignorant of the rules of writing histories, as I have in my other works acknowledged my self to be of the names and terms of art; I desired my Lord, that he would be pleased to let me have some elegant and learned historian to assist me: which request his Grace would not grant me; saying, that having never had any assistance in the writing of my former books, I should have no other in the writing of his life, but the informations from himself and his secretary, of the chief transactions and fortunes occuring in it, to the time he married me. I humbly answered, that without a learned assistant, the history would be defective. But he replied, that truth could not be defective. I said again, that rhetorick did adorn truth. And he answered, that rhetorick was fitter for falshoods than truths. Thus I was forced by his Graces commands, to write this history in my own plain style, without elegant flourishings, or exquisit method, relying intirely upon truth, in the expressing whereof, I have been very circumspect; as knowing well, that his Graces actions have so much glory of their own, that they need borrow none from any bodies industry....

---

1 William Cavendish (1592-1676), Duke, Marquis, and Earl of Newcastle; a prominent Royalist leader in the Civil War and a companion to Charles I.

... [B]eing, so much as I am, above base profit, or any preferment whatsoever, I cannot fear to be suspected of flattery, in declaring to the world the merits, wealth, power, loyalty, and fortunes of my noble Lord, who hath done great actions, suffered great losses, endured a long banishment, for his loyalty to his King and countrey;[1] and leads now, like another Scipio,[2] a quiet countrey-life. If notwithstanding all this, any should say, that those who write histories of themselves, and their own actions, or of their own party, or instruct and inform those that write them, are partial to themselves; I answer, that it is very improbable, worthy persons, who having done great, noble and hero-ick exploits, deserving to be recorded, should be so vain, as to write false histories; but if they do, it proves but their folly; for truth can never be concealed, and so it will be more for their disgrace, then for their honour or fame. I fear not any such blemishes in this present history, for I am not conscious of any such crime as partiality or fals-hood, but write it whilst my noble Lord is yet alive, and at such a time where truth may be declared, and falshood contradicted; and I challenge any one (although I be a woman) to contradict any thing that I have set down, or prove it to be otherwise then truth; for be there never so many contradictions, truth will conquer all at last.

iii. *The Life of the Thrice Noble, High, and Puissant Prince William Cavendishe*: 187-92

Of his Natural Humour and Disposition

My Lord may justly be compared to Titus the Deliciae of mankind, by reason of his sweet, gentle and obliging nature;[3] for ... he loves all that are his friends, and hates none that are his enemies. He is a loyal

---

1 The Duchess accompanied Queen Henrietta Maria into exile in Paris in 1645, at which time she met William Cavendish, then Marquis of Newcastle; they spent the next seventeen years in exile in Paris, Rotterdam, and Antwerp, an experience that recalls that of a fellow Royalist, Roger Manley.

2 Either Publius Cornelius Scipio Africanus (237?-183? B.C.), Roman General who defeated Hannibal, or Publius Cornelius Scipio Aemilianus Africanus Numantinus (184?-129? B.C.), Roman General and statesman who destroyed Carthage; adopted grandson of the elder Scipio.

3 Cavendish here suggests her husband's military prowess and his strength of charac-ter (his ability to inspire delight).

subject, a kind husband, a loving father, a generous master, and a constant friend....

He hates pride and loves humility; is civil to strangers, kind to his acquaintance, and respectful to all persons, according to their quality.... To the meanest person he'll put off his hat, and suffer every body to speak to him.

Of his Outward Shape and Behaviour

His shape is neat, and exactly proportioned; his stature of a middle size, and his complexion sanguine.

His behaviour is such, that it might be a pattern for all gentlemen; for it is courtly, civil, easie and free, without formality or constraint; and yet hath something in it of grandure, that causes an awful respect towards him.

Of his Discourse

His discourse is as free and unconcerned, as his behaviour, pleasant, witty, and instructive; he is quick in reparties or sudden answers, and hates dubious disputes, and premeditated speeches. He loves also to intermingle his discourse with some short pleasant stories, and witty sayings, and always names the author from whom he hath them; for he hates to make another man's wit his own.

2. Aphra Behn[1]

i. *Oroonoko: Or, The History of the Royal Slave* (1688): 1–8

I do not pretend, in giving you the history of this royal slave, to entertain my reader with adventures of a feigned hero, whose life and fortunes fancy may manage at the poet's pleasure; nor in relating the truth,[2] design to adorn it with any accidents, but such as arrived in

---

1   See Appendix G, p. 150, note 3.
2   Behn's best-known work of fiction continues to raise controversy over its truthfulness; however, since Ernest Bernbaum contended that Behn had never been to Surinam (see "Mrs. Behn's Biography a Fiction" *PMLA* XXVIII [1913] 432–53), scholars have, in the face of evidence to the contrary, largely come to accept her

earnest to him. And it shall come simply into the world, recommended by its own proper merits, and natural intrigues; there being enough of reality to support it, and to render it diverting, without the addition of invention.

I was myself an eye-witness to a great part of what you will find here set down; and what I could not be witness of, I received from the mouth of the chief actor in this history, the hero himself, who gave us the whole transactions of his youth: and though I shall omit, for brevity's sake, a thousand little accidents of his life, which, however pleasant to us, where history was scarce, and adventures very rare, yet might prove tedious and heavy to my reader, in a world where he finds diversions for every minute, new and strange. But we who were perfectly charmed with the character of this great man, were curious to gather every circumstance of his life....

I have often seen and conversed with this great man [Oroonoko], and been a witness to many of his mighty actions; and do assure my reader, the most illustrious Courts could not have produced a braver man, both for greatness of courage and mind, a judgment more solid, a wit more quick, and a conversation more sweet and diverting. He knew almost as much as if he had read much. He had heard of and admired the Romans. He had heard of the late Civil Wars in England, and the deplorable death of our great monarch;[1] and would discourse of it with all the sense and abhorrence of the injustice imaginable. He had an extreme good and graceful mien, and all the civility of a well-bred great man. He had nothing of barbarity in his nature, but in all points addressed himself as if his education had been in some European Court.

This great and just character of Oroonoko gave me an extreme curiosity to see him, especially when I knew he spoke French and English, and that I could talk with him. But though I had heard so much of him, I was as greatly surprized when I saw him, as if I had heard nothing of him; so beyond all report I found him.... His face

---

visit to the colony as fact. In any case, as Jane Spencer points out, "the autobiographical element [in *Oroonoko*] means that Behn's interest in the narrator's position develops into an examination of her own role as woman and as writer" (*The Rise of the Woman Novelist* 47).

1   Charles I, executed on 30 January 1649.

was not of that brown rusty black which most of that nation are, but of perfect ebony, or polished jett. His eyes were the most awful that could be seen, and very piercing; the white of 'em being like snow, as were his teeth. His nose was rising and *Roman*, instead of *African* and flat. His mouth the finest shaped that could be seen; far from those great turned lips, which are so natural to the rest of the Negroes.... There was no one grace wanting, that bears the standard of true beauty.... Nor did the perfections of his mind come short of those of his person; for his discourse was admirable upon almost any subject: and whoever had heard him speak, would have been convinced of their errors, that all fine wit is confined to the white men, especially to those of Christendom; and would have confessed that Oroonoko was as capable even of reigning well, and of governing as wisely, had as great a soul, as politick maxims, and was as sensible of power, as any Prince civilized in the most refined schools of humanity and learning, or the most illustrious Courts.

ii. *Oroonoko*: 40

I ought to tell you, that the Christians never buy any slaves but they give 'em some name of their own, their native ones being likely very barbarous, and hard to pronounce; so that Mr. Trefry[1] gave Oroonoko that of Caesar; which name will live in that country as long as that (scarce more) glorious one of the great Roman: for 'tis most evident he wanted no part of the personal courage of that Caesar, and acted things as memorable, had they been done in some part of the world replenished with people and historians, that might have given him his due. But his misfortune was, to fall in an obscure world, that afforded only a female pen to celebrate his fame; though I doubt not but it had lived from others endeavours, if the Dutch, who immediately after his time took that country,[2] had not killed, banished and dispersed all those that were capable of giving the world this great man's life, much better than I have done.

---

1 Oroonoko's master.
2 Surinam was ceded to the Dutch in February 1667; though reclaimed by the British in October, the Dutch regained possession with the Treaty of Breda.

You must know, that when the news was brought on Monday morning, that Caesar had betaken himself to the woods, and carried with him all the Negroes, we were possessed with extreme fear, which no persuasions could dissipate, that he would secure himself till night, and then, that he would come down and cut all our throats. This apprehension made all the females of us fly down the river, to be secured; and while we were away, they acted this cruelty; for I suppose I had authority and interest enough there, had I suspected any such thing, to have prevented it: but we had not gone many leagues, but the news overtook us, that Caesar was taken and whipped like a common slave....

He had learned to take tobacco; and when he was assured he should die, he desired they would give him a pipe in his mouth, ready lighted; which they did. And the executioner came, and first cut off his members, and threw them into the fire; after that, with an ill-favoured knife, they cut off his ears and his nose, and burned them; he still smoked on, as if nothing had touched him; then they hacked off one of his arms, and still he bore up, and held his pipe; but at the cutting off the other arm, his head sunk, and his pipe dropt and he gave up the ghost, without a groan, or a reproach. My mother and sister were by him all the while, but not suffered to save him; so rude and wild were the rabble, and so inhuman were the justices who stood by to see the execution, who after paid dearly enough for their insolence....

Thus died this great man, worthy of a better fate, and a more sublime wit than mine to write his praise. Yet, I hope, the reputation of my pen is considerable enough to make his glorious name to survive to all ages, with that of the brave, the beautiful, and the constant Imoinda."[1]

---

1   Oroonoko's wife.

iv. *Memoirs on the Life of Mrs. Behn* (1696):[1] n. pag.

My intimate acquaintance with the admirable Astrea, gave me, naturally, a very great esteem for her; for it both freed me from that folly
of my sex of envying or slighting excellencies I could not obtain; and
inspired me with a noble fire to celebrate that woman, who was an
honour and glory to our sex; and this re-printing her incomparable
novels, presented me with a lucky occasion of exerting that desire
into action.

She was a gentlewoman, by birth, of a good family in the city of
Canterbury, in Kent; her paternal name was Johnson,[2] whose relation
to the Lord Willoughby, drew him for the advantageous post of Lieu-
tenant-General of many isles, besides the continent of Surinam, from
his quiet retreat at Canterbury, to run the hazardous voyage of the
West-Indies; with him he took his chief riches, his wife and children;
and in that number Afra, his prominent darling, our future heroine,
and admired Astrea.... [B]esides the vivacity and wit of her conversation, at the first use almost of reason in discourse, she would write the
prettiest, soft-engaging verses in the world. Thus qualified, she
accompanied her parents in their long voyage to Surinam, leaving
behind her the sighs and tears of all her friends, and breaking hearts of
her lovers, that sighed to possess, what was scarce yet arrived to a
capacity of easing their pain, if she had been willing. But as she was
mistress of uncommon charms of body, as well as mind, she gave
infinite and raging desires, before she could know the least her self.

Her father lived not to see that land flowing with milk and honey;
that paradise, which she so admirably describes in *Oroonoko;* where
you may also find what adventures happened to her in that country,
the misfortunes of that Prince had been unknown to us, if the divine

---

1   Appearing at the beginning of the first edition of *The Histories and Novels of the Late
    Ingenious Mrs. Behn* (London: S. Briscoe, 1696), *Memoirs* claims to be written by
    "One of the Fair Sex." However, as Frederick M. Link points out, the author was
    probably Charles Gildon, who also wrote the brief preface to Behn's play *The
    Younger Brother*, which appeared earlier in the year. In Link's words, Gildon "was not
    above masquerading as a woman if he felt it to his advantage" (*Aphra Behn* 17).
2   According to Jane Jones ("New light on the background and early life of Aphra
    Behn" 311-13), Behn's father was probably Bartholomew Johnson, a Canterbury
    barber; he married Elizabeth Denham on 25 August 1638.

Astrea had not been there, and his sufferings had wanted that satisfaction which her pen has given 'em in the immortality of his virtues, and constancy; the very memory of which, move a generous pity in all, and a contempt of the brutal actors in that unfortunate tragedy. Here I can add nothing to what she has given the world already, but a vindication of her from some unjust aspersions I find, are insinuated about this town in relation to that Prince. I knew her intimately well; and I believe she would not have concealed any love-affair from me, being one of her own sex, whose friendship and secrecy she had experienced; which makes me assure the world, there was no affair between that Prince and Astrea, but what the whole plantation were witnesses of: a generous value for his uncommon virtues, every one that but hears 'em, finds in himself; and his presence gave her no more. Beside, his heart was too violently set on the everlasting charms of his Imoinda, to be shook with those more faint (in his eye) of a white beauty; and Astrea's relations, there present, had too watchful an eye over her to permit the frailty of her youth, if that had been powerful enough....

She was of a generous and open temper, something passionate, very serviceable to her friends in all that was in her power; and could sooner forgive an injury, than do one. She had wit, honour, good humour and judgment. She was mistress of all the pleasing arts of conversation, but used 'em not to any but those who loved not plain-dealing. She was a woman of sense, and by consequence a lover of pleasure, as indeed all, both men and women, are; but only some would be thought to be above the conditions of humanity, and place their chief pleasure in a proud, vain hypocrisie. For my part, I knew her intimately, and never saw ought unbecoming the just modesty of our sex, tho' more gay and free than the folly of the precise will allow. She was, I'm satisfied, a greater honour to our sex than all the canting tribe of dissemblers, that die with the false reputation of saints. This I may venture to say, because I'm unknown, and the revengeful censures of my sex will not reach me, since they will never be able to draw the veil, and discover the speaker of these bold truths. If I have done my dead friend any manner of justice, I am satisfied, having obtained my end. If not, the reader must remember that there are few Astrea's arise in our age; and till such a one does appear, all our endeavours in encomiums on the last, must be vain and impotent.

Works Cited/Recommended Reading

Aitken, George A. *The Life of Richard Steele.* 2 vols. New York: Haskell House, 1968.

Anderson, Paul Bunyan. "Delariviere Manley's Prose Fiction." *Philological Quarterly* 13(1934): 168-88.

———. "The History and Authorship of Mrs. Crackenthorpe's *Female Tatler*". *Modern Philology* 28(1931): 354-60.

———. "Mary de la Rivière Manley, a Cavalier's Daughter in Grub Street." Ph.D. thesis, Harvard University, 1931.

———. "Mistress Delariviere Manley's Biography." *Modern Philology* 33 (1936): 261-78.

Ashley, Maurice. *General Monck.* London: Jonathan Cape, 1977.

Ballaster, Rosalind. "Introduction." *New Atalantis.* Ed. Rosalind Ballaster. London: Pickering & Chatto, 1991. Harmondsworth: Penguin Books, 1992.

———. "Manl(e)y forms: sex and the female satirist." *Women, Texts and Histories 1575-1760.* Ed. Clare Brant and Diane Purkiss. London and New York: Routledge, 1992. 217-41.

———. *Seductive Forms: Women's Amatory Fiction from 1684 to 1740.* Oxford: Clarendon Press, 1992.

———. "Seizing the means of seduction: Fiction and feminine identity in Aphra Behn and Delarivier Manley." *Women, Writing, History: 1640-1740.* Ed. Isobel Grundy and Susan Wiseman. London: Batsford, 1992. 93-108.

Barash, Carol L. "Gender, Authority and the 'Life' of an Eighteenth-Century Woman Writer: Delarivière Manley's *Adventures of Rivella*." *Women's Studies International Forum* 10:2 (1987): 165-69.

Batchelor, John. "Women's Lives: The Unmapped Country." *The Art of Literary Biography.* Ed. John Batchelor. Oxford: Clarendon Press, 1995. 87-98.

Behn, Aphra. *Memoirs on the Life of Mrs. Behn. The Histories and Novels of the Late Ingenious Mrs. Behn.* London: S. Briscoe, 1696.

———. *Oroonoko: or, The Royal Slave.* London: Will. Canning, 1688.

Benstock, Shari, ed. *The Private Self: Theory and Practice of Women's Autobiographical Writings.* London: Routledge, 1988.

Blain, Virginia, Patricia Clements, and Isobel Grundy, eds. *The Feminist Companion to Literature in English: Women Writers from the Middle Ages to the Present.* New Haven: Yale University Press, 1990.

Blanchard, Rae, ed. *The Correspondence of Richard Steele*. Oxford: Clarendon Press, 1968. 425-39. [Contains selections from Manley's *The Lady's Paquet Broke Open*.]

Burney, Frances. *Camilla, or A Picture of Youth*. 1796. Ed. Edward A. Bloom and Lillian D. Bloom. Oxford: Oxford University Press, 1983.

Carter, Herbert. "Three Women Dramatists of the Restoration." *Bookman's Journal* 13 (1925): 91-97.

Cavendish, Margaret (Duchess of Newcastle). *A True Relation of my Birth, Breeding, and Life. The Lives of William Cavendishe, duke of Newcastle, and of his Wife, Margaret, duchess of Newcastle. Written by the thrice noble and illustrious princess, Margaret, duchess of Newcastle*. Ed. Mark Antony Lower. London: John Russell Smith, 1872.

———. *The Life of the Thrice Noble, High and Puissant Prince, William Cavendishe*. In *The Lives of William Cavendishe ... and of his Wife*. Ed. Mark Antony Lower. London: John Russell Smith, 1872.

Churchill, Winston. *Marlborough: His Life and Times*. 4 vols. London: George G. Harrap, 1947. Rpt. 1949.

Clark, Constance. *Three Augustan Women Playwrights*. New York: Peter Lang, 1986.

Cotton, Nancy. *Women Playwrights in England c.1363-1750*. London and Toronto: Associated University Presses, 1980.

[Curll, Edmund.] *An Impartial History of the Life, Character, Amours, Travels, and Transactions of Mr. John Barber, City-Printer, Common-Councilman, Alderman, and Lord Mayor of London*. London: E. Curll, 1741.

———. "Preface." *Mrs. Manley's History of her Own Life and Times*. London: E. Curll, 1725.

Davis, Lennard J. *Factual Fictions: The Origins of the English Novel*. New York: Columbia University Press, 1983.

Day, Robert Adams. *Told in Letters: Epistolary Fiction before Richardson*. Ann Arbor: University of Michigan Press, 1966.

Duff, Dolores Diane Clarke, "Materials toward a Biography of Mary Delariviere Manley." Ph.D. thesis, University of Indiana, 1965.

Duffy, Maureen. *The Passionate Shepherdess: Aphra Behn 1640-89*. London: Jonathan Cape, 1977.

Duncombe, John. *The Feminead; or, Female Genius, A Poem*. London: M. Cooper, 1754.

Ehrenpreis, Irvin. *Swift: The Man, His Works, and the Age*. Vol. 2. Cambridge: Harvard University Press, 1967. 3 vols.

Elwood, John R. "Swift's 'Corinna.'" *Notes and Queries*. CC (1955): 529-30.

Fabricant, Carole. "The Shared Worlds of Manley and Swift." *Pope, Swift, and Women Writers*. Ed. Donald C. Mell. Newark: University of Delaware Press; London: Associated University Presses, 1996. 154-78.

Farnham, Fern. *Madame Dacier: Scholar and Humanist*. Monterey, CA.: Angel Press, 1976.

The Female Wits; or, The Triumvirate of Poets at Rehearsal. In *The Female Wits: Women Playwrights on the London Stage 1660-1720*. Ed. Fidelis Morgan. London: Virago Press, 1981.

Fielding, Henry. *Joseph Andrews*. 1742. Ed. R.F. Brissenden. Harmondsworth: Penguin Books, 1977.

Finke, Laurie A. "The Satire of Women Writers in *The Female Wits*. *Restoration: Studies in English Literary Culture, 1660-1700* 8(1984): 64-71.

Foster, James R. *History of the Pre-Romantic Novel in England*. New York: Modern Language Association, 1949.

Gallagher, Catherine. *Nobody's Story: The Vanishing Acts of Women Writers in the Marketplace, 1670-1820*. Berkeley and Los Angeles: University of California Press, 1994.

[Gildon, Charles.] "Memoirs on the Life of Mrs. Behn. Written by a Gentlewoman of her Acquaintance." *The Histories and Novels of the Late Ingenious Mrs. Behn*. By Aphra Behn. London: S. Briscoe, 1696.

Gilmore, Leigh. "Policing Truth: Confession, Gender, and Autobiographical Authority." *Autobiography and Postmodernism*. Ed. Kathleen Ashley, Leigh Gilmore, and Gerald Peters. Amherst: University of Massachusetts Press, 1994. 54-78.

Gonda, Caroline. *Reading Daughters' Fictions 1709-1834: Novels and Society from Manley to Edgeworth*. Cambridge: Cambridge University Press, 1996.

Graham, Walter. "Thomas Baker, Mrs. Manley and the *Female Tatler*". *Modern Philology* 34 (1936-37): 267-72.

Hearne, Mary. *The Lover's Week*. 1718. Bound with *The Female Deserters* by Mary Hearne and *Love Intrigues* by Jane Barker. New York and London: Garland Publishing, 1973.

Heinemann, M. "Swift's 'Corinna' Again." *Notes and Queries* CCXVII (1972): 218-21.

Heinzelman, Susan Sage. "Women's Petty Treason: Feminism, Narrative, and the Law." *Journal of Narrative Technique* 20(1990): 87-106.

Hipwell, Daniel. "Mary de la Rivière Manley." *Notes and Queries*. Seventh Series, 8 (1889): 156-57. [A copy of Manley's will].

Hume, Robert D. *The Rakish Stage: Studies in English Drama, 1660-1800*. Carbondale and Edwardsville: Southern Illinois University Press, 1983.

Jacob, Giles. *The Poetical Register: or, the Lives and Characters of the English Dramatic Poets*. London: E. Curll, 1719.

Jelinek, Estelle C. *The Tradition of Women's Autobiography: From Antiquity to the Present*. Boston: Twayne, 1986.

Jerrold, Walter, and Clare Jerrold. *Five Queer Women*. New York: Brentano's, 1929.

Johnson, R. Brimley. *The Women Novelists*. Freeport, N.Y.: Books for Libraries Press, 1919. Rpt. 1967.

Jones, Jane. "New light on the background and early life of Aphra Behn." *Aphra Behn studies*. Ed. Janet Todd. Cambridge: Cambridge University Press, 1996. 310-20.

Kenyon, J.P. *Stuart England*. London: Penguin Books, 1978.

Köster, Patricia. "Delariviere Manley and the DNB: A Cautionary Tale About Following Black Sheep, with a Challenge to Cataloguers." *Eighteenth-Century Life* 3 (1977): 106-11.

——. "Introduction." *The Novels of Mary Delarivière Manley*. Ed. Patricia Köster, 2 vols. Gainesville, FL: Scholars' Facsimiles and Reprints, 1971.

Langbaine, Gerard. *The Lives and Characters of the English Dramatick Poets*. Completed by Charles Gildon. London: Turner, 1699.

Lapthorne, Richard. *The Portledge Papers being extracts from the letters of Richard Lapthorne, Gent, of Hatton Garden London, to Richard Coffin Esq. of Portledge, Bideford, Devon from December 10th 1687-August 7th 1697*. Ed. Russell J. Kerr & Ida Coffin Duncan. London: Jonathan Cape, 1928.

Lennox, Charlotte. *Sophia*. 1762. New York: Garland Publishing, 1974.

The Life and Character of John Barber, Esq; Late Lord-Mayor of London, Deceased. London: T. Cooper, 1741.

Link, Frederick M. *Aphra Behn*. New York: Twayne, 1968.

London, April. "Placing the Female: The Metonymic Garden in Amatory and Pious Narrative 1700-1740." *Fetter'd or Free? British Women Novelists 1670-1815*. Ed. Mary Anne Schofield and Cecilia Macheski. Athens, OH: Ohio University Press, 1986. 101-23.

Luttrell, Narcissus. *A Brief Historical Relation of State Affairs from September 1678 to April 1714*. 6 vols. Oxford: Oxford University Press, 1857.

Lyons, John O. *The Invention of the Self: The Hinge of Consciousness in the Eighteenth Century*. Carbondale: Southern Illinois University Press, 1978.

MacCarthy, Bridget. *Women Writers: Their Contribution to the English Novel 1621-1744*. Cork University Press, Oxford: B.H. Blackwell, 1945.

Manley, Delarivier. *The Adventures of Rivella*. London: (no publisher on title page) E. Curll, 1714.

———. "Letters to Mrs. De La Rivière Manley" [? Richard Steele] from *The Lady's Paquet Broke Open* [reissued as *Court Intrigues*].

———. *The Lost Lover; or, The Jealous Husband*. London: Bently et al., 1696.

———. *Lucius, The First Christian King of Britain*. Augustan Reprint Society 253-254. University of California, Los Angeles: William Andrews Clark Memorial Library, 1989.

———. *Mrs. Manley's History of her Own Life and Times*. London: E. Curll, 1725.

———. "Mrs. Manley's Will." *Notes and Queries*. Seventh Series, 8 (1889): 156-57.

———. *New Atalantis*. Ed. Rosalind Ballaster. London: Pickering & Chatto, 1991. Harmondsworth: Penguin Books, 1992.

———. *The Novels of Mary Delariviere Manley 1705-1714*. Ed. Patricia Köster. 2 vols. Gainesville, FL: Scholars' Facsimiles and Reprints, 1971.

———. *The Royal Mischief*. London: Bently et al., 1696.

———. "To the Author of *Agnes de Castro*." *Agnes de Castro*. By Catherine Trotter. London: H. Rhodes, 1696.

Montagu, Mary Wortley. *The Complete Letters of Lady Mary Wortley Montagu*. Ed. Robert Halsband. Vol. 1. Oxford: Clarendon Press, 1965. 3 vols.

———. "Saturday," from *Six Town Eclogues*. *Eighteenth-Century Women Poets*. Ed. Roger Lonsdale. Oxford: Oxford University Press, 1990.

Morgan, Fidelis. *A Woman of No Character: An Autobiography of Mrs. Manley*. London and Boston: Faber & Faber, 1986.

———. *The Female Wits: Women Playwrights on the London Stage 1660-1720*. London: Virago Press, 1981.

Needham, Gwendolyn B. "Mary de la Rivière Manley, Tory Defender." *Huntington Library Quarterly* 12 (1949): 253-88.

———. "Mrs. Manley: An Eighteenth-Century Wife of Bath." *Huntington Library Quarterly* 14 (1951): 259-84.

Nussbaum, Felicity A. *The Autobiographical Subject: Gender and Ideology in Eighteenth-Century England*. Baltimore and London: Johns Hopkins University Press, 1989.

Olney, James, ed. *Autobiography: Essays Theoretical and Critical*. Princeton: Princeton University Press, 1980.

Palomo, Dolores. "A Woman Writer and the Scholars: A Review of Mary Manley's Reputation." *Women and Literature* 6 (1978): 36-46.

Pearson, Jacqueline. *The Prostituted Muse: Images of Women and Women Dramatists 1642-1737*. New York: Harvester. Wheatsheaf, 1988.

Perry, Ruth. *The Celebrated Mary Astell: An Early English Feminist.* Chicago and London: University of Chicago Press, 1986.

Pix, Mary. "To Mrs. Manley, upon her tragedy called *The Royal Mischief.*" *The Royal Mischief.* By Delarivier Manley. London: Bently et al., 1696.

Pope, Alexander. *The Rape of the Lock. Alexander Pope: Selected Poetry and Prose.* Ed. William K. Wimsatt. 2nd ed. New York: Holt, Rinehart and Winston, 1972.

Rabb, Melinda Alliker. "The Manl(e)y Style: Delariviere Manley and Jonathan Swift." *Pope, Swift, and Women Writers.* Ed. Donald C. Mell. Newark: University of Delaware Press; London: Associated University Presses, 1996. 125-53.

Reeve, Clara. *The Progress of Romance through Times, Countries, and Manners.* 1785. Vol. 1. New York: Garland Publishing, 1970. 2 vols.

Richetti, John J. *Popular Fiction before Richardson: Narrative Patterns 1700-1739.* Oxford: Clarendon Press, 1969.

Rogers, Katharine M. *Feminism in Eighteenth-Century England.* Urbana: University of Illinois Press, 1982.

Ross, Deborah. *The Excellence of Falsehood: Romance, Realism, and Women's Contribution to the Novel.* Lexington: University Press of Kentucky, 1991.

Sergeant, Philip W. *Rogues and Scoundrels.* London: Hutchinson, 1924.

Sherburn, George, ed. *The Correspondence of Alexander Pope.* Vol. 1. Oxford: Oxford UP, 1956.

Shields, Carol. *The Stone Diaries.* Toronto: Random House, 1993.

Smith, Charlotte. *The Old Manor House.* 1793. Ed. Anne Henry Ehrenpreis. Oxford: Oxford University Press, 1989.

Smith, John Harrington. "Thomas Baker and *The Female Tatler*". *Modern Philology* 49 (1951-52): 182-88.

Smith, Sidonie. *A Poetics of Women's Autobiography: Marginality and the Fictions of Self-Representation.* Bloomington and Indianapolis: Indiana University Press, 1987.

Spacks, Patricia Meyer. *Gossip.* Chicago and London: University of Chicago Press, 1986.

———. *Imagining a Self: Autobiography and Novel in Eighteenth-Century England.* Cambridge: Harvard University Press, 1976.

Spencer, Jane. *The Rise of the Woman Novelist: From Aphra Behn to Jane Austen.* Oxford: Basil Blackwell, 1986.

Spender, Dale. *Living by the Pen: Early British Women Writers.* New York: Teachers College Press, 1992.

Stanley, Liz. *The auto/biographical I: The theory and practice of feminist auto/biography.* Manchester and New York: Manchester University Press; New York: St. Martin's Press, 1992.

Stanton, Domna C., ed. *The Female Autograph: Theory and Practice of Autobiography from the 10th to the 20th Century.* Chicago: University of Chicago Press, 1984.

Steele, Richard. *The Correspondence of Richard Steele.* Ed. Rae Blanchard. Oxford: Clarendon Press, 1941.

———. "Prologue." *Lucius, The First Christian King of Britain.* By Delariviere Manley. Augustan Reprint Society 253-254. University of California, Los Angeles: William Andrews Clark Memorial Library, 1989.

Straus, Ralph. *The Unspeakable Curll: Being Some Account of Edmund Curll, Bookseller to which is Added a Full List of his Books.* London: Chapman & Hall, 1927. New York: Augustus M. Kelley, 1970.

Swift, Jonathan. "Corinna." *Jonathan Swift: The Complete Poems.* Ed. Pat Rogers. New Haven and London: Yale University Press, 1983.

———. *Journal to Stella.* Ed. Harold Williams. 2 vols. Oxford: Clarendon Press, 1948.

Todd, Janet. "Life after sex: the fictional autobiography of Delarivier Manley." *Women's Studies* 15 (1988): 43-55.

———. *The Sign of Angellica: Women, Writing and Fiction, 1660-1800.* London: Virago Press, 1989.

Trevelyan, George Macaulay. *England under Queen Anne, iii: The Peace and the Protestant Succession.* London: Longmans, Green & Co., 1934.

———. *England under the Stuarts.* 7th ed. New York: G.P. Putnam's Sons; London: Methuen, 1916.

Trotter, Catherine. "To Mrs. Manley, by the Author of Agnes de Castro." *The Royal Mischief.* By Delarivier Manley. London: Bently et al., 1696.

Utter, Robert Palfrey, and Gwendolyn B. Needham. *Pamela's Daughters.* New York: Macmillan, 1936.

Ward, Adolphus William. *A History of English Dramatic Literature to the Death of Queen Anne.* Vol. 3. London: Macmillan, 1899. New York: Octagon, 1966. 3 vols.

Ward, Estelle Frances. *Christopher Monck Duke of Albemarle*. London: John Murray, 1915.

Williamson, Marilyn L. *Raising Their Voices: British Women Writers, 1650-1750*. Detroit: Wayne State University Press, 1990.